Backroom Confessions

Rose Jackson-Beavers

Published by Prioritybooks Publications

Missouri

This book is a work of fiction. The incidents, characters, and dialogue are products of the author's imagination and are not to be interpreted as real. Any resemblance to actual people, living or dead, is entirely coincidental.

Prioritybooks Publications

P.O. Box 2535

Florissant, Mo 63033

Manufactured in the United States of America

Library of Congress LCNN

2004093409

ISBN 0-9753634-1-7

Cover design by Majaluk CDMG

Edited by Jill Ronsley

www.suneditwrite.com

For information regarding discounts for bulk purchases, please contact Prioritybooks Publications at 1-314-741-6789 or ros-beav03@yahoo.com.

Others books by Rose Jackson-Beavers

Summin T' Say

Quilt Designs and Poetry Rhymes

A Hole in My Heart

Caught in the Net of Deceptions

Acknowledgements

To all those who support my writing and read my columns, you are the reason that I love what I do. Your support is appreciated. Thank you for being a fan. To my editor, Ishmael Sistrunk, thank you for all your hard work. To my parents, L. J. and Connie Booker, no love can ever be as strong as what I have for you. Your belief and faith in me have always given me the determination to succeed in everything I do. Thanks for the love and support you have given to me and to all my brothers and sisters. To Deborah Sistrunk, you have truly inspired and supported my writing. Thank you. Diane Page, you are a remarkable woman. To Edna Petty, this one is for you because you pushed me so hard to publish this one. To Cedric and my baby girl, Adeesha, God gave me the perfect family. I love you both dearly. I'm so blessed to have you both in my life. I give all thanks to the Almighty God. It is Your grace that has blessed me and given me the talents that I have, and without You in my life, I could do nothing.

Dedication

This book is dedicated to McKinley and Sylvester Jackson, both of whom taught me the meaning of love and family. Your memories will live on through your family.

Backroom Confessions

Rose Jackson-Beavers

Chapter 1

"Jerickca, why is it so difficult for you to understand that as the director, you must separate yourself from your employees. It's just not professional to mix business and friendship on a job," Anthony said.

"I'm not mixing friendship and business. I'm a supervisor who can talk and laugh with her staff but can walk away with the same expectations that you have of your staff and know that the job will get done." Jerickca was getting sick and tired of her husband's assumptions. She didn't have personal friends at work, but she made an effort to be seen by her staff as approachable.

"I still say that you need to treat your job as a job. When you start laughing and sitting around with your staff, they're going to slack off and not accomplish your goals." Anthony threw up his hands, exasperated.

"I don't see that happening. I've been managing people too long, and I can tell who can or cannot handle relationships. I know that some employees can't tell the difference between a co-worker and a personal friend. But there are only a few like that. It doesn't matter if it's with me or someone else. People who don't have business skills won't be able to fit into the job."

"Mark my words, Jerickca, you may be heading for trouble. It's best to separate your relationships. Keep your friends and job separate. You'll have less trouble and problems. You really need to stay away from backroom gossiping with your subordinates."

"Believe me, I do understand your concern, but people need to feel comfortable on the job. They need to know that they can laugh, talk, and spend positive time together. Happiness increases productivity," Jerickca said as she turned to walk away. "You run your company and let me do the same with mine."

"Forget it. I don't see why you are having such a hard time understanding this issue. Didn't you learn anything when you got your Master's degree?"

"Don't go there with me!" Jerickca screamed as she slammed the door to the bedroom. She lay across the bed and thought about her job. She wasn't doing anything wrong, but her husband, Anthony, was a successful businessman who knew what it took to get to the top of his profession. She knew that Anthony was only trying to help, but she enjoyed going to the backroom occasionally. Sometimes she needed the light banter and friendship that went on in that one little special room.

Jerickca knew that whenever she saw the door to the back office closed, a conference of some sort was going on. She would just gather up all her nerves and push the pine door open. Sometimes the staff were having a conference about something that they didn't like about the job: a new policy, lay-offs, or a grant ending. But most of the time, they were gossiping about a co-worker or talking about a current event. She also knew that if they were not talking about the job, it was about something private in someone's life, and they were not yet willing to discuss this with their supervisors—only with their peers.

Other topics included family, relationships, and sex. That was usually the topic of the day. If anyone wanted to know what to do about sex problems, all they had to do was head to the backroom and talk to one person. After five minutes or so, the backroom would be packed with all kinds of people, from the supervisors to the secretaries. Everyone wanted to hear the juicy conversation that was going on. When people wanted to share their concerns, they went to this room to get the support needed to face their problems. All the employees knew that when they needed emotional support or advice for their particular problems, all they had to do was walk toward the back of the building and push open the heavy wooden staff door. It was a pattern that had been established to solve any problem. As she lay on the bed, she turned because she heard the phone ringing. She picked it up.

"Hello, Deborah."

"What's up, girl?"

"Just feeling a little down lately. Anthony and I were at it again. We've been arguing a lot about our relationship and my business practices. You know how he hates that I spend time being personal with my employees."

"Maybe you and Anthony should keep your opinions about your jobs to yourselves—especially since the two of you don't see eye to eye on engaging workers."

"You're right about that!"

"Anyway, what is so special about that backroom?"

"It's just a place where staff go to communicate. It's their own little corner where they feel safe to have interesting conversations. You argue in the backroom, fight, make up, and sabotage or support each other."

But what Jerickca didn't say was that you also arranged dates for the single person, had birthday parties, housewarmings, wedding and baby showers, and going- away parties. Mostly, it was the place that you felt safe enough to tell a lie just to get out of a difficult situation, because you knew others would have your back if you didn't.

"Jerickca, you could create a problem by spending so much time with the workers. You're next in line to supervise hundreds of employees, even though I know you would prefer not to. Hanging out in that backroom could become an issue—all that gossiping could start problems between your workers."

"You're right about that. If I had my preference, I wouldn't take that promotion. Anyway that's in the future, so it's no use focusing on that."

"Just be careful. I know it's difficult to be professional all the time, but try to spend less time with your subordinates. As an attorney, I need to warn you that you could be promoting a hostile work environment."

"That would be true if I allowed staff to malign each other or hurt our clients, but I would never allow that to happen."

"Good. You know I told you that you need to emphasize taking care of yourself, Jerickca."

"It just seems that everyone wants a piece of me. I want my employees to be happy, but I don't want it to be at my expense. My relatives, employees, and even some of my friends treat my kindness like a revolving door. The more I give, the more they take."

"Then you are going to stop giving yourself to others and start taking care of yourself by doing something special. We're going to Clayton, to that spa I told you about tomorrow. Just be ready and I'll pick you up in the morning around ten."

"Alrighty, then! I'll see you at ten."

Jerickca wanted all her staff to enjoy working for her, but she took a special interest in those working the new PRIME Grant she recently received. To give them freedom to laugh away their stress, she allowed them to congregate in the backroom to ventilate bad feelings and just to enjoy good-old-fashioned conversation.

What was the backroom? It was a large area divided equally into four spaces, each about the size of a small bathroom. These spaces were nothing but a miniature cubicle with no walls attached, about six by twelve feet wide. Yet all four of the employees in the backroom knew their boundaries. There were no markers and no roped off area, but everyone knew where each area began and where it ended. The backroom had four large desks, each with a phone, a bookshelf, a chair for visitors, and a storage unit. Located in the far right corner was an enormous gray and white copy machine that stood at attention, waiting for someone to control it by pushing its buttons. The workers had insisted that the copier be put in their area to cut back travel time through the building to secure copies for their monthly mandatory paper work.

When it was really quiet, you could hear the hum of the dorm-size Sangus refrigerator in the left corner near a cherry wood four-shelf bookcase. But most of the time, you heard talking, whispering, and high-pitched laughter. It sounded as if the workers had completed their work and were now ready to get down to the serious business of the day—gossiping. This was simply the act of studying, investigating, and deciphering a person's character morally and emotionally to find out their motive for existing. Then workers would destroy whomever they were discussing at that time, rip them to shreds like a dishrag that is chopped and sliced up by a garbage disposal. Especially if that person had allowed himself or herself to get caught doing something that was forbidden, like dating someone's husband, or cheating, or not documenting their time when signing in and out appropriately to handle their personal affairs. Some of the workers were known for using the company and taking advantage of the flexible schedule.

Others were becoming bolder in leaving to pay their bills or meet doctors' appointments rather than working to earn their pay. Many of the workers would just leave and pretend to be in the field seeing clients without realizing that the supervisors and everyone else knew that when they had left the job, their hair was a mess—matted down and without curls—but when they returned, you would have thought they'd just left a professional model shoot, because their heads had been completely pampered and primped by a professional hair stylist.

The staff that was selected to work on the PRIME Grant often gathered to laugh and to discuss conversations about the good ole' days. One conversation that Jerickca could clearly recall was when she walked in the room and the janitor was telling about men having sex with chickens in the south when they couldn't get to a woman. It seemed crazy that educated and intelligent people participated in these off-the-wall conversations, but somehow the questions and answers that would be provoked would be funny and intriguing. Jerickca thought about the conversation on the chickens and why any man in his right mind would put his penis in a chicken. The janitor had responded. "Because it's hot and that's why men are so crazy about sex, hot holes for long poles." Jerickca just sort of smiled and walked out of the room, but she had a serious conversation for her mom who lived on a farm as a child. The chicken story was a little too hard to believe, so when Jerickca met her mom for lunch the next day, she told her about what she had heard. She remembered the conversation so vividly.

Lula Mae was an excellent conversationist. She knew the answer to most questions you asked her, and if she didn't, she would tell you. Jerickca had become a fountain of information passed from her great-grandmother to Lula Mae and down to her. Lula Mae was a woman of sixty who grew up in the Deep South with seven brothers and two sisters. She was kind, gifted, talented, and had many skills. One skill that she had mastered was cooking. She was one of the best cooks in the south.

She had a way with baked turkey, dressing, and sweet potato pies. Her turkey was so moist and tender, it would just fall off the bone. When visitors sat at her table to eat, as they tasted each item on their plate, they would hum and pat their feet while responding, "This is so good." Everybody who knew her was impressed and spent hours crying on her shoulders and many more got first-hand counseling information. People would travel miles to eat her good cooking or just to get counseling for a problem too difficult for them to handle. Although she was not educated academically, she was a brilliant thinker, seamstress, storyteller, homemaker, and listener. So it wasn't unusual to find Jerickca probing her mother's mind.

At Joe's Crab Shack that day, Jerickca told Lula Mae what she had heard at work about the chickens.

"Mama," Jerickca said, unsure whether she should have asked the question or whether it would make her look stupid, "Have you ever heard of a man having sex with a chicken?"

Lula Mae's eyes widened and she cocked her head to the side. Finally, she flashed her warm smile and said, "'Course I have. Remember I grew up on a farm. I remember one day my oldest brother Gerald was in the barn feeding the animals when I went to tell him that MuDear wanted him. After he went to talk to her, I didn't see him for a while. I was out playing when he first called my name and I went to look for him. I found him in the car, holding a chicken. He handed the dead chicken to me and told me to get another one and I took it to him. Later I saw him walking with the dead chicken and I asked my brother Sweet T, what he was doing to those chickens and he said that he was poking them. Back then, the boys said poking when they were talking about sex. So yes, I believe that the chicken story is true, though I never saw it directly," she said with a wide smile. "It could all be a myth but anyway, who told you about the chicken?"

"The janitor was discussing it on break with the workers and there was a big disagreement as to whether the story could be true." Jerickca said.

"You can never tell what is true or not but I believe that chicken story with all my heart," Lula Mae said with a low chuckle.

Although the Department of Adolescents and Children Resources had over two hundred employees, the social workers ruled the office. They were the sharpest and smartest group of people assembled in one company. With vast talents and skills, whatever they touched became gold, whatever they said was right, and whatever they did was seen in the most positive light. At least that was what many of the staff at the department thought. These twenty social workers were outstanding employees, and although brilliant and mostly positive, each carried his own baggage. Some of them were as tight as a baby swaddled securely in a warm blanket.

They were Megan, Phoenix, Patches, and Denver. Their supervisor, Jerickca, shared a special place in their hearts, because she was as cool as a summer's breeze in hot Arizona. She was smart, cute, and passionate about her work, and they loved her because she was always in their corner. No matter how bad or difficult they made things, Jerickca always found a way to justify their behavior without them having to suffer dire consequences for their actions.

The Applicants

Chapter 2

"Good morning. Thank you for calling the Department of Adolescent and Children Resources. This is Karen speaking. May I help you?"

"Hello. May I please speak to Mrs. Jerickca Parker?"

"I'm sorry, Ms. Parker is not available at the moment, but if …" Before Karen could finish what she was saying, she was rudely interrupted by Megan.

"Do you know what time she will be in?" Megan said as if she was upset.

"No, but as I was saying …" Interrupted again by the caller, Karen was trying hard to maintain her professionalism.

"I sent my resume and I have not heard anything. Do you know if she received it?"

"What is your name?"

"Megan."

"I don't recall that name, but if you leave your first and last name, I will leave her a message and I'm sure she will get in touch with you."

Karen moved the phone away from her ear as Megan slammed it hard back into its cradle. "I can't believe these people," she said to no one in particular. *Luckily, she didn't leave her full name because I would definitely tell Ms. Parker how she acted on the phone and she wouldn't give her the time of day*, she thought.

Megan picked up the phone and called her friend Cynthia. "Girl, I don't know why I'm even looking for a job 'cause I certainly don't need the money. I don't even have to work—you know what I mean?"

Cynthia just laughed at Megan. Although Megan irritated the hell out of her, Cynthia stayed in touch with her because she was the kind of person who you stayed one step ahead of, and if you didn't she would eat your butt alive. Cynthia would rather talk to her any day than become Megan's next target. When Megan focused on getting revenge, an ugly situation arose, one that you would rather not deal with. So most people just tolerated her.

"Did you mail your resume?" asked Cynthia.

"Hell yeah, I mailed that baby three weeks ago and I know she will call me because I probably have more experience than any of the people who are applying. I know that she will call eventually, but I have more things to do than to sit here waiting on some woman with an ugly name like Jerickca to call me."

"Girl, you know you ain't got no sense. Why you want to make fun of that woman's name? I think it's a strong name. It's cool." Cynthia laughed.

"You would think some shit like that. That heifer probably looks like a dude. Where you get a name like Jerickca from anyway? Some dude named Jeri?"

"You'd better not let her hear you say that," Cynthia stated.

"Why? What the bitch gone do? She ain't all that. You must know her or something?"

Cynthia wanted to get off the phone. This was a person she didn't like anyway. Why was she allowing this woman to invade her space and mess with her Christianity? Cynthia decided to get off the phone as quickly as she could. "Girl, I met her once. She seemed nice."

"What was she wearing? Did she have on designer clothes or

what?"

"I don't remember, but she was attractive."

"How you know? That last dude you went out with look like a bulldog in the face."

"Somebody's ringing my doorbell. I'll get with you later." Cynthia slammed the phone down. That woman really irked her and she would have to get her a caller identification box because she was not going to allow her to talk to her like that ever again. It was over with Megan. She meant it this time. That girl didn't respect anybody.

Out of all the staff that Ms. Parker would hire, Megan would become the leader of the pack. Tall and slim with long straight hair, she was beautiful and she knew it. Her hair was the color of copper with thin blond streaks. It looked so natural, as if the sun had changed her hair while she basked in it to give her skin a dark bronze tone. She was a medium caramel color before the powerful sunrays that tanned her skin to a bronze brown tone touched her. She had light hazel eyes and she walked with a strut. Everyone knew when she entered a room. Always the one dressed for success, she adorned herself in the most beautiful jewelry, each piece matching her designer garments carefully from necklace to earrings.

Megan was meticulous about fashions and was quick to criticize those who didn't meet her standards. Even though she was bitchy and talked too much, everyone who knew her was impressed with her stylish clothes. Whenever anyone met her, they would be in awe of her beauty, but especially her clothing. Thinking she was the boss, they would greet her as if she was Princess Diana and they were her loyal servants. Widowed without children, she looked as young as thirty but was all of forty-four years old. Her only wish in life was to be with a man who loved her and wasn't afraid to show it.

Megan did not have a Bachelor's degree in Social Work, but she had over twenty years of experience working as a social worker with other state agencies. Her main theme in life was to save her clients, because they simply needed her help to save them from their pitiful lives. She had to help them to become someone of importance, because if she didn't, who would? After all, she felt that she was the best social worker in a five hundred-mile radius. It would only be a small gesture to help someone else change his or her pitiful life to become better. Always the one to exaggerate her relationship with her clients, she made it seem as if they couldn't live without her daily intervention. She was the only one who could guide them through their problems and stop them from merely existing, because she would give them hope. In a way, her clients acted as though they couldn't live without her constant guidance. They wanted Megan's looks, money, and cars. Megan sported around in a cold black 2000 Jaguar. When she tired of that, she simply backed out of her garage in her white Range Rover, kindly given to her by her late husband, Richard, who had been a trial judge.

Richard lacked the ability to verbally tell Megan he loved her, because he never had a role model to teach him to express his feelings. His father and mother both died when he was a toddler. A mean aunt who never showed emotions raised him. He promised himself that his family would always know his love through his kind deeds. He tried to show his wife how much he loved her by purchasing her anything that money could buy. Before he died, he made sure that she was well cared for, by leaving her several large insurance policies.

Although she could easily have stayed home rather than go to some dreary job, she preferred to work. Otherwise, who would see all the fine things that she had purchased? She needed to hear people say, on a daily basis, how pretty she was and to compliment on her coordinated and beautiful clothes. Megan couldn't get enough accolades throughout the day because she never felt special at home. She had given Richard almost twenty-two years, all without a hint of heated passion. Sure, he had bought her everything, but all she'd wanted was her husband to whisper words of love to her.

For love, she would be willing to give up her Chanel suits and her 300 pairs of designer shoes by Gucci, Coach, Kenneth Cole, and others. With love, Megan wouldn't have time to embarrass or malign others; she would be too busy with her lover, if she had one. Megan's lifetime goal was to represent. She had to be the best dresser, worker, and lover. She would do anything to be the top dog—then sabotage her-co-workers.

Chapter 3

Phoenix was sitting around the table talking to her mom. "Mom, when I graduate from college, my life is going to be totally different from the way it is now. You have worked so hard, and what did it get you? Nothing but tired feet and gray hair. Not me! I want to see the world and go places I have never been and buy things without worrying about the cost."

Barbara looked at her daughter and feared for her. Phoenix had always wanted more than she could afford to obtain for her on her meager salary as a nurse's aide. She was the type of girl whose taste was far more sophisticated than Ms. Manners (the national expert on etiquette) and way out of reach for her fantasizing daughter. She would get her little butt in trouble if she didn't change her ways.

"Honey, Mama has told you about letting your eyes get you in trouble. You shouldn't think of life in terms of material things. Life has so much more to offer like friendship and spiritual relationships, love of family and a true love of your own. Wanting to have the best in life is fine, but you don't have to sacrifice your values and beliefs."

"Mama you act like I'm going to steal something," Phoenix said as if she was agitated.

"Phoenix, don't think I'm stupid. I know that you have been seeing that bigheaded, no-good boy, Quincy. I know that he slings dope."

"I've never seen it. He's never done that stuff around me. What I don't know can't hurt me."

Barbara shook her head slowly and said, "You can't play with fire and don't get burned. Everybody on this block knows that your boyfriend sells drugs. That stuff is breaking up families and causing people to die because of territorial issues. They are fighting over drugs and trying to stop each other from getting paid. If you are taking his money he will definitely want something in return."

"Mama, I'm not accepting anything from Quincy."

"Stop lying. Don't you think I see the expensive things that you are wearing? Who bought them? I didn't, and you certainly did not. So stop playing games and give that stuff back to that boy. I mean it girl. Don't let me see anything else come into this house that I didn't buy."

Phoenix sat at her country oak-styled kitchen table remembering that particular conversation with her mom. That's how conversations always went in the house between Phoenix and her mom. But Phoenix always had other plans. She wanted things by any means necessary. This was her first rule of prevention from being broke to dating a drug dealer. She would just figure out a way to sneak her new clothes into the house.

Phoenix was short and petite. She had a very large and toothy smile. Her teeth were perfectly even and very white. Her hair was of a medium length and worn in a mushroom or flip. Most people would say that the texture of her hair was good, meaning it did not need a permanent or chemical to straighten it. She never used chemicals to get her bouncy and controlled look. She, too, was professional and wore the latest designer styles. She and Megan were the tightest of the four. Each of their attire balanced the other's, and if Phoenix wore the wrong shirt with a suit, Megan was sure to scold her.

Phoenix was married and she had an infant daughter. Always the one who wanted to be seen with the richest and smartest, she was known as a "wannabe." This was a person who only associated with those who had made it or who everyone knew would achieve success eventually. These individuals had one noticeable asset: money. They either were born with money or had new money from investments. It didn't really matter so much how they got the money as long as they had it.

She felt that old money was better than new money because it came from an inheritance or from a trust fund. New money meant the person had lucked up on a good investment or made money by being a benefactor from someone's insurance policy. One main difference between the two types of money was how the owners acted. People who had old money were used to the lifestyle they had and would not run and spend the money unwisely, but folks who caught a break in getting money usually blew it quickly.

Although Phoenix was sweet and approachable, she had two major downfalls. One was the way she whined and kissed up to the supervisor to get ahead, and the other was that she was unhappy with her life and current financial status but unwilling to improve her situations through personal growth and development.

She was willing to kiss ass to move to the top. No butt was too bitter to pucker up to. If she couldn't make it on her looks and ability, she would get to the top the best way she could. She was sure of one thing, and that was that she would definitely reach the highest peak of any and all mountains and valleys that she pursued, one peak at a time.

Phoenix had a wild past. A product of a broken home, she had lived with her mother and three brothers in the Pruitt-Igo Housing Projects located in St. Louis, Missouri. Although the area she lived in was considered one of the worst places a person could ever live, it was not too far from the beautiful riverfront that not only housed quaint restaurants and other shops, but also the colossal Arch. When tourists visited St. Louis, they had to visit the Arch, one of the most impressive structures in the country.

Where Phoenix came from was nothing compared to the riverfront, which showcased so much beauty unlike her area. Her only view was of tall high-rises, with alive and dead rats and trash flung all through the halls, as well as human urine and feces. It was the lowest of the low in public housing. Living in some of the apartments was as bad as living on the streets under an abandoned, broken-down, wet, and rat-infested terminal. The murder rate in this area was higher than in all of St. Louis. There were only three ways out of this hellhole: making good money (legally or illegally), dying or seeing the place blown to pieces by the city, and being relocated to another complex.

Although the later avenue was taken, it couldn't have been soon enough. So when the city decided to blow up the dilapidated building and relocate its residents, it couldn't have happened soon enough for Phoenix. She decided she wanted better for herself and she wanted to show all the naysayers in her life that she could be anything she wanted.

Money had been tight for Phoenix and her family. Her mother Barbara worked as a nurse's aide in a local hospital. Barely able to make ends meet, oftentimes she and Phoenix would have to go to the food pantry so that the family could eat throughout the month. This only made Phoenix more determined to be someone who had made it in life. To be able to successfully "represent," her only hope would be education. After applying to several colleges, she was accepted at Clark Atlanta University. After completing many applications to get financial aid, she finally received two grants for minorities with special needs. Phoenix never dreamed that she would attend college, because she had found high school too difficult. No one believed that she was capable of going to college, and whenever she mentioned it, her so-called friends and relatives would laugh at her. They spent so much time putting her down because she came from the projects. She wanted to prove to the world that she was capable of being somebody. To accomplish her goals of obtaining a higher education, she did what she had to do to make good grades.

She made friends with Deborah Dennison, a future political

science major with a minor in sociology and one of the smartest girls in the whole school. She was also boring and unpopular. Deborah needed Phoenix as much as Phoenix needed her to reach her goals, which was to be accepted by the cool crowd. Deborah wanted to be popular and liked by everyone.

For Phoenix, enrolling in a good college was one sure fire way to meet a good college boy who was from parents who had old money, the very best kind one could have, because it would last. In the meantime, to dress the part of someone who had something, she dated Quincy because he had the money to buy her the kind of clothes that she could only dream of having as her own. To keep the expensive toys and trinkets coming, she became his love slave. Whatever it took to sexually satisfy him, she did it. Every time Quincy touched her, she felt nauseated. So many times, he did things that disgusted her and made her feel little. She could never confide to anyone about the time he took her from the behind forcing his penis in her anus. She fainted because the pain was atrocious.

When she returned to consciousness, he was lovingly kissing her and apologizing. To make up for the brutal act towards her he took her shopping and bought her several Ralph Lauren suits and her first Chanel purse. This made her forget how cruel he had been to her. Quincy knew how to please her, because he understood where she had come from. She had long ago confided in him about her childhood and how poor her family was.

She stayed with him for six long years because he could provide her with beautiful clothes, money, and a car, like the new Toyota Celica he had bought her. When she stepped into the high school or the college cafeteria in her new expensive clothes, she felt better than the others. She also drew friends to her side because they wanted to wear her clothes, and some just wanted to be in her presence. She learned early that if she wanted to get out of the low-income projects, she would have to meet someone with money. To date someone of that caliber and attract that kind of money, she needed to look like money.

Phoenix was very lucky because "her girl," Deborah, helped her all through high school by giving her answers to major tests that were critical for her to attend college. Deborah continued to help Phoenix even in college. Phoenix and Deborah attended the same college. Phoenix received much encouragement from the staff and support from her new friends, including the fine brothers who attended Moorehouse, whom she had met along the way. It took her five years of sweat and pain and manipulation to meet the graduation requirements for a degree in Social Work.

It had been years since she talked to Deborah. She could vividly remember their last conversation. Phoenix asked Deborah to help her on a test that would determine whether she graduated one semester earlier. She called her at her dormitory, and when Deborah picked up the phone, she asked her to sit next to her so that she would have a clear view on her test paper.

"Are you crazy?" There is absolutely no way that I'm risking being kicked out of school. If you need help, Phoenix, go over to the tutoring center and they will help you with your weak areas. I have already done all I can. You know I don't mind helping you, but I will never allow you to cheat off my paper, risking our education."

"You know what? You ain't shit. If it weren't for me, you wouldn't have any friends. I'm the reason people tolerated your boring ass. All I asked you to do was help me, and you can't even do that." Phoenix screamed into the phone.

"I have helped you throughout the past four years. I refuse to jeopardize my education. I have spent hours on hours with you, and if you haven't learned it by now, it's already too late. So if you are the reason that I have friends, then I don't need them, and I certainly don't need you!" Deborah responded.

She was hurt but knew that she would get through this problem. With that, Phoenix heard a loud dial tone. It was the wrong thing to do, because without Deborah, she ended up doing an extra year. She often felt she should call and apologize, but that was water under the bridge now.

Phoenix knew that she needed to get a Master's degree to get a better paying job in the field, but hell she could barely get the Bachelor's, so there was no way she was going back to school. She would have to keep trying to move up on her present job to get to the top of her field. The only way to do this would be to lie and cheat, because she lacked the skills to move higher into management. To make sure she achieved her goals of being financially successful, she went as low as to entice a prominent man from his friends and business by trying to make him fall in love with her.

Chapter 4

"What the hell are the women staring at? I don't have time for that shit now, Patches mumbled to himself."

Patches walked around the Edward Jones Dome with his hands in his pockets. He was excited because his football team at Hazelwood East was number one. Every game they played, they won hands down. Now they were at the finals, preparing to play for the championship. Everything was going just the way he had planned. His players continued to impress him, and he continued to impress the women. He saw the women staring and watching his every move. Usually, he liked the feeling he received when the ladies openly admired him. However, now he had a game to play, and their stares were a nuisance.

Patches was nervous. He was biting his nails down to the stubs. He was trying to be cool about it, but on the outside he showed courage. Yet inside, right there in the center of his chest, his heart beat a slow tune, as if Freddy Kruger was waiting in the woods to tear out his soul. He was frightened, trying hard to be in control. Yet Patches walked around the football stadium as if he owned it. He had the sway when he walked. He wouldn't let anyone see how nervous he was. Nobody could see him sweat.

Finally, James, the running back, secured a touchdown. Patches almost lost control because he was so excited. He was smiling so hard, you would have thought he was doing a toothpaste commercial. He was happy because they were winning by one touchdown.

Finally, they were in the last quarter and had only two minutes left to play. If the team continued to carry the football down the field while allowing the clock to run out, this game would be over and they would be the champs. As the quarterback reared back to find a target to throw the ball, he spotted Cecil, one of the fastest running backs in the city, and made immediate contact. The people in the stand were on their feet, screaming, "Run, Cecil! Run!" Patches stood up and watched. He couldn't move. His feet felt like lead, too heavy to move. Just as they won, he looked up and saw Stacey. She was a local reporter and she was gorgeous. He smiled at her and ran over to congratulate the players. They all headed to the locker room.

"You boys played a great game. Great job! What did I tell you all? Practice! Practice and play ball, and the feeling you get is beautiful, just beautiful. Teamwork makes great plays. I'm so happy I could kiss all ya'll. Shower and celebrate, but do it safe," he said as he walked away, doing a little happy dance.

"Coach, how you gonna play that?" asked Rodney, the quarterback.

"I'm 'a play like you play at home in the bed. Got that young boy?"

"Yeah, I got it like that," Rodney said as he gave his teammate a dap.

"Be safe, brothers. The assistant coaches are going back to the school with you. As I told you all earlier, I have something to do and I will see you guys on Monday. I'm out." Patches walked out of the stadium and bumped into the reporter.

"Hi, I'm Stacey," she said, reaching out to shake his hand.

Looking at her as if he could take her and lick her like a Popsicle, he smiled and took her hand. "I know who you are."

"You want to get together tonight?" she asked with a sexy look that penetrated his heart and made his penis feel a slow rise.

"Your place or mine?" asked Patches afraid that he was being played.

"Mine, of course." She took him by the hand and asked,

"Where's your car?"

She followed him and asked Patches to take her to her car, parked by the Embassy Suites Hotel. They said little while they rode. He was scared to say something, fearing that she might change her mind. Stacy sat quietly hoping he wouldn't say anything to make her change her mind. She had seen him at many of the games while on assignment as a general reporter. Not ready for a serious relationship, she just wanted to taste his sweetness with her moist tongue.

When they reached her car, she whispered, "Follow me."

How lucky could a brother get? This girl was beautiful; she had long thick hair that hung down her back, with cinnamon colored skin that was as smooth as a Lexus rolling down the street. He saw her nightly on TV. *Damn! How lucky could one man be?* Patches thought again to himself.

At her apartment, he barely looked around at his surroundings. They weren't important, anyway. He wanted to feel her body on his before the mood changed. Stacey went into the bathroom and turned on the shower. Calling Patches to the shower he stripped out of his clothes and entered. She was absolutely gorgeous, with flawless skin. He took the soap and created suds all over her body. He grabbed her and hungrily kissed her. She kissed him back, and then they did the famous dance. He kissed every part of her body as she moaned and arched her back toward the wall.

He wanted badly to penetrate her incredible body but didn't have any protection in the shower. So instead, he dropped to his knees and began the act of draining out her warm vagina juices by first sucking and then licking and lightly thrusting his tongue in her hidden area. She was gorgeous and he couldn't believe that he was having this opportunity to be this intimate with one of the most coveted reporters in the St. Louis area.

Finally, they moved to the bedroom. She was breathless, almost weak. He lifted her up into his arms and carried her to the bed, laid her down gently on her back and finished feasting on her weak and satisfied body. He felt her heart race and her moans increase, and slowly he reached for his pants and took out a condom. Sliding it on he entered her slowly as if he never wanted it to end, thinking that nobody would believe that he was with Stacey. He thrust her eagerly. It felt so good. They rocked and rolled until both were sweaty with stimulation. Stacey was raking her nails down his back, panting and moaning. She was sucking on his earlobe and moving her hips in a figure eight form. He was trying to hold back but it felt so good between her legs. She grabbed his butt, squeezed the cheeks together, and whimpered, "I'm coming." He could feel the heat of her body as her heart raced, she screamed again that she was having multiple orgasms and he could not hold himself any longer, he let himself explode.

"Damn! Damn! Damn!" he moaned.

"That was so good," Stacey whispered.

Patches lay back ready to enjoy the rest of the night when suddenly Stacey thanked him for the great sex and asked him to leave. This shocked him. *How could a woman this fine seek him out, fuck him into illusions, and then say you can leave?* he thought. Those were his damn words. This was fucking unbelievable.

"What do you mean, I can leave?"

"I'm finished with you. Get your clothes on and forget my address and name." Stacey stood up, handed him his clothes, and dared him with an evil look in her eyes not to make another move unless it was out her door.

Patches slid into his pants, put on his shirt and shoes and asked, "Stacey did I do something wrong?"

"Leave now," she hissed with a somewhat raised voice. "No

questions just leave my house."

"This shit is unbelievable. You fuck my brains and common sense out of my damn head and then you send me on my way. What kind of trick are you?"

"The same kind you are. Leave now before I call the cops."

"Fuck you bitch!" Patches walked out the door feeling used and dirty. He was used to getting any woman that he wanted, but millions watched this beautiful lady daily and she was a damn whore. She picked up men from games and probably bars too, and then she rode their dicks into oblivion just to send them packing. He laughed as he walked to his car. Turning to her, he screamed, "You fucking freak!"

"Takes one to fuck one," she said, right before she slammed and doubled locked the door. "Forget you ever met me."

This was an unusual event for Patches. Women never sent him packing. After all, he had something else planned tonight. He didn't have to be with her. He was the one that was always finding vulnerable women that he could fuck one night and come back to months later to tap that ass again for old time's sake. Things didn't happen like that to him. After all, he was Patches. He was extremely handsome, about five feet eight inches tall, and had a very muscular and tight body. He had gorgeous hazel eyes and the prettiest teeth that sort of beckoned you to kiss his smooth, lovable lips. He was also noted for his tight butt, because it was the perfect size for grabbing and holding. Patches knew that he was good looking and used his appearance to bed as many women as he could find. Single, his motto was "If you are sexy and fine, you could be mine, all mine." He lived up to his word.

His friends in the backroom could not understand the hold he seemed to have on women. Once he bedded them, they always came back for more. This intrigued more than his clique; Jerickca was beginning to notice how attractive he was. Especially since the meeting she had had with two of her employees who cried on her shoulders about his sexual abilities and how they couldn't get over him. *What did he do to those women?* she thought.

It was hard for Patches to pass a mirror without admiring himself. Patches was impressed with the face that stared back at him. As he would primp in the mirror, he always smiled. He couldn't believe the reflection that stared back at him. Sometimes Patches couldn't stand himself because he was so fine. He had the biggest broad shoulders that Jerickca had seen in a long time. *Short in stature but a real good looker,* he thought to himself with a smile as he prepared himself to meet Ms. Parker.

As he checked his appearance before going on his interview, he felt proud of himself. He looked great in his black Cerretti suit and white tuxedo, Van Heusan shirt, looking like he was one of the most popular African-American male models on the cover of GQ magazine. Patches said out loud, "Tyson don't have a thing on me." He felt satisfied. Patches was on cloud nine, because finally he was doing something with his life that made him feel good. "No," he said, "I feel damn good. Shit! How you like me now, dog?" He said it as if he were talking to someone in the room.

But he was alone. Yet, he was not really alone, because as an only child, he loved having time to himself; this was the way he found his peace away from all the woman he was dating.

Patches brushed the imaginary lint off his suit. He brushed from the front of his thighs down toward the knee. He did this on both sides, from left to right, finally turning to admire his backside. Checking to make sure that his black snakeskin boots completed his outfit, he lifted his leg to brush away any hint of dust from the hem of his pants. He felt and looked great. Patches was fine. He knew this all along. After all, even if he didn't think he was fine, someone else would surely tell him. They always did. Wherever Patches went, he was always noticed by the women and by all the jealous men who hated him. They didn't really hate him but they hated the fact that when he was in the room with them, he was the main attraction. The men around him would fade into the background like dreary paint hidden behind gorgeous wallpaper.

McNary was his given name, but everyone in his family called him Patches. McNary McAfee always stood out. When he was born, his mother looked at his light hazel eyes and wavy, dark, sandy hair and whispered, "You are going to break the women's hearts." She named him McNary after his dad, who was even better looking. His mother, Sinclair, nicknamed him Patches because once she told his dad, McNary McAfee Sr., that she was pregnant with his first child, he returned home immediately.

McNary Sr. had left his expecting wife for another woman. He told her he was just tired of the riffraff. No longer interested in Sinclair, he left their home with her best friend, CeCelia. He never called or visited her again until three months later, when she located him to tell him about her condition.

McNary Sr. had felt trapped in an unhappy marriage until he found out his wife was pregnant. He wanted a son so much that he decided to make his marriage work. McNary Jr.'s birth patched their troubled marriage back together, and they never broke up or separated again. Sinclair loved Patches because his premature entry into the world sealed her love for her husband, and she forgave him for running off with her old friend.

Patches was her love child, a child that she had wanted with all her heart, with or without the father. So whatever Patches wanted, he got. No matter what he did wrong, he was forgiven. From the time he was a small baby to when he became a grown man, Patches had the world in his hands, but all he wanted were the women.

After all, he was a ladies' man, only thinking about what he could gain and not how he had left each of his women brokenhearted and searching for love. The women he dated were supposed to be self-respecting and educated, and they couldn't pick out a scam artist if you pointed him out and walked up to his face. They were naïve and unsuspecting young women who he left clinging, crying, and pleading for one more chance to show him how much they loved him.

His intentions weren't to leave them broken-hearted and broken up, but he wanted to get his groove on. After all, didn't statisticians report that there were at least ten women for every man? Well, Patches wanted all of his ten, and he got them. He got them all, "by any means necessary." He didn't mean to leave them hurt. He just thought that he could bang them and leave. They were the ones who paged him all through the night, begging him to come back.

In most cases, he was even truthful with them, explaining to them that he didn't want a serious relationship, but the women thought that with the twitch of their ass and the wiggle of their hips, would keep him coming back to them. Many of his conquests felt they could change him to become the marrying type. But after every hit of sexual activity, it made him care less for them. There just weren't any challenges with most women. Most were so desperate for a good, employed man they would do anything to please. Clothes, dinners, watches, and other gifts of affections were just a small sample of what those loved-starved women would give to be cradled one night in the arms of a good-looking, single, successful man.

To top it off, he didn't have any responsibilities of children, because he always wore protection. He made sure that no woman would be able to pin an unwanted pregnancy on him. Patches was cautious. One thing he would never do was to mess with another man's wife. It wasn't worth the nuisance. He was a lover, not a fighter.

Patches was a ladies' man, with one positive thing going for him: he was an educated and hard-working social worker. His job was serious business to him. He would never consider doing anything to jeopardize it, especially dating a client. He didn't care if they had a perfect twenty-four lead crystal ass—he would never jeopardize his professional ethics to look at a client as anything but a person who needed his help to find resources and assistance to change their life for the better.

His decision to change jobs was because he had made one mistake, and that was to date his co-worker, Pauline. His mother, Sinclair, had warned him never to sleep where he made his bread. But he didn't listen, and now Pauline was spending more company time harassing his ass than earning her pay. She was a good lay but was overbearing and possessive. He couldn't look at another woman without her asking if he needed another neck, because she felt he was stretching the one he had to its limit watching every butt that passed. The only neck he felt he needed was to be at least one hundred miles from her stupid ass. He needed another job as bad as his next lay, and when Mr. Aaron, a friend he had met, told him about a new program he should look into, he immediately upgraded his resume and sent it to Ms. Jerickca Parker.

Chapter 5

Diane picked up the phone to call her daughter. She was getting tired of Denver acting as if she didn't have a problem or concern. She wanted Denver to stand on her own two feet and to feel comfortable deciding to do just that, while continuing to pursue her dreams.

"Hello Mom," said Denver.

"I haven't heard from you in a while. What's going on with you? I sent the application for law school. Did you fill out the paperwork?" Diane rushed through her conversation, afraid she wouldn't be able to get everything in before she made her daughter angry.

"Not yet, Mom. I haven't had the time. I've been writing a grant and trying to find a better paying job."

"Why are you even wasting your time looking for a job? I told you that I would pay your tuition, room, and board. So just complete that application package and mail it today."

"Yes, Ma'am. I'll take care of it today."

Denver hated when her mama made her feel so inadequate. She wanted to please her but was slowly trying to find the courage to go against her strong-willed mother. Her mother was very aggressive. She did everything in her power to achieve at the highest level and wanted her daughter to do the same. But Denver had other plans that she was too afraid to share. She wanted to be the life of the party but she was considered "too weak and meek" by her co-workers. She was seen as a person who lacked good communications skills and had difficulty explaining complex information, even though she could process complicated data.

She was of medium height and wore a size ten dress. She was

very attractive and most men wanted her simply because she was light skinned, or redbone, as they would call her. Her complexion was about three shades lighter than caramel candy and her hair was jet black, worn daily in a feathered bob. She dressed unprofessionally and only wore suits on special occasions. While Friday was the scheduled casual day, every day was casual for her.

Denver's daily attire included Capri pants or blue jeans with jackets or sweaters, depending on the time of the year. Her clothing was not of the designer persuasion; this made Denver feel out of place with the others. Whenever she spent time with her coworkers, she always said the wrong things and felt that they all thought she was stupid. She had decided that she would try to join their high society club by participating more in their office conversations. She knew that she didn't have anything in common with these women but frequently found herself trying to fit in, although she always felt like an outsider. She was indeed a token employee and a token part of the "in" group.

Denver was single, freely dating one married man, and enjoying every single minute she could get to see him. She was suffering from low self-esteem and an uncertainty about who she was and about her relationship with Latham Donovan, a businessman who traveled frequently as a buyer of retail products. Denver had made the ultimate mistake of falling in love with a married man. Even though deep down inside she knew that she would never truly have him, she didn't care, because being with him was better than being without a man.

She could be fun to be around once you got to know her and she felt comfortable with you. But most of the time, she was a major pushover. She would do anything for others, even when it meant sacrificing her beliefs and values. She couldn't say no to anyone. She spent most of her time trying desperately to fit in, to please others. Inwardly, she was not a happy person, because every ounce of her strength was used trying to make sure that no one was angry or disappointed by her endeavors. Denver was too soft-spoken and had a very meek voice. She was not a great communicator, and she spoke in a low tone that showed everyone in listening range that she lacked confidence in herself and her abilities. Her vocal tone was monotonous and dry.

Denver's quiet persona was deceiving because she was a very intelligent young lady. She had excelled in mathematics in high school and went on to college to major in Political Science. She wanted to be a lawyer for her mom's sake but was too timid and meek to even take the LSAT test. She felt that if she were a lawyer, no one would listen to her. So she gave up on obtaining a prominent profession, and she was stuck in a job that she happened to do well.

As the key writer of the PRIME Grant, she was given an opportunity to work with Jerickca Parker. In order for the Department of Adolescents and Children Resources to receive the very important "PRIME Grant" (which stood for Participants Reaching Into More Education), they had to collaborate with other agencies, the primary one being the Department of Human Resources. A smart political move was to employ one of their people, who happened to be Denver. On her last job, she was used mostly to help her supervisor complete budgeting and accounting for their proposals. She was so good at accounting practices and grant writing that Jerickca was trying to develop a job for her in that area.

Denver was allowed to hang with the girls in the back- room because she worked closely with their supervisor; to them it was a way to find out what was happening in the company. If the supervisor thought Denver was special, maybe she was. After all, Jerickca was certainly a hard act to follow. So Denver, who was as mild as an open bottle of hot sauce left unattended on a counter for many months after its expiration date, spent her life trying to please others. Yet she pretended to be a party animal because she thought that's what the girls needed her to be. Whenever her co-workers invited her out, which wasn't often, she would dance the night away, even though most of the time she was uncomfortable in her own skin.

The name Denver came from her mother, Diane. Diane had visited the city of Denver when she and a friend attended the wedding of another close friend. When Diane first stepped her foot in Denver, Colorado, she was impressed. It was so beautiful and so clean. The people that she met were very friendly, although she had previously heard that Denver was one of the most prejudiced places in the world. On this trip, she didn't see anything like that.

Diane was a very independent and complex person. She would often say that she needed a man, but when given the opportunity, she always seemed to make the man feel inept. She didn't want them to pull out her chair, nor to open a door for her. As a matter of fact, given the chance, she would do all those things for the man. She just felt manly most of the time—not gay or homosexual, but self-reliant. She didn't need a man to do but one thing for her, and that was to make her have an orgasm at least three times a week or anytime she felt like she wanted one.

Other than that, she was too busy to fall in love because it was too dangerous. Diane truly felt that if a man knew that you loved him, he would simply walk all over you. Not her! Never would she allow that to happen, because she would not give her heart to anyone, not even Denver's dad, whom she left when her daughter was a toddler.

Denver was almost a carbon copy of her mother in the looks department, but their personality traits were totally different. Diane was bold and sassy and Denver was very timid and unsure of herself. Both were of medium height and wore the same dress size. They were very attractive and could easily be considered model material but could only do print work because they lacked the height needed to get the assignments.

Their complexions were in the light caramel family, and both had slanted eyes set well upon their very high cheekbones. When they smiled with their small perky lips, you immediately noticed their perfect white teeth. Both had one deep dimple on their left cheek.

Mother and daughter dated frequently, her mother with many men, and Denver with married men. Diane loved playing the field; Denver hated being single. Whenever they dated, Diane left the man broken-hearted and Denver left with a broken heart. Sometimes Denver gave you the feeling that she was very cold emotionally. That was only to hide the uncomfortable, shy and meek person she had become. Those who knew her well understood that it was simply a cover to prevent her from feeling any pain.

When Denver was in high school, she was at the top in her class. It seemed like it was just yesterday that she read her Valedictorian speech. She clearly recalled how she said that she would be a lawyer. Although she could have easily made the grades in law school, it was clear to her that a lawyer she would not make. Research and case-finding would be easy for her, but going into the courtroom to challenge or fight for a client would simply be too much. Denver decided to major in political science and possibly teach on a college level. Even though teaching was her plan, deep in her heart, she didn't want to do that either.

Denver didn't know what she wanted out of life, but she remembered how happy she felt when she was in high school, dreaming of becoming a doctor. She took Political Science because her mother wanted her to become the next Matlock. All she wanted to do was heal people, but knew that would be impossible to achieve since her mother had always glamorized lawyers. She settled for something that would please her mother and not her. This was always how Denver made decisions. If it made Diane happy, then she could have a little happiness of her own, because her mother wouldn't pressure her as she was already following her instructions.

She was good with most technical things and was a master at troubleshooting computer problems. After graduating from college, Denver set out to find a job. It was a difficult task, because she quickly found that there were no top paying jobs in her field without a master's degree. After going back to the social service agency that she had trained at as an intern, she accepted a position as a research technician until a better position became available. Working now as an employee of Ms. Parker, she received extensive work as a writer and limited work as a caseworker.

After being notified that they had received a huge grant for which Denver had researched all statistical data and co-written the application, her immediate supervisor decided that she should benefit by being one of the first to apply for a position.

Denver had written in the proposal that their agency would collaborate with another social service agency by allowing them to case manage those clients who would enroll in the program. The goal of the project was to assist clients in becoming economically self-sufficient. Denver's supervisor had contacted Jerickca Denise Parker at the Department of Adolescent and Children Resources and asked her to be the agency in collaboration. Jerickca was definitely excited and didn't mind that she would have to hire Denver Anderson, who had no training in social work, but was very skilled in other areas. Although Jerickca would have to pay Denver a very good salary, it didn't matter because she would get her money back by putting Denver on her grant-writing team. Denver would be the youngest worker at the Department of Adolescent and Children Resources. Her biggest challenge would be trying desperately to fit in with the other workers.

Chapter 6

"Good morning, Anthony," Jerickca said while reaching to kiss him on his lips.

"Morning," Anthony replied.

"Come here, sweetheart, and give me a little something for breakfast," Jerickca said while gently rubbing Anthony's right nipple.

Taking Jerickca's hand and moving it off his chest Anthony responded, "I don't have time for that right now. I have to get going," he said while rising out of the bed.

"Dang! I just wanted a little bit, it wouldn't take long."

"Jerickca, I have a very important meeting and I told you that I don't like morning sex unless I don't have anything to do. Sex in the morning drains me and I have too much work today to start my day exhausted."

"Keep your shit to yourself then. I remember some time ago you didn't seem to have a problem. But go on to your little meeting." Jerickca jumped up and went into her personal bathroom to shower. Pushing the door closed, she looked at herself in the long mirror.

Jerickca was about 5 feet 4 inches tall. Although she was almost two hundred pounds, she was built. "I do need to lose some weight," she said. "Maybe that's why Anthony didn't want to make love this morning. Just maybe I'm losing my ability to turn him on because I've gained so much weight. I'm going to go on a diet," she said while slowing turning around and looking at herself in the mirror.

Although, her measurements were in equal increments, and

she looked as if she could easily fit into a fourteen, the sixteen she wore was now too tight. Most people felt that she could be a plus size model because she was a great dresser and knew how to impress with her clothes and hair, which she wore in a variety of the latest styled braids; sometimes she even wore them in a way that made it difficult to distinguish whether or not she actually had them in her hair. Jerickca couldn't imagine life without her braids. She was sure to wear only professional styles and would stay at her braider's house long hours to make sure they were always neat and professional.

Her braids had to be fresh with no new growth sticking out. Jerickca was also known for paying top dollars for her hairstyles, returning every four to six weeks to get a touch-up. She loved the variety you could get from wearing braids, often changing them into pixies singles, pinch, bobs, and others.

Jerickca had a beautiful personality. She was fair to all and would give her last dollar to help someone in need. She was fun-loving and sensitive. She would cry at movies, whether they were happy or sad. At work, she was considered a hard worker who played no games and expected paperwork to be complete and accurate. She was a good supervisor who wanted everything to be perfect at work and even at home with her family. Married to a pleasant and handsome man, she had one daughter who was twelve years old.

Jerickca was very lucky, because she had achieved so many of her childhood dreams: the house, beautiful cars, and plenty of hard cash. Her husband was president of his own computer firm, and he had invested his money well. Anthony and Jerickca were very private about their money and refrained from letting people know their true financial worth.

It took all she had to disguise her material things by pretending to be broke, even though she had an excessive taste for nice things. To look the part of an executive, she drove a nice car and wore beautiful suits. Other than that, she never wore jewelry or flashed any money. She never carried money around, and this gave the impression that she lacked money. This was a rule of safety for her. Jerickca and Anthony looked as if all their money was spent on cars and clothes, because they both dressed well and never entertained in their home.

They were considered a mystery couple, basically trying to keep to themselves. The Parkers had learned early in their marriage that if people thought for one minute that you had money, they wouldn't lift a finger to support you. She had lost many friends and potential promotions because people had made unkind and unsupported statements about them not needing anything. Yet with all the money and power she had, Jerickca was very unhappy.

She wanted to experience a perfect love. To her, that meant that Anthony would need to romance her the way he used to with wet kisses, hand holding, and sex talk. She loved when he talked to her during sex, and now he had become this perfectionist who never seemed to stray out of that role, not even to please his wife.

Jerickca was from a large family. She had two brothers and six sisters whom she loved dearly. They were also the source of her anxiety, because each of her siblings depended on her for support, both emotionally and financially. This really bothered her, because she needed her siblings to be more self-sufficient, rather than depending on her for all their needs. Jerickca had such a hard time trying to remove herself from their daily problems. One brother and one sister were on drugs, another brother was having marital problems, and another sister ignored her problems and just lived in a world that was not closely or remotely anything like this world. She made her own rules, laughed at her own jokes, and seemed to be very successful and happy.

Yet, Jerickca was worried about her extended family. It always seemed that something was wrong in her family. They couldn't seem to handle their problems without her input and intervention methods. Jerickca suffered because it was becoming more and more difficult to balance her own life while trying to help her brothers and sisters. She was tired because worrying kept her from resting. She was physically and emotionally drained. Lacking sleep during the night and stressed-out during the day, she decided to let them work out their own problems. No more money would she give out to her brother Jeremy so that he could just pass it to the drug dealer.

Another problem Jerickca had was that she wished she could have a good time, but she did not know how to do that without losing her Christianity. She was confused because she really didn't know how to enjoy life the way a Christian was supposed to. She wanted to serve God freely with commitment but found it difficult to do so because she was afraid that she was treading in places that would not be acceptable to her God. She had been taught that God didn't go into clubs and other places that were unacceptable to him, and this scared her, because she didn't want to go anywhere without God's protection of love and grace. She spent many of her weekends reading and imagining a fabulous life, rather than trying to enjoy what life had to offer. Without a real social life, she had no outlet, and this left her frustrated.

She had always been considered a good person, with parents who had raised their children strictly and close to the church. Her friends felt that she had missed out on a lot because she had married straight out of college, having dated only one other guy. Her relationship with her first boyfriend lasted from the age of thirteen to nineteen. Married since she was twenty, she was celebrating sixteen years of marriage, and she was just thirty-six years old.

Good friends were important to Jerickca. Without her best friends, Spencer and Deborah, she would be lost. Jerickca spent most of her free time with her girls, shopping, traveling, and pampering themselves. She rarely went to clubs because her conscious would not allow it. To her, that was like straddling the fence between being a good Christian or a party animal. It made her happy to see the four friends get together after work to have fun while bonding more closely, especially this group. The staff were known for going over and beyond their regular duties to assure success on the job.

Jerickca's staff were hard workers who loved to party and were sought out by other co-workers who wanted to hang out with them just to be seen as their friends at parties so they could get invitations to popular affairs. The four friends wore their popularity on their shoulders with pride and grace. Just to be invited to go somewhere with the group was a sign that you had made it and were considered a member of the "A" club.

Jerickca was an honorary member to the club and was often invited to parties with the group but declined because of work and religious ethics. She didn't want to be seen as a supervisor who mixed pleasure with business. She had already experienced that on more than one occasion when Megan and Phoenix couldn't separate business from something personal with her.

Once Jerickca walked in the backroom and found Megan and Phoenix laughing and talking about some guys they had met. Jerickca sat down and spent some quality time with her staff. They joked, and Jerickca became a member of their elite club. After that day, Phoenix and Megan would come and eat lunch with her sometimes. Twice after work she went shopping with the two of them. She invited Denver, Patches, Precious, Candy, and several other staff members, but they declined. She didn't want her staff to think that she had a special relationship with anyone.

Unfortunately, they both went back to work and acted as though they were best buds, exaggerating and telling others about their so-called activities with the supervisor after work hours. Phoenix even told Candy, who told Jerickca what she had heard about her spending time with two of her staff on the weekend. Although the staff felt left out, they never said a word, because they truly enjoyed their jobs. Phoenix and Megan were going back on a regular basis, trying to make the rest of the staff feel that they were giving advice to Jerickca and that many of her decisions about them were made by her two favorites.

Jerickca had heard the rumors and tried to tell her staff in many ways that she did not socialize after hours with people from work. She tried hard to show that through her daily relationships. Yet, they believed Megan and Phoenix. Eventually the staff just decided that they would be careful around Jerickca's girls; thus, several key staff, particularly Denver and other social workers throughout the agency, were alienated. No one challenged the authenticity of their statements, so there were never confirmations as to whether she was their friend. Jerickca worked hard to make staff feel that she cared about them all. She really did have their best interests in mind. Whenever the company hosted an activity for the workers, she would attend and spend time with the A group and the rest of the staff without feeling guilty. This way, she was not accused of spending time with the "social workers," because she was with all her staff. When she was around, it was one big happy staff. Everybody, including the A team, had a great time.

Jerickca suffered from panic attacks and the desire to be recognized for her skills, because sometimes she noticed that her subordinates would say anything around her, having become too comfortable. She was mixing a little too much in the backroom. She found herself heading to that area more than twice a day because of the conversation.

She also needed to lose weight badly to feel comfortable with her image. To lose weight Jerickca was filling her body with diet pills and overeating, only to put her fingers down her throat to throw it all back up. As she matured and progressed up the ladder of success, her priorities began to change. She found that money and material possessions meant absolutely nothing without a healthy sense of who you were mentally. Yet she was still doubtful about seeking mental health help because she worried it would somehow end up in her personnel files. She had another fear, and that was that she and Anthony would not be able to regain the passion they once had. When they first started dating, they couldn't keep their hands off each other. Their sex life was fantastic. Anthony was adept at making her reach high levels of orgasmic pleasure. She remembered when she met him. She was inexperienced and had only been with one other man.

Anthony cooked for her and pampered her, complete with candles, wine, and smooth talk. One month after meeting him, she could not hold back her desire for him any longer. He looked so good with his handsome self, and he had the body to match. When he touched her, his fingers set her skin on fire with desire. She could feel her vagina turning into a hot furnace, waiting to be extinguished.

The first time she was with him, he gave her so much pleasure with his tongue that she thought she would have to go the hospital to regain control of her breathing. She had never had an orgasm before, so it scared her yet felt so enjoyable. This confused her, because she couldn't understand how something like a penis and a man's touch could scare you yet give so much pleasure. This was the beginning of a first-rate sex life. After being married for sixteen years, it had finally lost its steam. She was worried that her weight was the reason. Most of the time, he was tired or she was too exhausted after a hard day at the office. There was not much time for sex that included foreplay, passion, and desire. Sex had become Anthony's sleeping pill. He only wanted a quickie, which was to the point, to help him end his day in a peaceful and restful state. She was left very unhappy and unsatisfied.

Chapter 7

Megan picked up the phone to call her old friend Cynthia. "Girl, I haven't heard from you in awhile. What's been happening with you?" she asked.

Cynthia responded, "Nothing much." She didn't want to say too much, because Megan had a knack for gossiping and starting problems, so when she called, it was best to basically listen. After their last conversation, she was being very careful with her words. "Have you heard from Ms. Parker yet?"

"Not yet. But she'll call soon. You know I got skills. Besides, if she doesn't call me, there won't be any skin off my back. After all, that's my least worry. I've got enough money left to pay my expenses for the next ten years or so, if I spend it wisely. I've had several offers, but I'm just not interested in working any old place."

"Well, I'm sure Ms. Parker will call sooner or later," Cynthia interjected. "Have you started dating yet?"

"Not yet. Men are such a trip. Every time I see one, all I hear is, 'You are so cute. You look so good.' Girl, I get tired of hearing that. I don't need someone to keep repeating that to me."

"It's nice to get compliments." Cynthia thought, *What could have happened to make her feel like she has to be above everyone else all the time?*

"I'm so ready to do something. I get sick of sitting around the house all the time. It would do my heart good to help some of those public aid recipients find a job or do something positive with their lives. I really like helping them achieve their goals."

"You are good working with people. Everybody really likes you," Cynthia said with a hint of jealousy.

"I know, girl. But I get tired of just being the pretty one. I need more stimulation. That's why I want this job so bad."

"Well, I'm sure you will get it. After all, you seem to get everything you want."

"You got that right. I am blessed." Megan smiled thinking about her life. She had been laid off from her job that she had held for ten years. She was frightened and concerned about how others would see her. She wasn't afraid of being broke because she had money, but she was embarrassed that something like that could happen to her. After all, she wanted the status of working hard like everyone else. Even though she lacked a college degree, she held many hours of training credits from various workshops throughout her community and had over nine hours in her chosen field. She was just as good and smart as someone who had a degree.

Megan was a trained and experienced social worker. She loved working with families who were considered generational welfare recipients. She felt really good when she could "save" one more person from a life of poverty and need.

Whatever she could do to help another sad soul, she would do, even if it meant going through her closets and giving the welfare recipients their first Chanel suit. She felt special when they hugged her neck and thanked her for believing in them. But what Megan really believed in was herself. She felt that she was given a certain power from someone higher because she had the ability to change people's lives. She could make people walk on water if she wanted them too. If they couldn't, it certainly wouldn't be because they didn't try.

Megan had a positive attitude most of the time, which was meant to impress Jerickca or her former bosses. But when her employers turned their backs, she became like Sybil, cussing and disrespecting the very people she wanted so badly to help. She sometimes hated her clients and disrespected them because they didn't want anything out of life. It bothered her that the only way they would move to get a job was by being threatened that their public assistance and food stamps would be taken away. She wanted them to do better because they wanted to, not because they were forced to do something about their lives.

When Megan was a child, she was adored and loved by both parents. After they both died in a house fire, when she was in the fourth grade, she felt like taking her own life to follow them. Without any brothers and sisters, she was frightened and confused. How could the God she had been taught to love and obey take something so precious from her? She was angry and was quickly becoming bitter. Her parents had excellent, high-powered jobs. Her father was president of First Financial Bank and Trust Company, and her mother was a professor at the state university. Sent to live with her maternal grandparents after her parents' death, Megan was broken in spirit and a sad, lonely child. Her grandparents were so loving and kind. They transferred the great love that they had for Megan's mother, who was their only child, to their beautiful and talented granddaughter. It would be the only way to bring the innocent spirit of their only grandchild back to life.

As a child, Megan had it all. She was sent to the most prestigious private schools and was allowed to participate in all kinds of extracurricular activities. To ease her pain from losing her parents, Megan was allowed to take swimming lessons, tap, and modern dance, and she played the violin with such grace that she would be asked often to play at weddings, receptions, and church functions. With such a busy life, the pain of losing her parents began to lessen while her anger with God diminished. She loved and missed her mother and dad but she found that she could go on because she had her grandparents, who loved her more than life itself.

When Megan wasn't shopping for more toys and new clothes, she was practicing the violin or taking swimming lessons. She wanted to be an Olympic swimmer, and if that failed, a dancer. She was kind to all people. Whatever she had, she would share with them. As a young girl, she was taught to help those who had less than she. Her parents and grandparents taught her to share, because as an only child, she had been truly blessed. Now that she was older and wiser, she believed that each man needed to take care of himself, because she wouldn't.

"Cynthia, you know I have truly been blessed and I thank God all the time. I've been through so much and God has truly helped me to overcome," Megan said with pride.

"I know what you mean. He has given you strength when you were weak."

"Yes, God did, especially when my parents died and then my grandparents." Megan became silent as she held the phone thinking about her grandparents.

Her grandparents owned several dry cleaners. They were popular people who attended church often. Jim and Willa felt that they doted too much on Megan and wondered if it would affect her later in life. But after much consideration, they felt she needed all the attention they could give her because she had indeed suffered such a great loss. Jim and Willa felt that since Megan had no one who was as close to her as her parents, there was nothing wrong with them being there for her.

When Megan was eighteen and in her first semester of college, her grandfather died of a massive heart attack. It brought back all the pain and misery that she had experienced when she lost her own parents. Grandma Willa was devastated. Megan decided to quit college to help her grandmother manage the dry cleaners. Grandma Willa died of natural causes two years after Grandpa Jim, and Megan took over the cleaners. Eventually, she became bored working in their business, sold the cleaners, and pursued other avenues.

She worked as a social worker until she received a lay-off notice that the organization she currently worked for would be merging with a larger one. Megan and her co-workers would be assisted with job placements through the human resource department. Megan thought long and hard. She could easily stop working because she had plenty of money, but she sought fulfillment through working with others whom she felt would need that extra push to succeed. Megan was great at getting people to move toward their goals. At least that's what she thought. Most of the time, they moved not because of her skills, but to get away from her self-promoting attitude and her projection that she was better than everyone else. Megan's clients quickly tired of her bragging about her clothes and money.

"Well girl, I guess I better get off this phone. It was nice talking to you. Thanks for listening," Megan said.

"You know you're welcome," Cynthia said as she hung up the receiver. Thinking about Megan, she said to herself, *She could be such a good person if she would just get her act together.*

While searching for a job, Megan's friend recommended her to the Department of Public Aid. Once she aced the test, which she felt was easy, her name was put at the top of the list of people to be called for the next available position. It took three months before she received her call to report to work. By that time, she had been offered another job with the Department of Adolescent and Children Resources.

On her first day of employment, it became apparent that the other workers envied her. They would always stare at her, and when she would catch them looking, they would quickly turn their heads. She recognized their looks of envy because she had seen it so many times before. Everybody, it seemed, wanted what she had: the cars, clothes, and money. For a social worker who did home visits, she was considered over-dressed and lacking in real social work skills. The other workers wondered if she really worked when she went into the homes of her clients. After all, some of the clients lacked good housecleaning and personal grooming skills and had no idea how to keep their children fresh, clean, and well groomed.

Staff sometimes wondered why Megan dressed the way she did, with the possibility of getting dirty during a home visit. None of their concerns mattered to Megan, because all her life, people perceived her differently from what she really was until they had a chance to get to know her. With time, they would all be eating out of her hands.

The Interviews
How it all started

Chapter 8

When Donna Sanders contacted Jerickca to inform her that she wanted to basically give her agency money through the collaboration, she was both thankful and happy. This grant would secure several of her current staff a job for the next six years. This was a research demonstration grant and based on their performance, they could be rewarded an even bigger amount of funding in the future. The first thing she needed to do was to read the proposal and develop job descriptions.

After reading and comprehending the purpose of the grant and meeting several times with Donna, Jerickca wrote five job descriptions. She wrote one for a trainer/group facilitator to train the clients in developing job-readiness skills, a social worker to assist clients in adjusting to their new jobs while losing their public assistance benefits, and a recruiter/job-developer to enroll clients and assist in finding employers who would hire individuals with limited skills. She also wrote one for a manager and one for a supervisor.

Next, Jerickca developed a hiring scale. She knew that a lot of people would be applying for available jobs, because the salaries posted were better than average. Those selected would be paid based on experience, and raises would be given to encourage job retention throughout the duration of the grant. She had to pay excellent salaries, because Denver had written in the initial proposal that these salaries would encourage employee satisfaction and retention. After all, she wanted the workers hired to attend to the client through the six-year grant period.

To assure that she would get the best workers, Jerickca developed the employment scale so it was similar to the civil service one. She knew that her intuition would be her best measure of a person's character, and this had not failed her yet. She developed an evaluation form that would be easy to rate and would document the categories should someone decide to challenge her decisions.

She knew that her scale would be based on experience, education, and location. Location was important, because those hired would receive higher points if they had lived or worked in the area previously. She scheduled the interviews to begin the following week.

Jerickca decided to conduct individual interviews. Those who were accepted during the first round would be scheduled for a group interview with other candidates, as well as several other supervisors. Her main goal was to find a group of people who could get along with each other while working to achieve common goals. She wanted to see how well they interacted with each other. She wanted to observe whether they assisted each other when they needed help and to watch their non-verbal communication. The first interview was with Denver. She knew Denver would meet her qualifications as well as her expectations since she had authored the proposal.

Chapter 9

The night before Denver's big interview, she lay next to Latham and gently caressed his body. His smooth silky skin was supple to her fingers. She bent over and kissed him by first taking her tongue and circling her lips. Then she plunged her tongue into the depths of his mouth while gently sliding her hands up the middle of his thighs to the trophy she wanted to win.

Latham moaned, "Baby you sure make me feel good."

Denver whispered, "Kiss me you fool."

Latham slid two of his fingers into the warmth of Denver's essence, while telling her how much he cared about her. Her center core tautened around his fingers, as they pumped deeper inside her searing, sticky, wet oven.

Almost losing her breath because of the intense passion rising in her chest, she begged him, "Please make love to me now."

"Baby you feel so good," he said as he glided his love tool into her toolbox.

Satiated and satisfied, Latham left Denver lying there fresh from screaming for her mama, daddy, and anyone else whose name she hollered out when she had her orgasms. His love made her weaker by the moment. She couldn't wait to become his wife someday, and he assured her that soon they would become man and wife. She couldn't wait until that happened, but for now, she would just go to the interview she had scheduled with Jerickca Parker.

When Denver walked into the interview, she was surprised to see an African-American who held such a high position in a large organization. Not only that, but Jerickca Parker was in her late thirties and appeared well educated based on the plaques that hung on the wall. She was articulate, and Denver was impressed with her the moment she met her. She knew immediately that she would learn a great deal from her. Denver received good vibes from Jerickca, not as a person who was pretentious or stuck-up or who thought she was better than others, but as one that projected confidence and commitment. Denver's former boss, Donna, said that Jerickca was good to people and she would be someone that would allow Denver to achieve at her highest level.

Jerickca introduced herself to Denver and extended her hand to shake. "Please have a seat," she said.

"Thank you." Denver smiled as she took her seat.

"Congratulations on writing such an excellent grant, Miss Anderson. The research was outstanding, and I was very impressed with the benchmarks you developed to measure the success of the program. What made you decide to target parents with children thirteen and under and those who did not have a GED or high school education?"

Denver adjusted her skirt by pulling it down. She looked directly into Jerickca's friendly eyes and said, "I was interested in parents with children thirteen and under because I knew that those were the clients who would be losing their assistance when their child reached eighteen. I wanted to see those parents who didn't have an education have an opportunity to get one by working long-term with social workers who were also skilled in job placement and counseling. Since the federal government decided on time-limited benefits and many of those recipients would be losing their benefits within five years, this targeted population would be the persons who needed help now to develop skills to find a job. At the same time, they would pursue their GED so that they could become more marketable. I also know that these are the people who have received public assistance the longest and thus would need to be motivated to move forward."

Jerickca responded, "I'm very impressed with your writing skills and would like to include you on our grant-writing team. Would that be something that you would be interested in doing?"

"Yes, Ms. Parker. I would be happy to be included," said Denver.

Jerickca paused briefly and finally said, "Well, I do have one question about case management. I see that you have limited skills in this area. How do you feel about making home visits?"

Denver looked down at her shoes and then at Jerickca. "I do like visiting families to find out more about their living arrangements and to see how they interact with their children and other family members. I believe that if you really want to make an accurate assessment of your clients, you have to go to their homes, where they are most comfortable. I have absolutely no problems with doing home visits."

Jerickca looked into Denver's eyes while she spoke, and she felt that Denver appeared somewhat uneasy. Jerickca wouldn't hold this against Denver. In her experience as a manager, most people started off uncomfortable when they first met families, because they didn't know what they were facing. They were walking into the unknown. So to make Denver more comfortable, she asked her how she would handle a family that had no food.

"I would contact a local food bank or make a referral to the American Red Cross or other organizations in the community that have various resources." Denver responded. "I would also find out why the family had no food and address that issue, either through food and budget planning or teaching the parent how to stretch their food stamp allotment."

Jerickca was pleased with that answer and decided that she liked Denver. She knew that Denver was giving off vibes of some timidity, but felt that she could help her to overcome that problem with time. She then asked Denver her last question, which was, "What do you like to do for fun?"

Denver eyes glowed and she smiled. "I enjoy reading and taking long walks. I really like peaceful times," Denver hesitantly stated.

"Well, Denver," Jerickca said. "I'm sure that will come in handy once you start working here, because it will be hectic starting a new program. I will be calling you again next week so that you can sit in with other candidates during the group interview. This will give you a chance to see how we process information. However, you will officially start working here in three weeks, which is the beginning of our new pay period. Do you have any questions?"

Denver thought about that question but was unsure how to proceed because she had heard that you shouldn't inquire about benefits until you actually had the job, but she decided to risk it and said, "Only one. What are the benefits and how often do we get paid?"

"As far as your pay goes, I can only offer you thirty five thousand to start. This is the same figure that you wrote in the budget for the person who would get this position," Jerickca said while looking up with a raised eye.

Denver smiled, "That will be great!"

Jerickca pulled out a manila envelope and handed her one white sheet of paper. Then she spoke, "On your first day of employment here you will go through an orientation with our personnel director. In the meantime, this will give you all the holidays that we celebrate and, as you will notice, they are most of the major ones. We also accumulate one sick day a month. We are paid on the fifteenth and thirtieth or thirty-first of each month. Your insurance benefits, which include health and dental, will start on your thirty-first day of employment."

"Thank you," said Denver.

"I'll be in touch with you by letter. It will give you other instructions for bringing in documentation, such as a driver's license and insurance card, because you will need car insurance to go out in the field. Also, you will need to get a physical and a TB skin test, because you will be working with families and their children." As Jerickca spoke, she stood up and said, "I am looking forward to working with you."

Denver felt great and showed her beautiful white teeth as she stood up and prepared to leave the interview. She picked up her Coach city bag, extended her hand to Jerickca, and made sure her handshake was firm. She said, "Thank you for your time. I'll await your letter," before she walked out of the office.

Denver thought, *I'm so glad that I wore my only designer navy blue Jones of New York double-breasted suit and my low heel Nickels because I could tell that Ms. Parker had good taste. I think she was impressed with me. This interview was really an experience for me. I think she could see right through my spirit and knew that I was a little too timid. I know I need to change and become more assertive, but how? I've been like this all my life. Yet, I didn't feel that she would hold it against me. I think I am really going to like working for Ms. Parker. I was very impressed with her. I need to go and let Donna know how the interview went. I really do feel good about working for this organization. I'm happy that I put that salary in for myself. It really is a good starting salary in this area for a first time employee.*

Chapter 10

Jerickca had scheduled two more interviews for that evening. She was very impressed with Denver, but knew that she would be stronger and more valuable as a grant writer and fund developer. However, there was no money in this grant for a position of that nature, so Jerickca decided that she would allow Denver to work as a social worker with less than an average caseload and increase her duties in other programmatic areas. Jerickca went back to her office to make a few phone calls and to complete her evaluation forms on Denver. It would be easy to score Denver in with the rating scale she developed.

Just before lunch, Jerickca received a call from her sister Pamela. Pamela was a drug abuser and had dropped out of school when she was in the eleventh grade. She was smart, and even though she had dropped out of school, she was still able to carry a decent grade point average because her grades had been perfect in all her classes. When the school notified their mother that Pamela was ditching school on a regular basis, her mother had her evaluated by a mental health therapist. The therapist found that Pamela was suffering from depression. Pamela was immediately put on medication, but she never returned to school. She also unsuccessfully tried to commit suicide. In a ten-year period, Pamela had three children, whom she loved dearly, but unfortunately, she could not break her drug habit to take care of them. Pamela had been in treatment three times and tried hard to quit, but once back on the street, she used drugs more than before she had gone for treatment.

Jerickca asked Pamela what she needed.

Pamela said, "I need you to dig deep down in your heart and help me get off drugs."

"You dig deep into your own damn heart because you're the only one who can help yourself," Jerickca said.

"Why can't you just help me?" cried Pamela.

"Pammie, please understand that I love you, but getting off drugs will take self control, will power, and desire. I would love to help you stop abusing your body. Remember, I'm the one who keeps finding rehab places for you to go to, and then I send money to take care of you while you are there. But I'm tired baby. You have got to do this for yourself."

Pamela became so infuriated that she screamed, "You make me sick with your higher than mighty self!" She slammed the phone as hard as she could in Jerickca's ear.

Jerickca took the phone and looked at the mouthpiece and thought, *That little bitch hung up on me. I have too much work to do today to let that crap bother me. I just wish that she could get herself together, because this is really getting old and I'm tired of constantly worrying about her safety.*

Jerickca called her girlfriend, Deborah, and asked her to meet her at the Yung Chinese Restaurant. Once there, the waiter seated her and asked if she would be dining alone. She said, "I'm expecting another party."

Jerickca gazed at the menu. When she looked up to signal the waiter that she was ready to order, she saw Deborah and waved to her so that she would know where they were seated.

"Hey girl, what's shaking?" Deborah asked with a smile.

"Girl, ain't nothing shaking but the leaves on the trees. Other than the fact that I'm interviewing staff for that grant I told you about. Remember the girl I told you about who wrote that grant? Well, she seems to be a sharp young lady, but I don't think she knows it," Jerickca sighed.

Looking up from the menu, Deborah asked, "What do you mean?"

"She seemed to have the saddest eyes that I've ever seen, and she had trouble making eye contact throughout the interview. Her former employer hired her directly out of college because she had strong work ethics and had interned with her for two semesters. She had great things to say about her, and honestly, I was impressed. But you know me, Deborah! My antenna went up and my social worker skills smelled low self-esteem."

"Well, if she has the reputation of being a good worker, maybe you could help her with the other problems," Deborah stated with the utmost confidence.

"Let's order. I have to get back because I'm interviewing two more people this afternoon. How's Danny, Deb?"

"Same as always. Still tripping." Deborah hunched her shoulders and sipped her water. "I'm tired, Jerickca. I think I'm going to let him go. I'm so tired of trying to please him and he's still not happy. I feel like he's using me because I have been so good to him, but not good enough since he doesn't want to get married. I'm tired of the weak excuses like he doesn't believe in the institution of marriage, yet his ass lays up on me taking all my good pussy and doesn't want to make a life-long commitment to me."

Jerickca felt so bad for her friend. They met when they were in the third grade. They were both walking down the street and saw each other and just stopped and started talking. They found out that they attended different schools and lived across a major highway from each other. Jerickca was only on that side of the highway because she was with her brother who had stopped to talk to some friends. From that first meeting, they hit it off and spent most of their time together. They had become so tight, you would have to take a tire wrench to pull them apart. Each became the other's closest and dearest friend, and they could talk to each other about anything.

Jerickca wanted desperately for Deborah to be happy and to

find a man who would appreciate how kind and sweet she is to everyone. "You know what is best for you, but before you break up with him, talk to him because it's hard out there without a man. Just let Danny know how important marriage is to you. Then if he doesn't agree, you will have all the information you need to let him go and move on. You know what they say. As soon as you let that man go, another woman will be waiting to call him hers." Jerickca leaned in close. "Deborah, please make sure that you can handle being without Danny. Talk to him and try to really let him know your feelings—how much it hurts you to feel that you are good enough to shack up, with but not to be his wife. I know how much you love him. You and I both know what happens to you when you aren't with him, how depressed and moody you become. Please make sure that leaving him will be something that you can handle and know that I will be here for you no matter what you choose to do. No man is worth it, especially if he is using you."

Deborah smiled. She was so happy to have Jerickca in her life, because she didn't have any siblings and always felt like part of her best friend's family. Ever since they were old enough to understand friendship, they had been together, and from past experience, they knew that they could always count on each other for trust and support. Looking up at Jerickca, she said, "Thank you for always being in my corner, girl. I wouldn't know what to do without you in my life."

"I love you, too." Jerickca said with a toothy smile.

When Jerickca arrived at the office, she informed her secretary that she was back and that she should have the applicants complete the paperwork when they arrived. Jerickca continued her paperwork while awaiting the next interview. So far, everything was going smoothly.

Chapter 11

Today was a special day for Megan, and she could barely contain her excitement because she had landed an interview with the Department of Adolescent and Children Resource. Megan had been laid off from her previous job for three months, and she was not excited about looking for another job. It wasn't that she needed to work for financial reasons, but she desired to because it gave her status. All the smartest and successful sisters had careers, and she wasn't about to stay home and live off insurance benefits from her deceased husband. This is why this interview was so important to her. She needed to have a reason to dress up and she needed a place to go.

It was April 15, a bright and beautiful morning, when Megan arrived at the Department. The building was brand new, which made Megan feel good. She wouldn't tolerate being seen working in an old, broken-down looking building. As she waited for the receptionist to call her, she thought about her life.

It really had been a good life. She had been provided with all kinds of wonderful material things. She owned clothing from top designers like Versace, Gucci, Coach, and others. She drove a sleek black Jag and a Range Rover. Life was indeed good. But Megan wasn't fulfilled, and she never had been. It was so easy for her to find fault in everyone around her, but she closed her eyes to her own problems. Although beautiful, she lacked positive self-esteem. Not only that, but she couldn't find a man to hold her and whisper beautiful soft words in her ears.

Megan was lonely when Richard was alive, and she was even lonelier now that he was gone. The only suitors who had approached her couldn't get a hard on if they bought one. They were all "old men" looking for company, and she was not the one. So all her hopes and desires fell on making her co-workers feel as if they needed her guidance to help them in their own pitiful lives. This kept her busy and made her feel a sense of importance.

While waiting in the reception area, Megan noticed a somewhat heavy, well-dressed, attractive woman pass her. They both looked at each other and smiled. Megan thought that for a woman who is fat, she sure is dressed well. That suit she is wearing looks like a Ralph Lauren. She continued to stare at the woman and smiled to herself, thinking, *I sure hope she is my boss. She certainly does have good taste in clothes.*

Several minutes later, Ms. Parker came out of the large double doors and extended her hand to Megan. "Good afternoon. I'm Ms. Parker and you are Megan DuPree. Please come into my office."

"Yes, I'm Megan. Thank you for taking time to interview me for the position of social worker," she said while following Ms. Parker into the interviewing area.

Jerickca asked her to take a seat. She noticed that Ms. DuPree was a very beautiful woman who did not look more than thirty-five, but she noticed from her resume that she should be about forty-four based on her graduation date from high school. She was thin and tall with long brown hair with blond highlights. She appeared to be quite bubbly.

"You were recently laid off from the mental heath center where you worked as a social worker," Jerickca said. "Exactly, what did you do in that position?"

Megan held her fingers tightly. She really wanted this job, and it seemed to her that the people here were very friendly. She noticed that everybody who came anywhere near her stopped and talked to her, and even asked if she needed anything. The office was located in a nice area in the middle of the community that she lived in. She thought intensely about this question and the answer she would give, because there was no way she would blow this interview. Megan decided to exaggerate her work experience.

Finally, Megan said, "I worked with clients who had been through our Substance Abuse Inpatient Program. I counseled and encouraged them to remain drug-and alcohol-free. I referred them to available services in the community when they could not keep their utilities on and linked them to other community services for their children to assure that their needs were met. I visited them in their homes, counseled them on preventive health care issues, and many times, I took them to doctor appointments. I also took them to the grocery store and basically made myself available to help them handle problems so that they would not get frustrated and go back to using drugs." Megan smiled as she concluded her last statement. She knew that she had scored big with Ms. Parker. Hell, she even liked that answer herself.

"Great." Jerickca said. "How many people did you carry on your caseload?"

"I carried thirty people, but I also assisted their family members when needed. I helped them to find jobs and assisted them in completing forms when they wanted to return to school to get a General Education Diploma. So, my caseload would really increase to large numbers at times because I had to document all my interactions with the total family," Megan said.

Lifting her eyes up from reading Megan's application, Jerickca said, "I worked with many of your co-workers from the Mental Health Center, so I am aware of the reasons that so many people were laid off. I was wondering, since you had been employed there for so many years, why didn't you take the transfer to the Child Development Administration?"

"Well," Megan responded. "As you can see, I do not have a college degree, and most of the available positions required one. So I decided to take some time off to decide my next career move. I have many career goals I would like to achieve. I enjoy working with people and helping them to become all that they can become, because it inspires and gives me the courage to succeed myself.

This is why it was important to take my time and decide my next career move."

"Do you plan on obtaining a degree or going back to school?" Jerickca looked at Megan with a quizzical look.

"I do plan on going back eventually, but I'm not ready at this moment because I recently lost my husband and I'm just barely handling his death." Megan held her head down and hoped that Ms. Parker would drop the subject. She didn't like talking about death because she loved to live. Talking about death brought back too many sad memories, and she needed to be happy.

"I'm sorry to hear about your loss Megan. When do you think you could start working if I should hire you?" asked Jerickca.

"Today!" smiled Megan.

"Well, before I actually hire the staff for this grant, applicants that I am interested in will be called back for a second interview. At that time, they will have an opportunity to ask additional questions and participate in a question and answer session about the positions and what would be expected if they were made an offer. I'm inviting you to participate in the second round of interviews that will be held next week. I will send you a letter with the time and date of the interview," stated Jerickca.

"Thank you, Mrs. Parker, for inviting me to participate in the second round of interviews. I look forward to coming back and hope to begin employment shortly after the interview." Megan thought showing confidence should be worth about ten more points. She thought, *For someone who hasn't had an interview in more than ten years, I did pretty good, if I do say so myself.*

She hoped that Jerickca would never find out that she was going to be terminated from her previous position for talking down to clients, so she quickly accepted the lay-off before anyone could say they fired her. She figured out how to sneak around, listen to management, and find out what was going on by turning the volume down low and pushing on the speaker button on her phone. Other employees never knew that she was listening to their conversation until someone would ask management if something that Megan told them was true. She could have lost her job many times, but she made it clear that she would never go down by herself. Megan was thinking back to other situations when she heard Ms. Parker's voice.

"Then I shall see you next week." Jerickca extended her hand to Megan and gave her a firm handshake. She had good vibes about Megan. Although she was a little overdressed for the position, she didn't come across as snooty. She thought Megan was rather pleasant and demonstrated a great personality, which would be important to clients having a hard time with problems.

Jerickca couldn't wait for the group interview. The real test of how these applicants would respond to others would be more visible, and this was extremely important to the program's success. That would be the time to identify problems while monitoring how the applicants supported each other. Jerickca would watch to see who would be team players and who would try to make others look bad so that they could come across as the best person for the job. Jerickca wasn't looking for a show-off or someone who would be selfish. She wanted to see potential workers supporting each other, laughing together, and getting along, because she needed staff who could work together to achieve common goals in some of the worst environments in the metropolitan community.

Jerickca went back to her office to complete her paper work on Megan. She was sure that Megan would make it through the next step. She received more points on the criteria for location and experience on the rating scale, which made her points higher than everyone interviewed so far.

After meeting with an applicant by the name of Kevin Danners, Jerickca did not invite him to the group interview. She was not impressed. He did not have any social work experience and had only completed an internship at the East St. Louis Housing Authority as an aid to the Activity Director. She needed someone who had field experience. Although he seemed to be a nice person, he was not the right person for this job.

Jerickca had met with ten applicants and so far, she was impressed with only Denver and Megan. She had two interviews left. Tomorrow, she would meet with Phoenix Harrington and McNary McAfee. She couldn't wait until the interviews were over so that she could recommend her selections to the Personnel Director, who would then do the necessary background checks and other pertinent paper work to qualify them for the jobs. Now, all she looked forward to was seeing her husband and her daughter and getting a good night's sleep.

When Jerickca pulled her car into the garage, she could smell the chicken her husband was frying. He was a husband who not only contributed to his family financially, but also supported her work by helping with their only child, Daphnie. Most of the time, he would begin dinner since Jerickca didn't get home until 6:30 p.m. They both agreed early in their marriage that whoever made it home first would start dinner. It had been a good system, because in the beginning it was Jerickca who did all the cooking and cleaning. Her husband was definitely important in her climb up the ladder to management. If it had not been for his support, she would never have made it to the top in her field, because she had to put in long hours.

She opened the garage door and pushed the garage keypad to let the door down.

"Hi honey," she said. He nodded his head. Jerickca thought, *He has one flaw: he seldom talks.* "Where is Daphnie?"

There was no response from him. It bothered her that she could never talk to her husband about their day, but she learned to just let the sadness roll off and kept going. Actually, they barely ever talked. He didn't seem mad or anything, but Jerickca knew when to leave him alone. She went upstairs, calling Daphnie. Once upstairs, she found her daughter sleeping and bent down to kiss her cheek. Daphnie turned over and said, "Hi Mom."

Jerickca loved this child and had been accused by a lot of people of letting her get away with too much. But to her, Daphnie was an only child, and she knew her limits.

"Hi, baby. Did you have a good day at school?"

"It was okay," Daphnie said as she swung her legs over the side of the bed to get up. "I have math and English for homework," she frowned.

"Well, go down to the kitchen table and get started. I will come down to help you with the math when I finish changing into something more comfortable," Jerickca said as she took off her jacket.

"Mom, can I please study at my desk today?" moaned Daphnie.

"No, you have too many distractions in your room. You would try to sneak and look at television or something, so just go to the kitchen." Jerickca could not let Daphnie study in her room, because she had tried to trust Daphnie on too many occasions and returned later to find her watching television or listening to music with her earphones. She wanted Daphnie to put learning first, but Daphnie had other plans like singing or modeling.

Jerickca changed into a knitted, sleeveless yellow dress, and her black comfortable house shoes. She walked into the kitchen to help Anthony with dinner. As she prepared everyone's plate, they all settled down to eat. During the entire meal, Anthony and Jerickca never discussed anything. This was not unusual to either Jerickca or Daphnie, because they both knew that Anthony never really talked unless there was something he needed to say. Although Jerickca accepted his shy persona, she was getting older and needed more stimulation. After all, at work she was well respected, but at home she felt invisible.

After dinner, Jerickca told Daphnie to finish her homework. Daphnie still hadn't found her independence and expected Jerickca to sit at the table with her until she completed her work. This frustrated Jerickca even more, because she never felt like she was off from work. It was beginning to drain her of all her energy to come home and still have to motivate and encourage her family to complete tasks.

Once Daphnie's homework had been checked and corrected, they prepared for the next day by getting their clothes ready. Jerickca and Anthony decided to go to bed early.

The next morning, when Jerickca felt the bed move, she knew that Anthony was responding to his 5:00 a.m. alarm. She heard the sounds of an old school tune, "Whip Appeal," sung by Babyface. She hummed along with the song, and after it ended, she quickly fell back to sleep. When she awoke again, it was because of Anthony's 6:30 call to wake her up. Usually this would be the time they discussed issues that needed to be addressed. It was weird the way they communicated. Jerickca never could understand why Anthony talked more to her when he was away from home than when they were together.

"Jerickca, I noticed that you spent over your monthly expense limit. What did you need to buy that couldn't wait? I don't understand you. We could have much more money in the bank if you would just stop this unnecessary spending," Anthony said.

"How much more money do we need, Anthony? We have a large portfolio and other securities. We already have enough to retire on three times each," Jerickca said with her voice beginning to rise from anger. "I just don't have time for this right now. We'll talk this evening."

"I don't care what we have and I'm finished talking," Anthony whispered as if someone had stepped into his office.

"I'll see you this evening," she said.

Anthony hung up the phone without saying goodbye. Jerickca knew that all she had to do was call him at work and tell him that she loved him and would try to stop spending so much money and he would be okay until next week. It had become a weekly ritual for Anthony to check the balances of the credit cards to know in advance how much money he would have to pay that month to avoid monthly finance charges. He always paid the entire credit balances, never wanting to owe anyone a dime or pay interest rates.

After twisting her micro braids into a French roll and pinning them tight, Jerickca looked through the closet and pulled out a navy blue suit by Preston and York. This was one of her favorite suits, because this designer always had petite clothing. Although she wore a size sixteen, she wore petite clothing because she had short arms and legs. She searched her closet, where she found and put on a cream silk camisole. Finally, she pulled out her navy blue leather pumps and slid her feet into them. Once she had completed her outfit with a small, thin string of pearls, she was ready to go to work and finish her interviews so she could concentrate on training and implementing the new program.

Today was going to be a power day for her. She checked to make sure that all the lights were out while briefly retracing her steps through the house. She walked through four bedrooms, three full bathrooms, and a laundry room. She then walked through her master bedroom suite, which contained a fireplace, coffered ceiling, two large walk-in closets, and a luxurious private bathroom with a whirlpool and a separate shower. Her home even had a terrific recreation room with built-in bookshelves and can lighting. Jerickca walked down the eighteen-step flight of stairs to the first level. On this level, she walked down the hall, crossed the marble-floored entry, and passed through the living room to her elegant dining room. She finally went into the dining room, crossed the hardwood floor with its gorgeous moldings, and went into her family room to turn off the lights.

Occasionally, Anthony would miss turning off a light in the living room or dining room on his way out to the garage prior to his leaving in the morning. Since Anthony arrived home before dark most days, they never left any lights on in the house. Jerickca walked through the dining room into the kitchen. She set her purse down on the kitchen table. This was one of her favorite places in her whole house. She glanced around and admired her updated eat-in kitchen with its off-white walls, quality cabinetry, Corian counters, double ovens with the gas cook-top, built-in microwave, and walk-in pantry. She had personally decorated this room with a touch of country. Anthony had bordered the walls in beautiful wallpaper accentuated with beautiful white and blue ducks walking through a field of daisies. Jerickca was lucky to have found a beautiful oil painting of ducks looking through a white wooden country fence. It was a perfect match for the ducks on the wallpaper. Her kitchen table, which she kept dressed for guests and comfortably seated eight people, was made of oak wood.

On the table was a stunning centerpiece made with a variety of silk and dried flowers. Far in the corner was a Hewlett computer and matching oak stand that Daphnie used most of the time when she could get Anthony off the Internet. Her home was her private fantasy, which she rarely invited others to enter.

Jerickca walked to the kitchen sink and reached for her medication. She took Vitamin B-12, a water pill, Vitamin D, and Paxil, which helped to control her panic attacks. This had become a daily routine. Sometimes, she would eliminate the water pill, especially when she had to leave the building. Jerickca would never take any medication that would cause her to use someone else's bathroom, because that was so unhealthy to her. That's why she occasionally omitted the water pill.

After taking her medication, Jerickca reached into the refrigerator to get her lunch. Finally, she was ready to go. She grabbed her dark Coach brief case and her purse. She opened the kitchen door that led to the garage and decided to drive her black Lexus sedan. She was always the last to leave the house. Daphnie usually left thirty minutes earlier to take the school bus. Using the remote, she opened the garage door and set the house alarm that was located on the inside wall.

After putting everything into the trunk, Jerickca was ready to go. She got into the car, turned on the radio, and searched the stations for some music. She decided to leave the station on 104.9 to hear Stacey Static's entertainment minute.

She enjoyed listening to the Breakfast Crew, which consisted of long time disc jockeys Tony Scott, Stacey, and Tossing Ted. They had the best station of all in metropolitan St. Louis, but mostly she enjoyed the friendly bantering of the jocks. They seemed to keep abreast of the people in the know. After listening for a while to the Breakfast Crew, Jerickca slid in her disc of the new gospel group, Mary Mary. This group was sensational and young, but they had the spirit to sing, and sing is what they did.

Jerickca searched and pushed number 5 and listened to "Can't Give Up Now." This song always seemed to mellow her before she got to work. Every morning, she made absolutely sure this song was played. Without it, she most certainly would have a bad day.

Turning on to highway I-70, she played the song four times before getting to work. She sang with deep emotions, and sometimes she could feel the spirit so strongly she would pull on the parking lot to her office in tears, happy because God had been so good to her. On a good day, her daily trip to the office took approximately thirty minutes. This was when it wasn't snowing. It was another story when snowflakes hit the ground in the Midwest. People went crazy, having accidents and sliding all over the place. Most of them acted as if they had never seen snow and lost their minds, as if they didn't know what to do when all the fluffy, white snow fell gently on their cars and roads. Jerickca hated the snow.

She had experienced two major accidents because of someone else. Once she was left in a ditch at the side of the road until a Good Samaritan happened by and pulled out both her and her car. The second time, she was in an accident in which another driver lost control and ran into her head-on. She hit her head hard on the steering wheel. After that accident, she had a bad attitude toward other drivers. She basically did not trust most of them. She watched how they behaved whenever the roads became wet with rain, sleet, or snow.

Once she arrived at the office, she got out of the car and opened the trunk to get her briefcase. She hit the button on her key chain to activate the alarm on her car. Walking toward the building, she spoke to several workers. Kelvin, the janitor, opened the door and gave her a pleasant "Hello." She responded with her own pleasant greeting.

As she took out her keys to open her office door, Candy, the receptionist, handed her messages from the previous workday. They briefly spoke before getting started for the day. Once settled in her office, Jerickca picked up the phone and dialed her secretary, Karen, at extension 2001. She informed Karen, that her interviews for the day would begin at 9:00 a.m. She then unpacked her briefcase and made files on the last two candidates for the positions.

At 8:45 a.m., her first interview for the day walked in. She heard voices and feet shuffling around. When she heard several women giggling, she walked toward the front to see what was going on. As she neared the front door, she saw Candy, Karen, and a childcare worker standing around a young man. When the daycare worker and Candy saw Jerickca, they immediately scattered. Karen turned to let Jerickca know that her nine o'clock interview had arrived. Jerickca looked at him, and he introduced himself to her as McNary McAfee. She asked him to complete the application in the conference room and said she would return shortly. She then told Karen to assist Mr. McAfee and to inform her the minute he had completed the application.

As Jerickca turned to walk back to her office, she said, "Karen, I would appreciate it if you would continue to be professional at all times when we have guests in the office."

Karen responded, "Sorry. He was so fine. I just got carried away."

"Make sure that it doesn't happen again," Jerickca said with a smile.

Karen felt somewhat bad, because it wasn't often that she behaved in that manner. *But that boy was so fine,* she thought. Karen couldn't wait to check on McNary McAfee. He was a breath of fresh air to her right now, especially since she was on the outs with her latest friend. Just maybe he wasn't married and she could try to get with him. *Mmhhh! He looks good enough to eat,* she thought.

Chapter 12

McNary felt uncomfortable receiving so much attention on a day when he was trying to impress management with his skills. He was very serious about his career and didn't appreciate how those women had gloated and surrounded him. Although he could clearly see how gorgeous each of them was, the last thing he would ever do is sleep where he made his bread again. He had decided that was a serious taboo and he wouldn't allow any woman—red-bone, thick in the waist, long bouncy hair, big legs and butt, pretty as Halle Berry or fine as Angela Bassett (all attributes that he loved)—to sway him from getting this job. He had done that before and said he would never do something that stupid again.

He couldn't believe how they almost attacked him. All they had to do was throw him on the floor and take him. They were that close to his manhood, breathing in his ear and gently touching his arm. If Ms. Parker hadn't walked up the hall when she did, he wasn't sure what would have happened. He couldn't believe it. Ms. Parker was young, a little on the plump side, which he found attractive, and well dressed. He preferred his women thick with a little meat on their bones, but what he found most attractive was her position of authority. He saw the way all the staff jetted back to their workstations when she appeared. This intrigued him. He loved women who were well bred and educated. He could easily see that she was like a bear with a baby cub touch. This, in his opinion, simply meant that Jerickca was a woman who could make a decision without hesitation, and ruled with a light touch, yet he thought she would be gentle in bed. She was indeed one good-looking woman, and he couldn't wait to impress her with his skills.

Jerickca felt an uncontrollable anger within herself the moment she walked into the hall and saw those women surrounding Mr. McAfee. She wasn't sure at first who he was, but she remembered that she had a 9:00 a.m. appointment with a young man. She was about to lose control with her secretary and the receptionist because they knew what her expectations were. *How dare they act like heathens on the job!* she thought. Her employees knew that she was a professional who expected the best out of them. So when she saw them huddled around Mr. McAfee, she immediately had to count to ten. She had learned that technique from her friend, Dr. Spencer DeAndre, one of the top mental health professionals in the country.

Jerickca had met Spencer in Washington D.C. ten years earlier, while attending a conference on women and their children. She was there to lobby for a program she supervised, which was about to end due to a funding cut. When she walked into the General Session, the room was already packed and there were no seats available anywhere. As she stood in the back of the room waiting for the hotel attendants to bring in more chairs, a tall woman with a short close cut fro kept looking in her direction. They smiled at each other. When the chairs arrived, they ended up sitting next to each other and immediately felt comfortable talking to each other.

They spent the entire conference together shopping, dining, and touring all over the capital. That weekend, she made a close professional friend, who not only had a cool persona, but was also educated and very down to earth. Whenever Jerickca felt stressed, Spencer told her to stop and count to ten before she did anything else.

It really did help her, and since that time, Spencer had been trying to get Jerickca involved with Yoga. She thought Yoga would further help Jerickca to relax and stop stressing over her family and professional issues. When Jerickca needed counseling, she always called Spencer, who resided less than six hours away in Chicago. Oftentimes, she and Spencer would vacation together. During these times, Jerickca would share everything about her job, family, and friends with her friend. Since the day they met, they talked on the phone at least once a week. Thinking about Spencer always had a calming effect on Jerickca, because as a psychologist, Spencer knew how to put you in check with your inner spirit. Now, she had to get back to work, because Mr. McAfee was waiting.

Jerickca smiled as she exhaled, because it was time to meet with Mr. McAfee. She walked down the hall, turned the corner to her right, and entered the conference room. The room was painted light mauve and was furnished with a burgundy conference table and matching padded chairs. It was a beautiful room that was decorated to make you feel comfortable, alive, and in charge. McNary was sitting on the left side of the conference table, and when Jerickca walked through the door, he smiled, showing beautiful, perpendicular white teeth. She smiled back and extended her hand to him.

"Good morning, Mr. McAfee. Thank you for waiting. Would you like anything? Coffee? Water?" Jerickca asked.

"No thank you, I'm fine," McNary said, again showing those pearly whites.

"Mr. McAfee, how did you find out about this position?"

"I saw it in the employment ads of the St. Louis American," McAfee said.

Jerickca quickly glanced over his application and said, "I notice that you are a substitute teacher for the Hazelwood Missouri School system and you worked with the social service agency, Lutheran Services."

"Yes, that's true. I also serve as a coach for the football team at Hazelwood East High School," McNary said.

"Football is my passion, whether we are losing or winning. I like the teamwork concept. Although I'm active in sports, it doesn't affect my professional work. I enjoy being a social worker and a coach, but I need both to sustain me. It is who I am."

McNary hoped that he wasn't saying the wrong things because he really did want this job. When he had spoken to Ms. Parker over the phone, she explained the whole job to him, and he was certainly impressed. So he made absolutely sure that Jerickca knew that he took his career seriously.

Jerickca could tell that McNary had a great passion for both jobs. As he talked, it was easy to see the glitter in his light-colored eyes. His passion was crystal clear for coaching, as well as social work. He was even built like a football player. He had a thick neck and a large round head, a trait that many football players shared. He was in shape and had those square shoulders and large hands with neatly manicured nails.

He glowed with excitement and spoke quickly and fluently about both of his jobs. Jerickca had the feeling that if she hired this young man, he would be the draw that would bring in his female clients' husbands, boyfriends, and fathers. The city desperately needed a male involvement specialist, and with his sports background, he could be key in that area.

Jerickca thought for a second and finally asked McNary if he could work a full-time, flexible schedule, because they would not only have day activities, but sometimes evenings and weekends.

McNary sat up straight and leaned forward. "I am flexible and can work whenever you need me. However, I would prefer to work flexible hours during the football and basketball seasons. If I could arrive earlier in the morning and leave about a half hour earlier, I would still be able to coach. I can also see myself bringing in many young men and children to see professional as well as high school and other league games. My love for sports can only enhance my ability to reach the families. As a matter of fact, I'm pretty sure that using sports will draw fathers who have not been in their children's lives by involving them in something that they and their children are mutually interested in, which is sports."

He is right, Jerickca thought. She decided to let him drag the interview out, because she didn't want him to think that he had impressed her so quickly, although he had.

Jerickca excitedly asked him, "What are some other things that you would do to bring fathers into the program?"

McNary smiled, pulled an outline from his thin burgundy leather portfolio, and said, "I took the liberty to write an outline, because I wanted to discuss the male involvement crisis in this community, as well as throughout the metropolitan area." The metropolitan area included Greater St. Louis, Missouri, East St. Louis, Illinois, and all the other cities that surrounded St. Clair County.

McNary continued, "I thought that having a focus group of men from these communities and allowing them to plan their own activities might give them the push they need to become more involved with their families. To do this, we could plan an orientation just for the men, serve them food, and give them an opportunity to express themselves. Also, we could then take their opinions and allow them a chance to organize and plan quarterly activities. We could have football nights, rap sessions, and workshops on grooming, as well as job fairs and resume development sessions. Although many of these activities would be fun-filled, we would make sure that the fathers learn skills while developing positive self-esteem that will help them to understand why they should be good, involved parents."

Jerickca could barely contain herself. She was very impressed and bit gently down on her bottom lip before she responded. "Those are some excellent ideas, and I'm sure the fathers and other significant males would enjoy participating. As I stated earlier, I will be hosting a second interview and am inviting you to attend. This job will be intensive and comprehensive in addressing the families' needs, and it will also be paper-driven. The paperwork alone is over sixty percent of the job, because the funding sources expect to look at this program critically to determine how families, with all the benefit of services and resources, will compare to those who do not receive benefits and services. The purpose of this grant is to determine which group will fail or become successful and economically self-sufficient. We need staff who are as good at completing their paperwork as they are in making successful contacts with families," Jerickca responded. McNary assured her that he was up to the challenge.

Once Jerickca completed her interview with McNary, she finalized her paperwork and reminded her secretary to send out letters to the final candidates. She was pretty sure that she would hire Megan, Denver, and McNary. She prepared her questions for the final interview and invited two other supervisors from two other programs to assist her in the group interview.

After Jerickca cleaned and organized her desk in preparation for ending her workday, the switchboard operator informed her that she had a call waiting on line two. She picked up the phone and said, "Good evening. This is Ms. Parker."

"Hey girl, you got a minute before you leave the office?" Deborah asked.

Jerickca could almost feel Deborah's unhappiness coming through the phone lines. She felt as if Deborah's emotions could travel as fast as a virus, infecting thousand of computers in a single moment, when she heard her voice. She wanted her friend to be happy and it pained her to know that her heart was aching.

"Yes, I always have time for you, girl. What is it?"

Deborah's breathing became labored, and she was stuttering. "Danny tried to hit me this morning."

"What?" Jerickca asked.

"We got into an argument because he came home late last night. I waited until this morning to ask him where he'd been, and he just freaked. He was screaming that I shouldn't ask questions and that I wasn't his wife. When I started packing my things, he turned toward me and shook me very hard. He was so angry that he was foaming in the corners of his mouth as he told me that if I left he would break my neck."

"Did you say he hit you? Because if that bastard did, you get out now and I will call the police!" screamed Jerickca. "Deborah what is wrong with him? Why is he acting this mean?"

"He didn't actually hit me but he grabbed me and shook me very hard. I just don't know, Jeri. Lately, he's been acting weird. He acts as if I'm the problem. I know I put pressure on him to get married, but we have been living together for a year, and I just don't want to do this anymore," cried Deborah.

"Have you and Danny really sat down to talk about your feelings?"

"Yes, and he said he is not ready to get married."

They both held the phone, not saying a word. Jerickca was trying hard not to hurt her friend any more than she already had been, but she knew she had to say something.

Finally Jerickca spoke. "Debbie, you need to leave Danny. If he grabbed, shook, and threatened you, he could be dangerous, especially since he said he didn't want to get married right now. I am so afraid for you. The next time, he may hit you and really hurt you."

Deborah thought about it a second and felt that maybe she shouldn't have concerned her best friend, but she had to talk to someone. Being careful with her response, she said, "Jeri, I really don't think he would hit me. Yes, he has been acting weird, staying out late, but he says that it's because of me and that I'm turning into nag."

Jerickca said quickly before she lost her nerve, "Honey, I have a friend in the Domestic Violence field, and I'm going to get some literature and other information for you to read. Right now, I really think you should come stay with me a while and look for an apartment. You can't make a man marry you if he doesn't want to. Anyway, I don't think you should be thinking about marriage now."

Deborah raised her voice loudly and said, "I don't want to leave! I love him."

"I know, but think about what I said, and be careful. Stop pressuring him to marry you. You don't have to do that, because you are a beautiful, smart, and successful lawyer, and you certainly don't need the hassle," said Jerickca.

Deborah laughed gently. "I know I don't need the hassle, but I need the love."

"Girl, get a grip on your hormones. Anybody can fulfill your needs, but I know you want that man. I'm not a Sammy sausage head, you know," Jerickca interjected.

"I gotta go. Danny is back," said Deborah.

"Be careful, girl. I love you," Jerickca said before hesitating and finally hanging up the phone.

Jerickca sat staring at the receiver. She hated when Deborah had man problems. She was so successful in her career, yet so vulnerable in her love life. She remembered when Deborah first met Danny Burton. They were at the Missouri Black Expo, an annual event to promote African American businesses. There were also seminars on self-help, finding jobs, and changing careers, concerts by popular artists, comedians like D. L. Hughley, plenty of beautiful African-American people, and fine Danny Burton.

Deborah was the first to see him, and she turned to Jerickca. She grabbed her by the arm gently and whispered, "Girl, look at my husband," with a sly and greedy smile. They both laughed and quickly turned their heads when it seemed as if they would make eye contact with him. They didn't want to make eye contact at that moment, because they were laughing with their mouths wide open. Deborah hoped and prayed that he would say something to her or that the two of them would meet down at vendors' row, which is exactly what happened. Deborah was reading the back of *Sumthin T'Say*, a poetry and essay book. She flipped through the pages, found a poem, and turned to Jerickca to read it to her. It was called "Man Blues."

Man Blues

Sitting here so alone,

Without a man to call my own,

Watching the time fly by,

It makes me wonder "why,"

I have no man by my side

Someone that my mother can call her son,

Or maybe a man who would call and just say Hi.

Then I won't have to hear those words, Good Bye.

I have Man Blues,

No gold, gray, or other colors of the Sky,

Man Blues and I don't know why!

Have you ever had Man Blues?

If you have, you would really miss those dudes,

Man, Boy, Dude or Guy,

It doesn't matter what you call them,

I just know that I want a piece of that pie!

They both giggled because they understood clearly the author's words. "Who wrote this book?" asked Deborah.

"Someone by the name of Rose Jackson-Beavers. She's new, but I like her poetry, and look at this fabulous book cover." Jerickca turned to talk to Deborah and bumped hard into Danny.

"Excuse me. I'm sorry. I didn't mean to bump into you," Jerickca quickly interjected.

"No problem if you tell me who that gorgeous woman is with you," he smiled.

"Who?" Jerickca thought she would humor herself, because she knew he could only be talking about her best friend, Deborah. Today, Deborah was wearing a black suit and a cream-colored silk camisole, with a thin strand of white pearls and small pearl earrings. Her hair, which was shoulder length, was done in a fabulous French roll, with wisps of hair tenderly falling around her face and neck. One long, thin strand of hair fell softly on both sides of her cheeks. She had high cheekbones and dark eyes, which she made up with smoky black eyeliner. She had on a pair of black pumps and carried a black Coach camera bag with a black agenda book. Everyone who knew Deborah knew that she was a big Coach fan. She always preferred their bags, because you could put more stuff in them. She said the leather stretched easily.

She was gentle, sweet, and not pretentious. She worked hard making her own money at one of the top law firms in the metropolitan Missouri area. She was a criminal attorney who worked diligently to free her clients. Although young, she had a thirty-and-zero winning streak. She never lost, because she was quick at finding details and analyzing complex information. She had always been the one to look at the whole picture and not just some parts of it. So if you came to her, you had better come straight.

At that moment, Deborah walked up to Jerickca after purchasing two copies of the book, *Summin T' Say*. Jerickca winked at her friend and said, "This is my best friend Deborah."

Danny was all smiles, "Hi Deborah. I'm Danny, and it is nice to meet you. I didn't get your friend's name, but she was kind enough to talk to me."

"This is my girl, Jerickca, and it's nice to meet you. Are you enjoying the Expo?" Deborah was so nervous and she couldn't think of anything else to say.

"Yes, I am. There are some great speakers here and the banquet was great. It's turning out to be beneficial, and I'm especially glad I attended." He gave Deborah a sexy half-smile that revealed deep dimples in his cheeks. "Are you going to attend the concert at the Savvis Center, Deborah?"

"I didn't plan to," she responded.

"I would be very happy if you and your friend, Jerickca, would be my guests," he said as he pulled out three tickets. Jerickca knew that it didn't matter who was heading this concert, because she could see the pleading look in her friend's eyes to accept. So they both said they would meet him at the front door around 6:35 that evening. They shook his hand and returned to the fair.

That's how it all started. Danny started romancing Deborah the moment he saw her, and whenever Jerickca was with her girl, she received benefits too. Even though she could pay her way anywhere she wanted to go, she was happy her friend had finally found love. Since that first meeting, she and Danny were always together. If he was abusing her friend, she would personally see him arrested and behind bars before he hurt one strand of hair on her friend's head.

Chapter 13

When Phoenix arrived for her interview, she felt nervous, because this would be her chance to prove that she could do something on her own for once. Everything in her life had been a byproduct of someone else's success, such as passing exams, wearing others' clothes to impress, and getting into college. She had even had help graduating. The only thing that she had ever done on her own was to get Juan DeFrance to allow her to be his mistress. She only married her husband Devante because she wanted security and knew that he would provide for her. Although he was a good father to their daughter Simone, Phoenix didn't love him. She had faked so many orgasms that when she finally experienced her first one with Juan, she felt as if she would have a heart attack.

She remembered their first time together as if it had happened yesterday, but it had been almost a year ago and he still made her weak in the knees. That first orgasm almost blew her mind. When his lips slowly moved down towards her sizzling, impatient pussy, she almost passed out. Her husband, Devante, was boring in bed and didn't want to experience anything different. He never wanted to go downtown, because he thought it was unsanitary.

Whenever she asked him to, he would refuse, saying that women's vaginas were stinky and he wasn't about to put his lips where people released "waste from their bodies." If it weren't for his damn job at Gateway Computer Systems, she would have dumped his boring, no-sex ass a long time ago. His job kept him away from home because he had to travel, and this gave Phoenix plenty of time to see Juan. When she was intimate with Juan, he always made her cry out as if he were taking her very breath every time he touched her. If he had wanted to marry her, she would have left Devante at the snap of the fingers, in two seconds flat.

She was working hard, trying her best to blow his mind in the bedroom, as well as stimulate him intellectually so that he would want her to be his wife. So far, he hadn't even discussed marrying her. Now she was about to be interviewed for this job. She had to find something better than what she had, because she wasn't sure she could continue to lay next to her cold-fish husband.

When Phoenix walked up to the desk, she told the receptionist her name and was given the application to complete. Smiling and showing the gold tooth in the front of her mouth, the receptionist said, "My name is Candy. When you complete the application, bring it back to me and I'll let Ms. Parker know that you are ready."

"Thank you," Phoenix said as she walked away. She was thinking that somebody should have told the receptionist to get that gold out of her mouth, because it was so ugly. After all, the receptionist was sort of attractive, with long, auburn-colored hair that she wore in a wrap. She had pretty features, including almond-shaped eyes and high cheekbones.

As Phoenix completed the application, she glanced around the area and thought about how nice it would be to work in this place. It was a stunning red-brick building that was almost half a block long. The building had incredible windows all around the front and about twelve doors from the front to the back. It must be no more than two years old, if that. She looked at the workers, who where walking around smiling. Those who walked close enough to her spoke to her.

One young lady, who looked to be in her twenties, stopped and talked to her. She introduced herself and said that her name was Karen Thomas and she was the secretary to Ms. Parker. She asked if Phoenix was ready to see Ms. Parker, and Phoenix answered "Yes." Karen was wearing a navy blue suit with a navy blue and white shell. She looked very professional. Phoenix figured that she had to make some good money, because her suit looked like it was a Valerie Stevens, and her navy blue pumps were the same ones that Phoenix had purchased at Famous Barr to match her navy blue suit by Preston and York. *Good,* she thought. *If the staff dress that way, then I won't have to deal with jealous women talking behind my back, and this will be a smooth transition for me.* She had long ago tired of working with African American women, because if you dressed better or looked better than those around you, there would be hell to pay. Phoenix was so tired of the drama.

Karen escorted her to an office that was beautifully decorated in burgundy and sky blue. There were beautiful pictures on the wall, and she noticed that Annie Lee had done most of them.

"Good afternoon," Ms. Parker said as she stood and extended her hand.

"Good afternoon. I'm Phoenix Harrington, and I'm happy to meet you. Thank you so much for seeing me today."

After all the pleasantries were done, they settled down to get to know each other. The interview lasted about one hour. Although, Phoenix interviewed satisfactory, she did not overly impress Jerickca. She had limited skills as a caseworker but demonstrated, through her interview questions, that she was willing to learn. Jerickca noticed during the interview that Phoenix was extremely nervous and constantly folded or rubbed her hands together, as if she didn't know what to do with them.

She decided to give the poor woman the break that she seemed to need at the moment. If by any chance she didn't work out, she could be dismissed before her ninety-day probation ended. Jerickca couldn't totally read Phoenix, because she seemed very nervous and somewhat careful about what she was saying. This didn't necessary mean she had something to hide, but for some reason it bothered Jerickca. She didn't know why, but she decided to hire Phoenix and train her to handle the position.

Chapter 14

After the final group interview, Jerickca had her secretary call and offer jobs to Phoenix, Megan, Denver, and McNary. They had demonstrated the most cohesiveness out of all the candidates. Not only that, but they actually helped each other answer questions to ensure that the person who was speaking answered the question to Jerickca's satisfaction. They laughed together and supported each other as if they were the best of friends, even though they did not know each other. Jerickca was definitely impressed.

The following day, everyone contacted her and confirmed their salaries and start date. Other letters were mailed to those interviewees who had not been selected, thanking them for participating in the interviews. Jerickca personally wanted to notify each candidate, because she hated when someone applied for a job and never heard any response.

It was now time to start the program and get to work. In the next two weeks, Jerickca wasn't sure what to expect. She knew that her hiring skills had always been above average, but lately she had been so exhausted that she didn't know whether she was going or coming.

It started with a sluggish feeling and then escalated to an increased feeling of hopelessness and worthlessness, which caused her to lose her ability to concentrate. Jerickca was also having a difficult time sleeping and was spending a lot of time in the bathroom reading. This was the one place that she could find some peace. She seemed to concentrate better in her bathroom. It was like her intimate library with books, ink pens, highlighters, and other reading materials. Sometimes she would stay in the bathroom hours at time thinking, reading, and trying her best to become sleepy so she could retire to bed. Most mornings, she would finally drop off to sleep around 2:00. This was probably why her body was worn down. She needed to go to the doctor, because now her head was hurting more than ever.

Jerickca had already planned the orientation and was ready to get down to business. The people she had hired would be easy to train. The training program was basically an orientation to the agency, its mission, and other services. Other training would include the actual program they would be working in and the paper flow. This included writing case notes, completing assessments, and learning how to broker and refer clients throughout the metropolitan community for specific services, including food, clothing, money for utilities, and mental health services.

When Jerickca had completed her paperwork and forwarded it to the personnel office, Karen called to inform her that her sister, Pamela, was there to see her. Jerickca immediately stood up and walked the long hallway to the front to greet her sister. When Jerickca saw Pammie, she smiled, because she was pleased to see that she had dressed nicely to come to her job.

Although she used drugs, Pammie was not your average crackhead. She was beautiful and smart, and most of the time, she dressed immaculately. This was how she lured her businessmen, who had unknowingly given her money to keep her supply of drugs available. Since she was so beautiful, they never suspected that she was using drugs. In actuality, she had been using them for more than six years and was one of the most skilled manipulators anyone would ever meet.

"Jeri girl, I gotta talk to you about something important, and I hope that you won't be disappointed in me," Pammie said while looking deep into Jerickca's eyes. Usually if Pammie showed up at Jerickca's job, it was to ask for money. So Jerickca was always prepared to make her explain in full detail what she needed money for, and if she wasn't satisfied with the response, she wouldn't give her a dime. Sometimes, just because she loved her sister, she would give her half of whatever amount she had initially asked for.

"Why would I be disappointed in you? What have you done?"

"Jeri, I'll tell you that when I get over to your house. I hope you don't mind but I want to bring a friend over to your house this evening and we can talk then. Okay?"

"I don't have any money, and you know how I feel about your bringing your thuggish ass friends over to my house, so if you're coming over to beg, stay home," Jerickca said as a matter of fact.

"Please make sure that your husband is there, too. I have some coins that he might want to look at," Pammie said, as if she had this great amount of coins that some lucky guy would be able to cash in and thus become a millionaire.

"I don't play that shit. Don't bring any stolen goods to my house. Do you understand that?"

"Yeah, but these coins were given to me by a friend who I did a favor for, and I don't have to steal," she sneered while putting both of her hands on her tiny waist and imitating Mae West. "A man will give my fine butt anything I want, and don't ever forget that."

"Pammie, I'll see your crazy butt tonight. And don't stand me up!"

"All right. Later," Pammie responded, as cool as ever.

As Jerickca's sister walked away, she looked as if her skin was melting into her bones. She was so thin. Although Pammie had never weighed more than 120 pounds, it was easy to tell when she was using drugs again, because her weight plummeted to 100 pounds and below. No matter how small Pammie would get, she still looked good. She was built like a "brick shit house," as they said in the hood.

Jerickca wondered what her sister had to tell her. Usually, she wanted to beg for money or something. But rarely did she just want to talk, because she was simply too busy looking for her next piece of crack. Jerickca would just wait until she saw her sister again to see what she was up to now.

The day had been long and Jerickca was extremely tired. She looked forward to getting home tonight so that she could go to bed. Once she got into her car, she felt a need to hear some gospel music. So she looked through her CD case and found Yolanda Adams, "Mountains on High," and went straight to number five. This was the jam, "In the Midst," and after listening to it, she skipped to number seven and heard the uplifting, soul-stirring ballad, "Open my Heart." This Yolanda chick could really blow, and Jerickca could rock along with her. Jerickca had that smooth, second soprano voice that could easily shift to alto when needed.

However, most of her singing was so closely related to gospel singer Helen Baylor, it was scary. When Jerickca put her CD in the CD player and started to hit those notes, you couldn't tell who was singing, Jerickca or Helen. Jerickca could rock a house, too, especially if she did the one thing her brother told her to do, and that was to look real ugly when she "s-a-n-g." But Jerickca refused to make all those ugly faces; after all, you get the same voice no matter how many ways you twist your face. Her brother was adamant that people felt your spirit better when you looked ugly while singing. Well that was his opinion, one she wasn't willing to experiment with to find out.

When Jerickca walked through the house, she went through her usual routine with her husband. They spoke while he made dinner and Jerickca changed clothes. She asked Daphnie how her day was and she simply stated fine.

"Daphnie, do you have any homework?"

"Yes, Mommy, I have homework in English, math and science. Oh yeah, I have spelling too, but I finished that in study hall."

"Well, sweetheart, get your homework completed early tonight so that I can check it. Mommy is really tired and she wants to go to bed early. Okay?"

"Okay, Mommy!" Daphnie said.

After dinner, Jerickca checked her daughter's homework and told her that she had done a good job. They made a few corrections after Jerickca explained what Daphnie had done wrong. The door-bell rang and Anthony got up to answer it.

"Hey Pam," he said with slight agitation in his voice.

"What's up Anthony? This is my friend, Jamie," she said.

"Nice meeting you," Anthony said, barely audible.

"Where's my sis?" Pammie asked. As she walked through the house with Jamie close behind, she turned and said, "Jamie, I told you that my sister had a badass house. Ain't it tough?"

"It sure is," Jamie said as she glanced around. "I love her color scheme. This mauve and off-white is kicking."

"Hi," Jerickca said. "I'm Jeri."

"I'm Jamie, Pammie's friend."

Jerickca smile and said, "Nice meeting you."

"You and your family have a beautiful home," Jamie exclaimed.

"Thank you. My husband pretty much decorated it. I'm terrible at planning colors, and I don't have the patience to match pieces. He is very patient, almost to an extreme, but I appreciate how he handled things like an expert interior decorator." Jeri looked at Anthony, who made a face. "Would you like something to drink? A soda, wine, or something?"

"A soda would be great," Jamie stated.

"Let's sit in the kitchen. It is very comfortable there."

They all walked toward the kitchen and sat down at the circular oak wood table. Jerickca prepared sodas for everyone while Jamie and Pammie chatted. Finally, Jerickca sat down after serving the drinks.

"Now, what's so important that it couldn't wait?"

Pammie looked intensely at Jerickca. Her eyes danced around as if she was having a difficult time trying to find a place to park them. Then she said, "Jeri, I hope this doesn't disappoint you, but Jamie is my lover."

"Really!" Jerickca said as if she was surprised. Her mom had already told her the 411 on this story. It was no surprise to Jerickca or the rest of the family. Pammie had always gotten into trouble for giving away her things like clothing and watches, which she did while trying to impress her friends.

Pammie broke the silence by saying, "I hope that you are not disappointed in me, because I need your support in my life."

"The last thing you have to worry about is losing my support. If you are happy with Jamie, then I'm happy for you. Jamie, I do have a question for you. Are you aware that Pammie is a drug addict?"

"Yes, I'm aware of that. In my previous occupation, I was an Affirmative Action Officer who dealt with people morning, noon, and evening. It didn't take long for me to figure that out. I have taken classes in substance abuse, and I'm going to try and help her kick the habit." Jamie smiled.

"What do you do now?" Jerickca inquired.

"I'm an engineer."

"Well," Jerickca sighed, "I'll be very frank with you. Before you help Pammie kick her habit, if you are not using drugs, then you will be by hanging around her. I hope you both understand that kicking addiction is difficult and you need more than love to quit. You need treatment in a facility and you need Jesus."

"Yeah, we know. But she's doing great right now and she is not using drugs," Jamie said as she smiled at Pammie.

Pammie got up and went into the living room to inform Anthony of their conversation about her new love, Jamie. Jerickca thought Jamie must have some money because Pammie fell in love too quickly. It never took much for Pammie to find someone with money she could use to pay for her drugs. So, this could possibly be the same kind of situation.

Jamie and Jerickca discussed their careers and talked about their families. Jerickca found out that Jamie was the youngest child in a very rich and prominent family in the city. She had an older sister and brother. Pammie was only thirty-one years old, but Jamie was forty-three. She was older than Jerickca by a few years.

After they had all talked, everyone said their goodbyes while welcoming Jamie to the family. After they left, Jerickca asked Anthony what Pammie had said to him, and he laughed. "She told me that Jamie had the best tongue technique she had ever felt."

"Gross!" Jerickca shrieked.

"A lot of women are going that way now. You see them holding hands in the clubs, grocery stores—everywhere," said Anthony.

"I don't get it. I know the world is coming to an end now, because the Bible said that men and women will become lovers of themselves, but I thought that meant people would be masturbating all over the place. Now, I think it means the same sex will date, or most likely that is what it means. I can't explain that any other way," Jerickca said as she shook her head.

"There you go again with the world is coming to end," Anthony said as he went up stairs.

Jerickca knew it was. It had to be. Too much stuff was happening right out of the book of Revelation, like earthquakes, tornadoes, floods, wars, loose morals and killings. All these things seemed to be happening suddenly around Jerickca.

Jerickca went upstairs to shower and retire to bed. Before turning off the lights, she got on her knees to pray. "Lord help us," she said. "Help us all, because we are all sinners and need you to forgive us. Please help us to become more Christ-like, and forgive us for our many sins. Please don't punish Pammie and Jamie for their ways, but show them the way to your kingdom, or give them the desire to thirst about your Word, and then they can learn about your love. I ask that you bless Anthony and Daphnie, so that we will always know your love, and bless us as we sleep tonight. Please forgive us for our sins. Bless my mother, father, sisters, and brothers as well as Anthony's family. Bless the sick, those who are frightened and hungry, and the meek. Help us to do those things that would please you. I ask that you bless everyone tonight, no matter what their problems or concerns, and that you will help them with their needs. Thank you for blessing my family, and please, Lord, send an angel to guard us as we sleep. I love you for sending your Son to earth so that we may live. Amen."

Jerickca never went to bed without thanking God for her life. Anthony also prayed daily. Most times, they both were on their knees at the same time. Jerickca really believed the saying that "a family who prayed together, stayed together." At least that was her hope.

As she lay in bed next to Anthony, she threw her leg gently over his body. He felt hot and comfortable to Jerickca and this was so soothing to her. She couldn't sleep if he wasn't in bed with her, because she found the bed to be cold and unfriendly. So she loved it when they did not have to travel, because then she wouldn't have to sleep without him beside her, keeping her body toasty and warm.

First, she draped her legs over his lower body to feel his heat. She tenderly lift her legs and turned her backside to him spooning herself against his genitals. She reached behind and caressed his penis. He was becoming harder, so she increased the rhythm of her hand going up and down his shaft. She turned to face him and kissed his lips, his ears, and his eyelid. Then she sucked his nipples while still stroking his penis.

As she continued to massage his erect dick, he slid his finger inside her lubricated walls. She moaned as he slid his finger in and out. As he fingered her, she positioned her body so that he could enter her. Moving his hand, she straddled him and slid his penis inside her. She rode him as if she was on a horse, trying hard to gallop back to the ranch before a storm. Finally, he hit that spot and she screamed out, "Fuck me Anthony." He grabbed her ass and squeezed her cheeks together as he moaned and pumped inside of her. Finally, they collapsed. "Damn that was good," she said. Anthony grabbed her and gave her a deep French kiss. Afterwards, they cuddled until they fell asleep. This was how it had always been with them, loving each other as if it was their first time together.

One of the things that Jerickca always loved about Anthony was that he had always satisfied her from the day they met until about nine months ago. Now he was not as passionate. In the past, he never went to bed without making her have an orgasm. That's one of the reasons she loved him so much—because he was so unselfish and it seemed as if he really loved his family. He took good care, made their lives comfortable, and assured them that he was a loving father and husband.

Lately, he had changed. She noticed less than a year ago that sex was becoming secondary. Now, he wasn't as tender as he had been. He was just pacifying her to avoid an argument. He made sure that he had sex with Jerickca often enough to avoid a confrontation. Jerickca was so frustrated, but she loved him, and as the long-suffering wife, she tried to adjust to his new way of having sex. But it was tough.

The Gathering

Chapter 15

It didn't take long for the staff to bond. After several months, they had become as close as fingers in a pair of gloves. Whenever any activities were scheduled for families in the program, they would all assist in the planning and the implementation of the events. They were hard workers and very good at what they did. These were indeed some of best social workers that you could find, because they truly loved their jobs and the people they served. Even though the pay was better than average, they could always use more money, but they were really happy with the company.

Jerickca knew that this job provided them with so many benefits that money just couldn't buy. This job provided the workers with freedom, flexibility, and laughter. Although they worked hard to accomplish their goals, they spent an equal amount of time laughing about the world and sex issues, as well as life on the job.

Jerickca was concerned about one staff person: Denver. She just didn't bond well with the others. She tried, but her remarks only made her look stupid. She even laughed at the wrong times when someone was telling a joke. Now, Jerickca could clearly see why this girl was so good at writing proposals—because she was so bad at talking face to face with people. She felt more comfortable handling paperwork than she did people. She was surely going to be a hard nut to crack, harder than a hazelnut. Jerickca was really worried about Denver and was trying to find some assertive classes to send her to. She needed to do it in a hurry. Denver even looked out of place.

When Denver saw the door in the backroom closed, she wouldn't get up to see what was happening. Most of the discussions would include all staff, but Denver seemed intimidated by her co-workers and remained in her office during many of the backroom discussions.

Denver spent a lot of time thinking about issues but never really saying anything. She was fast becoming invisible to her peers. Jerickca knew that she would have to encourage others to work closely with Denver, because she didn't want her to feel alienated. It would take some work, but she had to try.

Jerickca had learned many years ago that it was painful not to be accepted by others. She remembered it so clearly. She would see this girl named Angela standing at her locker crying, with her pom-pom hairballs lying on the floor. Pom-poms were hair shaped in big round curly balls. Angela had very short hair and she often wore wigs to feel better about herself. But there was a girl named Denise who would harass Angela, and sometimes she snatched her wig pieces off while laughing with others. Angela would just stand at the locker crying until one day Jerickca decided to take action. She walked up to Angela, picked up her wig piece, and hugged her. They walked to the bathroom and Jerickca helped fix her hair while comforting her.

Then one day, she boldly walked up to Denise and said that if she ever snatched another hairpiece off of her friend's head, she should consider her ass personally kicked by Jerickca. Denise saw the anger and hurt in Jerickca's face and never touched Angela again.

This set up a long friendship between Jerickca and Angela. Jerickca had an affinity for rescuing underdogs. This is probably the reason she initially went into social work. So it was really important that she help Denver as much as possible.

As she walked down the hall carrying her briefcase and homemade lunch, she passed the backroom. It wasn't unusual for the door to be closed in the morning, because Jerickca always informed staff that they should always keep their conversations away from the clients, particularly if the staff was discussing a client's case. This morning, though, Jerickca heard the laughter, walked toward the door, and pushed it opened. “Good morning,” she said.

"Jerickca," Phoenix said, "I wanted to discuss a case with you. I have talked about it with my co-workers because they had already heard about it. Come in and shut the door."

"What is it?"

"Last night I got a call from my client, Tabitha. She lives in the Orr Weathers housing projects with her four children." The Orr Weathers was low-income public housing that was notorious for crime, drugs, and gangs.

Jerickca asked, "Is she the twenty-year-old?"

"Yeah, that's the one. Well, she told me that "Top Cop," Glenn Burts, had her dancing at a strip club and she was so in love with him that she was only doing it to please him. The problem is, she doesn't want to dance anymore because the patrons are touching and grabbing on her while she is dancing."

"Phoenix, do you believe her?"

Before Phoenix could respond, Megan jumped in and said, "Yeah, I do and I don't. I believe that the cop is messing around with her because he is a dirty dog. But no, she doesn't want to quit dancing because she likes doing that stuff. I know her for her work, and that is the kind of thing that Tabitha does. I know she is dancing because she wants to. That heifer was probably stripping before she met that cop. That's why he doesn't want her to quit dancing. He ain't forcing her trifling ass to do nothing. She's probably angry with him because he dates other women. That cop is messing with all kinds of women. As a matter of fact, his wife of twenty years just broke up with him and moved out of the area. He is a big-time whore."

Everybody knew that if Megan said it, it was probably true. She knew everybody in the city and could get the scoop on anybody, plus she was so nosy that she would contact people in the know to find out what they knew about the situation. She had the perfect nose for digging into others' business.

"Please don't speak about our clients in that tone and use that kind of language, because if it were not for them, we wouldn't need you. I don't appreciate it."

"I realize that and I am sorry," said Megan, "but these clients make me angry when they lie."

Jerickca responded, "You need to learn how to separate your personal feelings from your job, plus we don't know what the truth is until we speak to Tabitha."

"You're right, Jerickca. I will definitely work on my attitude."

Jerickca asked Phoenix, "What is your plan for Tabitha? I know that she is grown and makes her own decisions, but what about her children? Have you noticed anything different about them, seen any marks, any bruising, signs of hunger, a dirty house, or the kids without proper clothing?"

"Nothing. The kids are healthy and happy. The house is clean and they seem well-adjusted."

Jerickca said, "Who keeps the children while she is dancing?"

"Her sister."

"Well, the only thing that you can do is to remind her that you are a mandated reporter, and that if you see anything going on that could hurt or affect the children, you will have to report it. Also, inform her that she has rights, and if this cop is forcing her to dance at the strip club against her will, she should make an official report to the police department, as well as to the state office. Make absolutely sure that she understands that if she is lying, she could ruin someone's reputation and job. But if she is telling the truth, there are steps she can take to get help. Even before making a report to the law authorities, she can go to a domestic violence shelter and they will assist her and guide her through the process of getting her life back. Let me know what happens after you meet with her."

Phoenix stated that she had a scheduled home visit and would let Jerickca know something today. When Jerickca walked out the door, she could hear Megan talking. She was once again in the backroom talking negatively about the client. Jerickca knew that she would have to do something about Megan's behavior soon. She heard Megan say as a reminder to everyone, "Those public aid recipients are always telling lies, and you have to be careful because they have motives for messing around with married men. Just tread lightly because the bitch is lying. I know her for her work and she ain't right."

The one thing that Jerickca hated the most about Megan was how she talked about the clients. Although she didn't always put them down in front of Jerickca, often others told her about Megan's comical putdowns of the clients. Jerickca had spoken to Megan twice, and she assured Jerickca that at no time in the past or present had she discussed clients when someone other then staff was around; and she further stated that she was offended that anyone would say that she had. She also said that she loved the clients and had never put them down to anyone. As Megan continued to talk about the client, Jerickca pushed the door open and everyone in the room looked up.

"What did I tell you, Megan, about talking about the clients?"

"I'm sorry, Jerickca. I got carried away."

"This is the last time that I will warn you not to talk negatively about the clients," Jerickca said angrily.

One thing Jerickca was sure of was that if the client needed something, Megan was the first to respond, no matter what. Megan would hug the clients tightly and assure them that she would handle everything for them. The clients trusted her with their lives.

She had two faces, one of comfort and support and one of a snotty better-than-thou. Yet most of her clients were only aware of one of Megan's faces—the face of support and comfort.

Megan was the staffer that received the most invitations to baby showers, parties, and weddings. She was very successful in helping clients make positive changes in their lives. As a matter of fact, she had the highest success rate of clients who were gainfully employed, and her clients' salaries surpassed minimum wage by almost forty percent. Jerickca vowed to herself to help Megan control her personal opinions and work for the clients, because they paid her salary no matter what she thought about them personally. Megan must always respect the clients, or Jerickca would have to let her go.

Another situation happened that day that pissed Jerickca off. One of her workers from another department had asked to meet with her in confidence. Before Jerickca had a chance to find out what the situation was, she agreed to handle the conversation confidentially.

Precious Anderson stated that Candy, the receptionist, was sleeping with McNary. She said that she had stayed late one day last week and had walked in on them having intercourse. Candy was lying on the desk and they were having sex in the office. She said that they didn't see her because she tiptoed out before they finished. Jerickca didn't know what to do because she promised Precious that she wouldn't divulge the content of their conversation. But now, she wished she had not made such a promise. Should she confront him and risk being considered untrustworthy? She felt trapped, and she decided to call Spencer.

When Spencer answered the phone, she listened to her dear friend complain about how she felt trapped with such a delicate situation. Spencer just listened. She knew that Jerickca was stressed-out because she was trying to handle too many things. She had told Jerickca previously to settle down, because she couldn't be all things to all people, and that she needed to slow her role. She basically told Jerickca to slow down and think before she acted.

"What is your policy on dating co-workers?" Spencer asked.

"It basically states that we cannot fraternize on the job." Jerickca said as she tried to visualize the policy in her mind. "I guess I can just go over the policy again and elaborate on that one point without singling out anyone."

Spencer said that was a great idea. "But next time, girl, don't agree to something until you have enough information. Make sure that you let people who ask for a confidential meeting know that you specifically state that if it is something that can harm a person or hurt the company, you will have to address it as the director of the program. Make sure you set those boundaries. You know you could have fired both of them for inappropriate behavior on the job. There could have been other problems if someone made rape accusations or if those two workers were not consenting to sex or something else was happening. But the young lady clearly told you that they were dating, right?"

"She sure did. As a matter of fact, I have heard other unconfirmed rumors that McNary was dating several women here at the agency." Jerickca laughed. "He must be a hottie, girl."

"I can't wait to see this guy. He must be more attractive than you said," Spencer laughed.

"Yeah, he is fine, but you know I try not to look too hard. I don't want to put myself in a bad position. Well, I have got to get back to work. I'll talk to you this weekend."

Spencer reminded Jerickca to stay professional. "It's hard, Jerickca, to lead a staff when you are too close to them," she stated.

"I know and I'll be careful. I'll talk to you this weekend. Bye, girl." Jerickca hung up the phone and planned a meeting for the following day. She wanted to cover the field trip that they were planning for the families. They were going to take them to the Saint Louis Zoo in about two weeks, and she wanted to be sure that each person had handled the assignments, the monies had been allocated appropriately, and all the families had been contacted. She sent out a memo informing staff to bring complete information on their assignments for the zoo trip to the meeting the following day. Jerickca felt better after finishing this task.

She had to pull herself together, but how? Lately, she hadn't been as sharp mentally as she usually was. Her intuition was way off. Normally she could head off problems before they were noticeable to others, but lately she was definitely missing the mark. She didn't even know what was wrong with her. She was disappointed by her weight, because she was getting pretty close to the two hundred-pound mark, and she was slowly losing control with her eating disorder. Yet this wasn't a new problem. Once before, she had gained more than fifty pounds but lost them by eating right and exercising. She had always been able to handle her weight issue, but now things were getting worse with that and with her perceptions of herself. Jerickca had a big secret. She was bulimic.

Jerickca was having a difficult time with eating. Although she never physically felt hunger, she always thought she was hungry and constantly found herself stuffing her mouth with foods that she didn't need. Jerickca could barely eat a meal and keep it down, because five minutes after eating she would feel so stuffed that she would have to dash off to the bathroom to stop from vomiting all over herself. She had been sticking her fingers down her throat so long that now she could just do it without any physical involvement with her hands. She basically could stand over a toilet and just throw up. Strange thing, though, was that she wasn't getting any smaller—just more miserable, because now she was frightened for her health.

She knew she was in trouble but couldn't find the strength to seek help. She had tried to tell her doctor that she always felt too full, even when eating small portions, but her doctor just told her to decrease the amount. Since she didn't take the hint, Jerickca kept silent. Now she was totally out of control. She was finding herself throwing up after every meal. She would go to the store, buy all kinds of junk food, and eat it all, just so that she could throw it up. This was so stupid. She was harming her body and she was wasting money. Jerickca knew all about people who were bulimic.

She knew that she could easily die from the force of constant vomiting and could burst her esophagus. But she would silently pray and ask God not to let her die like that. She would never want anyone to find out she had died while throwing up her food because she had overeaten and felt too stuffed to keep her food down. Jerickca decided that either she would have to get help to find out why she ate too much or she would have to have stomach surgery, which she feared terribly.

She knew two people who had had the surgery with some degree of success. Jerickca also had read in the local newspaper about a prominent and wealthy man who had just died from the same surgery. So she had a lot to consider. One thing she was sure of was that if the weight stayed, she would never find true happiness with herself. She was planning on going on a diet, but every day, she changed the date before she started.

Jerickca had worked as a counselor before and received specialized training in eating disorders, so she knew the damage that she was doing to her body. Her dear friend, Spencer, was also a counselor, therapist, and psychologist who had experience in this area, but she was too embarrassed to tell anyone her secret, even a good friend. Even though she tried hard to keep her secret, she was beginning to feel that Daphnie was picking up on her problem. Daphnie had confessed to Jerickca that she had a friend at school who was bulimic and that they were really trying to be supportive of her. Jerickca thought about that conversation with her daughter.

Daphnie thought the girl was stupid to eat and throw up after every meal. She said, "I think her mom is putting a lot of pressure on her daughter because she doesn't want her to be fat."

Jerickca knew that Daphnie was far smarter than her years and she was very proud of her. She didn't want her to find out the truth and often wondered if there was a friend or Daphnie was telling her to let her know she knew her secret. Whatever Daphnie knew or didn't know, it seemed that she wanted her mom to be aware that she knew the signs of a person who was bulimic.

Daphnie told Jerickca that when their friend became bulimic, their health teacher had talked to the whole class about the subject. Great emphasis in their conversation was placed on making the students familiar with signs and symptoms, so that they would be able to identify friends who might have the disease.

Daphnie told her mom that compulsive overeaters were often caught in a vicious cycle of binging and depression. She said that people use food as a coping mechanism to help deal with feelings. Daphnie went on to say that binge eating temporarily relieves the stress of bad feelings, but depression, guilt, shame, and more depression follow it. People who binge always eat more in private. They constantly think of being fat with a fear of gaining weight. They have a problem with body image. They eat large amounts of food in a short period of time. They sneak food, lie about eating habits, fast, induce vomiting, abuse laxatives and diuretics, and exercise compulsively. Daphnie was talking so fast that she couldn't even catch her breath.

Jerickca remembered telling Daphnie to slow down. She was talking fast and needed to take a moment to breathe. Finally, she asked her how she had remembered all that information. Daphnie told her it was easy because her friend had all the symptoms.

She was happy that her daughter understood this problem that was now affecting so many young girls.

After their conversation, Daphnie happily walked away. She was excited that she could remember all that information. She wanted to help people get better, and she knew that she wanted to be a doctor some day, so she always paid close attention when they discussed diseases in the class.

Jerickca was so happy that her child was bright and able to comprehend complex information. It made her feel proud that putting her through the Christian school system was paying off. Mostly, this was because the teachers had more time to spend with their students and because there was a smaller number of students per teacher. This is why Jerickca had picked that particular school. Jerickca laughed, thinking about that conversation and how cocky Daphnie was acting.

Now, all Jerickca had to do was make sure that Daphnie never found out about her problem. This wouldn't be easy, because she knew so much about binging. Jerickca needed help, but she was unsure what her next step needed to be.

After the meeting, Jerickca went to her office to call Spencer to tell her what had happened. After several rings, Spencer picked up the phone.

"Hey girl! Were you busy with a client?" Jerickca asked, hoping she could talk to Spencer.

"No, I just walked into the office. How did your meeting go?"

"It went fine. I gave out assignments and took everyone's suggestions from the field trip. We discussed some of the clients' concerns and problems. Then we briefly went over the personnel handbook to cover some changes. I made sure to cover the fraternizing section and made sure that they understood the company policy on office romance. I told them not to ever get their butter where they made their bread," Jerickca said, laughing.

"How did they respond?"

"Megan and Phoenix said that there wasn't anyone at the company that was fine enough for them. So we didn't have too worry about them messing around with a co-worker. But I'm almost sure that if McNary were to say anything to them, they would both jump at the chance to hit the sheets with him."

Spencer laughed, "Well, at least you made sure they understood company policy. If they choose to ignore it, they will have to deal with the consequences. What's going on with Pammie?"

"Actually, nothing. Since she met this woman, she has been laying kind of low. Hopefully, she really is getting her act together."

Spencer hesitated. "Jerickca, does it bother you that Pammie is exploring the same sex?"

"Not really. It's her life. If she is happy with this woman, I'm happy for her. But I do worry about her soul. After all, the Bible says we should not become lovers of ourselves, even though that confuses me because I'm not sure if it means masturbation or having sex with the same gender," Jerickca said, sounding as if she was confused.

"Maybe you should ask your pastor."

I'd rather not. He may think I'm asking the question for myself."

"How often do you think about that?"

"Spencer, I'm not crazy, and I certainly don't need counseling about my sister's choices. Yes, I'd rather she was with a man, but I accept her for who she is. Her sexual choice doesn't make me love her any less than I would if she was straight. My love for her is totally unconditional," Jerickca said loudly in a high-pitched tone.

"I just know you, Jerickca. You always worry, and I don't want to see you get sick trying to put out all the fires. You're my friend, and I don't want you to get hurt."

"I know that I worry, but she is my sister and I just want the best for her." Jerickca became silent as she held the phone to her left ear. Then she shifted the phone to the right ear and sighed heavily.

"Is there something else you want to talk about?"

Jerickca knew that she should tell her that she was having a food problem because her friend could help her, but shame and fear stopped her.

"No, I guess I'll talk to you later in the week. Take care, girl. I love you," Spencer said.

"I'll call you later. Love you, too."

After they hung up, Jerickca sat quietly. Soon she would have to tell her friend. She couldn't keep this secret much longer.

Chapter 16

Denver picked up the phone to call her mother, Diane. She hadn't talked to her in more than three months. Ever since Denver graduated from high school at the top of her class, Diane treated her indifferently. She knew that her mom was disappointed in her because she didn't want to become a full-fledged attorney, but that seemed like eons ago. Yet, their relationship was strained more now than ever. Denver was disappointed in her mom because she spent most of her time hopping from one man's bed to another's. Whenever she confronted Diane, her mom just told her to mind her own business.

This response left Denver feeling worse. Why couldn't she have a regular mom whom she could talk to? All her life she had been left at her mom's grandparents' house or a friend's home while she traveled with her new boyfriends. Diane never really acted like a mom that a daughter could go to with problems. Denver always felt alone. That's why she had a hard time developing relationships. How could she do that when her own mom never had time for her?

"Hello Mom. I was calling to check up on you since you haven't tried to reach me." Denver really felt like cursing the witch out because she sometimes hated her.

"Hi baby. What's going on?" Diane tried to act interested, but as usual, Denver had called right in the middle of her lovemaking session with her new beau.

Denver sighed. "Nothing is wrong. I just wanted to tell you that I have a good job."

"Denver, you know that good isn't enough. Are you an attorney yet? Because if you are not, I don't want to talk about jobs until you are in the courtroom defending somebody," Diane said, talking quickly in a loud, agitated voice.

"You know what Mom? I shouldn't have called you. You should have been defending me, but all you ever did was expect me to be and do what you wanted. Why can't you just accept me, Mommy?" Denver started crying. Her mom always did this to her. They could never talk without screaming at each other.

"I just want you to be more than I am. I never got a chance to go away to college because I got pregnant."

"Please don't blame me for that. You could have continued school."

"Denver, it would have been impossible for me to do that with a small kid and no job."

Denver was still crying. "Mom, please accept who I am. Please!"

"I'm sorry. I'll do better sweetheart, I promise, but do me a favor and go to law school."

Denver slammed the phone down. "Fuck her!" she whispered. Denver couldn't believe Diane. Why was she so impossible to deal with?

Sitting at the cherry wood table with tears streaming down her face, she cried a bowl of tears. Suddenly, the quiet and tranquil room was filled with the loud, intrusive sound of the phone ringing. She allowed it to ring more than six times. She didn't want to talk to anyone, especially her mother since Diane had just made her feel miserable about her career choices. If she picked up the phone, it could be Lathan Donovan, the married man that she was dating. She didn't want to be cuddled up in the arms of anyone except her mother, because she longed for her to hold her and say that she loved her. She knew that that wouldn't happen, not today or tomorrow, because it had never happened in the past. The phone stopped ringing as quickly as it had started.

Denver thought about her relationship with her mother. She remembered every detail about her parents' relationship, both good and bad. Diane had always been a free spirit. She was the life of the party, with so many friends who enjoyed her company immensely. She was bold and sexy and had many unique qualities. She was as aggressive as a cock-strong man, gentle as Caress soap, and pushy like six musclemen shoving a disabled car off the street. Yet everyone, especially men, was drawn to her like a magnet. Diane married straight out of high school because she was pregnant with Denver. The first six months of her marriage, as well as her pregnancy, were the most difficult that she would have to face in her young life. Her husband, Jonathan, had already selected the college of his choice and registered to attend the University of Illinois in Champaign. Prior to finding out that Diane was pregnant, he was prepared to leave to start his life as a freshman in college. He was excited, and his parents were overwhelmed with joy, because he would be the first Cannon to attend college.

Diane had selected Illinois State, a college located in Normal, which was less than two hundred miles from East St. Louis. They were both very excited about attending college and looked forward to majoring in their prospective disciplines. Diane wanted to major in journalism, while Jonathan had chosen electrical engineering. Their parents couldn't wait for them to leave, because this would provide the lovers with a needed break from each other. They had grown too close to each other. When they were apart, which was rarely, their friends compared their separation to a baby without his umbilical cord still attached to its lifeline.

Diane and Jonathan were just like that, needing and wanting each other as if they couldn't live, couldn't breathe, unless their very lives depended on their love. Something changed all that. It was "The Prom." Prom night was the first and only time that they had become intimate while in high school. They both agreed that no love could be as strong as what they had for each other. They planned to make this night their bridge to adulthood. They rented a room in the Holiday Inn in downtown St. Louis. It was just a hop and skip away from the East St. Louis area. All one had to do was drive across the bridge over the Mississippi River and he would be in the state of Missouri.

Once they had registered at the hotel, they returned to East St. Louis and went to the Walgreen's on Collinsville Avenue to purchase two bottles of Asti Spumante. Like the rest of their bright-eyed peers, they attended the prom, which was held at the Augustine's Restaurant, a popular dinner-dance club that most schools used for their anticipated evening of glamour and seduction.

After the prom and breakfast at Denny's, Diane and Jonathan went back to St. Louis. Once they entered the hotel, their passion exploded. Jonathan was all over Diane. He wanted her so badly. He couldn't stand the wait. Jonathan almost tore her beautiful white gown off. Diane had dressed to impress him. She wanted him to desire her with an intensity so enormous that she imagined he would do everything in his power to be inside of her hot and boiling body.

Once their clothes were off their sweaty and tense bodies felt as if they would explode from their desperate desire for each other. Jonathan struggled to possess her. He tried with all the strength that he could muster to put his whole body into Diane's thin, virginal frame. Once he was inside the love of his life, her body raised high to meet him and they became one. They screamed out in passion as their bodies pounded each other. For Diane it was the ultimate proclamation of their love for each other. When they reached their orgasm at the same time, Diane swore that it was the moment she conceived Denver, because at that moment, her heart seemed to melt like butter on a hot grill.

Diane told Denver that that night changed their love forever. They were forced to marry right before Jonathan left for college.

They married before the Justice of the Peace at City Hall. That August, when Diane was three months pregnant, she went to the train station to see her new husband off to college. They had decided that he had to go to college so that he would be able to provide for his new family. College life was beautiful, and Jonathan loved it. He saw so many gorgeous young women from all corners of the world. He wanted to explore, date, and enjoy his life as a young man, but he couldn't because he was eighteen with a pregnant eighteen-year-old wife, and this made him feel miserable. When he came home on the weekends, he took his frustrations out on Diane. He became physically violent with her because he blamed her for his life being in a shambles. He punched and kicked her, and left her with black eyes and swollen jaws every weekend. Diane's parents didn't care that she was being beaten, because they, too, were disappointed in her for ruining her life. Their beautiful, talented, smart daughter was a total embarrassment to her family. All through her pregnancy, Diane was beaten and abused. It took her friends to pull her out of this bad situation. Finally, she divorced Jonathan and sued him for child support.

Diane went to college eventually, but she never became the journalist that she fantasized she would be. She ended up working in retail sales as a clothing buyer. It was an okay job with a great salary, but she traveled a lot, having to leave her small daughter with her mother. This made Diane want her daughter to acquire those skills that would make her excel and reach great heights. That's why she wanted Denver to become an attorney. Denver could have the career that her mother had missed because of her pregnancy.

Denver knew the story well, because her mom had told her about it often to ensure that she would never forget it and lose her focus while striving to achieve her goals.

The phone rang again. Denver held her head up and picked up the phone. As if coming out of a deep sleep, she whispered,

"Hello."

"Baby, I was worried about you when you didn't pick up the phone. I'll be right over," Lathan said before hanging up the phone.

Denver didn't have a chance to tell him that she didn't want any company, because he hung up the phone so quickly. *Now what am I going to do?* she thought. *I don't feel like being bothered with his married ass tonight.*

She got up from the table and went to the bathroom to shower and reinvigorate. Right now, whether she could admit it to herself or not, he was the person she needed to see. At least she loved and needed him, but this whole relationship confused her. One minute she wanted him, and the next, she hated him. She really did love him, even though he still had not asked his wife for the divorce. He said that he wanted to wait until his children graduated from high school.

Lathan had told Denver that he needed her to be patient. He didn't love his wife anymore because they had grown apart. They had two children. He had used the excuse that he needed to stay in the marriage for his kids.

"They need their father, and I need to be with them," he constantly told Denver. She just wanted him for herself. She had needs, too. Deep down, if she allowed herself to think about it long enough, she would realize that the shit about him not loving his wife was a lie. If a man really didn't love his wife, he would leave her ass. No one had to stay with someone that he didn't love, no matter what he said. Hell, a man would leave a miserable life and change his whole persona to find happiness. Why couldn't Lathan? Denver knew he was still having sex with his wife, because sometimes when he came over, she could smell another woman on him. Since she was dating a married man, she assumed it was his wife's scent. If he was so miserable, why was he still sleeping with the mother of his children?

The doorbell rang. She walked over and looked through the peephole in the colossal oak wood door. It was Lathan, looking as good as ever with his "foine" self. He was about forty-five and stood six feet three inches tall. He basically towered over her. When he entered the door, he grabbed her and hungrily kissed her. His kiss felt so good that she could feel her knees weaken. She didn't have a moment to protest, because he lifted her up and carried her straight to the bedroom. He laid her down while kissing her and sliding his hand gently down her legs.

She could feel the chill bumps intensifying all over her, except she wasn't cold. If you touched her body, it oozed with passion, heat, and seduction. He kissed her ears, slid his tongue down her neck and down to her breast where he let his mouth open and close gently around her puckered nipples. She was losing her breath, because it was too intense. The passion was rising through her chest and she could feel herself become weak. She shifted her body because she wanted him to be inside of her before she exploded. He was massaging her pulsating vagina. Her vagina was so moist that it felt as if it had released a flood of pussy juice that was running down her legs. She took his hand and moved it away from her hungry, anxiously awaiting hairy bush, because she wanted to slow it down. She pulled his face up close to hers and gave him a deep, wet kiss. Slowly she grabbed his manhood and helped to guide it inside her hot juicy pussy. He pumped his strong, thick dick into her with eagerness. She responded by gyrating her hips and using her kegel muscle to squeeze his penis inside of her. Every time she gripped his penis with her muscle, he moaned, "Fuck me." Their bodies were singing like a canary, making a joyful sound. Lathan couldn't contain his emotions. He whispered, "Do it, girl. Shit, work it baby." The more he talked dirty to her, the more she rolled her hips. His deep voice turned her on. She begged him to fuck her rough. He responded with deep and hard thrusts. She had never felt like this in the arms of any other man.

"Baby you feel so damn good." Lathan bent down and kissed

her full on her lips.

Denver responded, “I love you, Lathan. I love you so much.”

He didn’t respond. Grabbing his waist and holding him tightly she thrust her pelvis into him so she could feel the fullness of his penis. When she did this, he pumped harder. Finally, she screamed as her body went into multiple orgasms. He responded by releasing his semen into her. In the end, they both lay there, shaking. Their lovemaking was so powerful and all too consuming. Lathan was tired, so he fell asleep while Denver lay there thinking.

He didn't say he loved me back. He has never said that to me. She realized that he was just getting him a booty call. This wasn’t how it was suppose to be, because she really did love him. She would try harder to make him love her back. She would take the pressure off him and just let him seek her out. She would stop paging him and begging him to come over as she had done so many times before. But first, she wanted him inside her again. She tried to wake him by nibbling on his ears. Then she played gently with his nipples. She pulled at his penis. He didn’t budge. Frustrated, she finally turned over and went to sleep.

That morning when Lathan awoke, he looked at Denver. She was gorgeous. Her petite body looked about a size six or eight to him. She reminded him of his wife when they first met each other. As a matter of fact, that is what attracted him to Denver. She looked and acted so much like his wife, it was as if he was dating her all over again. Seeing her was simply an act of trying to recapture what he had with his own wife before the kids and everything else that goes with getting old. He could remember how he once loved his wife and would never ever have considered leaving her, not even for this young “thang” lying beautifully next to him. But life had a way of changing you, even when you didn’t want to change. It was just plain good sex.

Denver was not the first woman he had slept with while married. It was all about sex and meeting that physical need. Not one woman he had touched could make him feel what he felt for his wife. She was the love of his life. Unfortunately, no one ever told him that after being married so long, the body would not become as stimulated to have sex as it did when he was younger. No one said that he would need new meat to get a hard on. So now, sex was all about releasing that tension and pressure and feeling the warmth that surrounded his penis.

He loved his wife because she was his first love, and when he really thought about her and what they had once had, his heart ached with emotion. Sexually, she would never do in bed to him what these young tricks would do. So now, he just took all the loving he could stand. Feeling sexually free, he was content that he could have a piece of ass and go back home without the fuss and stuff. Nothing more, nothing to look forward to in the future—just the here and now, and then he would go back home.

His love thought he was on a business trip, and here he was with a young woman who was just four years older than his own daughter. It wouldn't be long before he stopped seeing Denver. She meant nothing to him, and after a while, sex was nothing unless you loved the woman you were with. But right now, he just wanted another piece of this beautiful supple body that was snuggling so close to him. He gently kissed her lips and she responded.

Chapter 17

Patches was sleeping with more than seven women. He couldn't help himself, because he genuinely loved women. They could be tall, dark, short, brown-skinned, light or redbone, skinny, on the heavy side, a project chick, or a professional. Each of them brought something new and different to his bed, and he loved it. What he found so fascinating was how easy they all were. They were so hungry and starved for affection. They would take anything from a man just to have a warm body to cuddle with. He didn't want to hurt women, but if he could have them sexually when he wanted them, he would be less than a man to turn them down.

Almost every night of the week, he was with a different woman. They had to be really great and daring in bed before he would see them again in the same month. He had mentioned to several of his co-workers and to Jerickca that he was oversexed. As a matter of fact, once when they were in the backroom discussing sex, Jerickca told him that he might have a white liver. She said that her mother had told her that men who couldn't get enough sex and wanted it every day had that disorder. Lula Mae said that in the south it was said that men who had sex more than once a day were oversexed or that they had white liver. It was considered a disorder that needed professional treatment. Women with this problem were nymphomaniacs. Jerickca said he should see a counselor, because he had once confided in her about sometimes feeling overwhelmed, trying to keep up with all the women he was sleeping with. But why should he go see a counselor when he was so happy?

What was even more amazing was the fact that these women would take anything he did to them sexually. He always did the best he could to please them in bed, because that way it was always easy to go back. But it was getting more and more difficult to keep the two ladies apart that he was seeing at work. Besides, he felt that Precious was running her damn mouth about them, and if that was true, he would make sure she wouldn't get another piece of his shit—something he damn well knew that she would regret.

Tonight, he and his boy, Drew, were going to hit Club Brioni, which was usually packed wall-to-wall with loved-starved women. He knew he could expect to hit on a cute honey and get his dick sucked. Grabbing his keys, he walked out the door to meet Drew at the club.

While he was sitting at the bar, he felt a tap on his shoulder. He slowly turned around and was shocked to see Toi Sanders, a young, fine honey that he slept with at least twice a month.

"What's up Toi?"

"Nothing much. I'm surprised to see you here. Why didn't you call me to tell me you were coming, because we could have saved gas and rode together?" she asked as if she was his woman.

"Me and my boy Drew decided to come out tonight—boys' night out."

Patches was pissed off to the highest level of pistation. He knew that pistation wasn't a word, but for the moment, it was the only way that could express how angry he really was. He didn't appreciate a woman approaching him, telling him what to do. Now he would have to take her home with him. He thought, *Women think they're running things, trying to act as though they could control him. What this woman didn't know was that he was controlling her.*

Toi grabbed a bar stool and pulled it close to Patches. They were talking and laughing when this ghetto fabulous girl walked up. Toi looked at the woman and immediately rolled her eyes at her, asking Patches, "Who is this bitch?" Patches ignored her.

"What's up Patches?" the woman asked. She moved less than two inches from his face, and then she whispered in his ear, "I know you ain't up in here with no other woman, are you?"

Patches couldn't believe his damn luck. He ran the show and no woman, no matter who she was, would ever confront him anywhere. Who the hell do they think they are, anyway? Tammy Winters was definitely a project girl. He had met her in this motorcycle club in East St. Louis, and when he wanted rough and tough sex, she was the person he called. Plus she was always trying to give him her public aid check. He never took her money, because she had two kids but he didn't mind taking her body. Those project girls knew how to turn a man on. Patches pulled up a stool that had suddenly became vacant and told Tammy to sit her ass down.

"Let's get something straight," he said as he pulled Toi's barstool close so that she could hear the conversation. "Don't ever confront me like that again. Didn't I tell both of you that I was dating because I ain't married to no one yet?"

Toi was the first to speak. "I didn't say anything, did I?"

"No you didn't, but I know you wanted to."

"Who is this bitch?" Tammy said trying to get loud.

"Tammy, if you are going to act a fool, you can step now. Or we can sit here like people with sense and come up with a workable plan," Patches said while totally mesmerizing both of the women.

"I don't want to lose you to her," Toi said.

Patches let out his breath as if he was agitated. "How we gone work this out? I have a plan. Toi, on Tuesdays I will see you, and on Wednesdays I'll see you, Tammy."

"I don't want no damn Wednesday," said Tammy.

"Take it or leave it," Patches said with his chest sticking straight out.

"All right, then," she said. She stood there looking strange and asked, "Are you taking her with you tonight?" Tammy was clearly getting on his last nerves.

"Don't worry about who I'm taking. You worry about seeing me on Wednesday and that's all I got to say." With that, he got up from the bar and grabbed Drew. "Let's roll up from here."

Drew was shocked by what he had heard. "Man, I can't believe them bitches let you get away with that shit man. What, you scheduling dates with them and they are letting you get away with that shit? I can't believe that. You are a bad mother."

"Man, I got it like that, but I gotta admit, I didn't think that shit would work."

Drew said women sure are desperate. They will let a brother do anything to them. They both left and went to Club Illusion, because that was how life was for Patches. He was definitely having illusions, and it felt good.

Chapter 18

Megan was tired after participating in so many program activities. It was frustrating for her, because she was the oldest of the staff and she wanted them to respect her. She did everything she could to make them do what she wanted. For instance, she made sure that each of them thought that she and the boss were tight as a lid on a sealed pickle jar. She would eavesdrop on Jerickca when she was having business meetings. She would stand outside the door and pretend that she was using the copier or the fax machine. It was so easy. She would stand as close to the door as possible and pretend that she was reading something that she needed to copy.

She would get an ear full as Jerickca discussed raises, transfers, promotions, or anything else with the Comptroller. She would schedule a meeting shortly after hearing Jerickca's conversation and pretended to have a problem with a client. Once inside Jerickca's office, she would make it appear that they were just cooling out to the observers. After the meeting, she would go to the backroom and proceed to tell everyone a secret.

"Hey everybody, I got something to tell you all, and don't tell no one else," Megan would say.

"What, girl?" asked Phoenix?

Megan leaned in and whispered, "Don't say that I don't support you all. Jerickca asked me about ya'll's performance because ya'll know we cool, and I told her what ya'll are doing in the field. She was so impressed that she told me she would be giving all of us a ten percent raise. Ya'll know I really be trying hard to get us raises and promotions."

Patches would then interject, "How'd you and her get so close?"

"Ya'll know I just get along with everybody. I have so many

friends, and people always tell me how smart and pretty I am. I just attract a lot of people around me because I have such a good personality. It's been like this all my life," she said with a serious look on her face.

"Thanks for looking out, girl," Denver said, smiling.

"Yeah girl, you my dog," chirped Phoenix.

Megan was always tricking people. She suffered from low self-esteem but didn't seem to realize it. She spent most of her time talking about everybody's business and gossiping. She thought she was smart and brilliant because she could make you believe that a cat could bark if you weren't careful. Her greatest skill was manipulation, which she did all the time without anyone being suspicious.

What people didn't notice, however, were her lonely eyes. If you looked really hard, you could see straight through her and tell that she was weak and lonely. Jerickca had already peeked her hole. She knew that Megan suffered from low self-esteem, and that was why she spent time with her whenever she interrupted her to talk. Jerickca did not believe in meeting with a subordinate without her immediate supervisor's knowledge. She would often invite the supervisor in when she talked to her staff out of respect for management protocol, even when the talks were nothing but chatting. Since Jerickca had an open door policy, she allowed the staff to talk to her as long as it wasn't about work that their supervisor needed to sit in on.

Megan spent most of her time in the evenings on the phone. She didn't have a man but was fiercely pursuing Jeri Taylor, who was the City Manager. She would often call his secretary, whom she knew from high school, to find out what was going on in his office. She would ask questions about where he spent his leisure hours or where he went to cool out, and would make ever effort to be at the same place he was.

It didn't take long for her to get with him. He saw her at Club Illusion one Friday night and noticed how beautiful she was. She was thin the way he liked his women, and she had the most beautiful hazel eyes he had ever seen. He couldn't stand it any longer and walked right up to her and asked for a dance.

"Dance with me," he said.

Megan walked out to the dance floor and looked at her three co-workers to let them know that she always got what she wanted. While dancing with Jeri, they talked about everything from sports to work. They spent most of the night dancing and talking. Megan had a great time, and she couldn't wait to get with him.

It had been almost two weeks since Megan had seen Jeri. He did not call her, though he had said he would, and this was a big disappointment for her. She had made sure he had her home, work, and pager number. She had even given him her cell number to make sure that she could be reached. She couldn't understand why he hadn't called. Surely, there was no one prettier than she was. She saw the way that he looked into her eyes and how he almost forgot where he was while they were slow dancing. He had even kissed her neck. *So why hadn't he called?*

Megan had to get in touch with him. All her coworkers were asking if they had gone out, and she was so tired of making up excuses for Jeri. Every time she walked into the backroom and there was a gathering, his name would come up. This time she would give them something to talk about. When she walked into her office Monday morning, the conversation had already started about men.

"How was your weekend, Megan?" Phoenix asked.

"I didn't do much. Just stayed home and rested," Megan said, agitated.

"Don't tell me that you didn't get with Jeri," Phoenix said, leaning forward as if she was about to hear some juicy information.

"Tell us the gossip," asked Denver. "What happened between you two?"

"I don't have any info this time. Jeri said that he had to go out of town on a business trip. But he did call me and said that he couldn't wait to get with me, so we are planning to have a good time when he comes back from Chicago," Megan said while unpacking her briefcase. She then asked them, "What did you guys do this past weekend?"

"Girl, we went clubbing in St. Louis," Phoenix responded.

Suddenly the intercom system buzzed and the receptionist informed Megan that she had a call. When Megan picked up the phone, as always, she spoke loud enough for everyone to hear her conversation with her client, Bertha Macklin.

"Why did it take you so long to return my phone call? I don't have time to play with you. Either you will take the job or I am going to report you to the Department of Human Service, and you know they are going to sanction you. Don't you know what that means, young lady? It means you and your children will have nothing to eat and no money to pay bills, because they are going to stop your financial assistance."

Bertha was very agitated and became furious at the way Megan was talking to her. She said, "You don't have to holler at me. I don't have a hearing problem. I want to speak to your supervisor."

"Fine you can talk to her, and she will tell you the same thing. We are sick and tired of you welfare recipients living off our taxes. You need to get a job. Then you won't have to worry about how I'm talking to you." Megan said loud enough for the other social workers to hear.

"Hey ya'll, that whore hung up on me," Megan stated as if she was surprised.

Everyone in the room was looking at Megan as if she had lost her mind. Finally, Patches said very courageously, "You shouldn't talk to the clients like that. It's disrespectful. If they report it, you could lose your job. You're asking for it Megan. You need to be careful. You need to stop disrespecting these clients."

"Boy, fuck you," Megan said. "Jerickca is my dog. She ain't gone believe no unemployed drug addict over me, and you best believe that!"

Phoenix and Denver just looked at each other in amazement, because they knew that if Jerickca heard the way that Megan was talking to that client, she would fire her. They didn't care what she said. They knew Jerickca would never lose millions of dollars on something like disrespecting the very clients who needed us. Plus she really cared about the people in the program.

Megan thought about the way she had spoken to her client and knew that if Jerickca believed Bertha, she would be in deep trouble. She knew that her mouth usually got her in trouble, but sometimes, those people just made her so angry. They wouldn't go to scheduled interviews, knowing that their assistance was short-term. They were messing up her statistics, because she always met her placement goals. Every week, Jerickca checked their client caseloads to see who was working and what progress was being made, either by clients going to school or doing something that would improve their lives, and Megan always had the best statistics. She just wasn't going to play with people who didn't want to do anything but make excuses. She went to work every day, and they could do the same if they had someone to push them. And that was all she was doing. She was motivating them to get a job. Sure, she threatened them, but those threats were what made the difference between failure and success. Everybody could just kiss her ass where it split, because she didn't believe Jerickca would fire her best social worker.

Suddenly, the door opened. Jerickca walked in and said, "Megan please come to my office."

Everyone looked at Megan as if to say, *We told you so*. Megan stood up, gathered a pen and notepad, and walked out the door with a fake smile, because she had no idea what she was about to face. Bertha had reported her, and now she had some explaining to do. She just hoped Jerickca would buy her part of the story.

As they walked through the hallway towards Jerickca's office, Megan began to wonder why this meeting was called in the first place. *Jerickca should know by now that the clients always complain when their monthly welfare checks were threatened. This was not so unusual, so why did she call me to her office? After all, she could have spoken to me in front of my road dogs. That way, I would have support about my side of the story.*

Jerickca was thinking, *This is getting old. Megan is receiving far too many complaints from her clients. I just don't understand why they dislike her so much, yet her clients are progressing far better than those of any other social worker. Her clients are getting jobs, promotions, married, new homes, and great benefits but they continue to complain about Megan. Maybe I should look at this picture differently and just accept Megan's better-than-thou attitude, but then I would be selling out the people who needed us the most just for statistics.*

"Sit down, Megan. I need to talk to you about your clients. First of all, I must be honest with you, because I am rather perplexed at how well your clients are progressing toward becoming economically self-sufficient. Yet you seemed to have the most complaints that we have seen here in the past year. Can you enlighten me as to what's going on?"

"Sure, Ms. Parker. I realize that I have been receiving a lot of complaints, and I believe that it is because out of all the workers, I expect more out of my clients. I don't buy into their excuses the way my co-workers do, because I know that they can achieve anything if they believe in themselves. I expect them to do well, and when they fall short, I don't accept excuses. Unlike the other workers, I know how to handle my clients because I'm older and wiser, while my counterparts are young and sometimes don't know what to do. My clients know what I want them to do and they don't like it, but when they see how their lives have changed, they always come back and thank me. I couldn't be the best worker you have if I allowed my clients to do what they want to do."

"Megan, I'm happy that you believe in your clients, but I really don't need you to evaluate my staff. As you know, I deal with each of you differently. But please don't ever come in here and try to knock your peers, because they, too, are doing a great job. As a matter of fact, I measure success by more than caseloads. I also look at attitudes, relationships, and respect. Performance here is measured in more ways than just having a job. You have to be happy with yourself, as well as with the type of job you have chosen. It is important that we allow our families to have a voice in their own lives, because the choices that they make are the ones that only they have to live with. It is true that your statistics are higher than the other workers' as far as jobs go, but you must realize that I measure success in the way we respond to our clients' needs, as well as how they relate to us. If they don't relate well, when they have a problem, they won't feel comfortable reporting it or telling their concerns about their lives and jobs to us. This would prevent us from intervening to assist them. Don't get me wrong! I'm happy that your clients are doing well, which is a main goal of the agency, but please remember that they'll remain happy if we treat them with the utmost respect. Let's decrease your complaints by showing your clients respect and concern. And remember that without clients, there is no need for social workers. I totally expect you to treat them with the highest level of respect, and I will not take anything less than that."

"I understand that Jerickca, and I will do everything I can to ensure that the clients know that I'm in their corner. It's only my love that makes me work so hard for them. Also, I was wondering whether or not we are going to recognize our families with a banquet or something, because if we do, I would like to serve as the chairperson."

"Megan, I think that's a great idea. We'll schedule a meeting and select committees to plan the program. I appreciate your work and want you to continue to strive for success in job placements, client satisfaction, and client relationships. And please always show our clients respect. As I stated before, no client will be talked down to or disrespected in any way. Please change your methods of dealing with them or I will have to deal with you. Do I make myself clear?"

Megan looked as if Jerickca had hit her in the face with a bat. Finally, she responded, "Yes, you have made yourself crystal clear."

As Megan walked out of Jerickca's office, she thought about the meeting she had just had, and she became angry. *How dare that bitch not give me my props when I have worked my butt off trying to get these lazy folks a decent job? She'd better ask somebody about me, because I know that I'm good at what I do. Jerickca may have all those degrees but I have experience, with many years of work over her. I know these clients, and she is too young to understand them the way I do. She needs to follow my lead, because I'm the reason that everyone likes her, anyway. Yeah, I heard her, crystal clear.* She laughed, thinking about one of Jerikca's favorite phrases.

Jerickca was thinking, *If Megan continues to disrespect the clients, she would have to let her go. Statistics won't mean a thing if we lose our contracts because of so many complaints. One thing I can do is schedule more training on developing positive relationships with our clients,* Jerickca thought.

Chapter 19

Phoenix picked up the phone to dial Juan's number at DeFrance Construction Company. He had started his company almost fifteen years ago and was now on the African American Business list of 100 successful African Americans' businesses. His company was number twenty-five and still edging toward the top with the forty million dollar development deal he had just won after putting in the most reasonable bid. That is why Phoenix wanted him so bad, besides the fact that he was good in bed.

This was the first time she had come so close to having money. Every time she was with him, he would leave money on the nightstand for her. To most people, a man leaving money on the table after a wild night of sex would have made a normal person feel like a prostitute, but not Phoenix. She would have been very angry if he didn't leave any money. After all, her precious stuff was exclusive. No amount of cash would be sufficient to have one night with her most valuable treasure.

That was the reason that she wanted Mr. Juan DeFrance in the first place. She had gone to the Gene Lynn's nightclub in downtown St. Louis. She knew that Gene Lynn's was a place that older men with money frequented. She went there because she had overheard some ladies in the Galleria Mall talking about the club as a place where their husbands went when they wanted to chill out. She was glad she had gone, because she saw several Cardinals baseball players and two Rams football players there. Although the players looked good to her, she could tell that they were young, and she was not interested in teaching a young boy new tricks. She wanted a man who knew his way around a woman's body without her saying one word.

Juan sent a drink to her and shortly after came over to introduce himself. He was so handsome—medium-brown with brown chestnut-colored eyes and a touch of gray on his temples. He was broad shouldered and stood six feet tall. She looked into those chestnut-colored eyes and if he had asked, she would have gone to a hotel that night. But he didn't. They just talked and really enjoyed each other's company. She admitted to being married, saying that she was unhappy.

Although Phoenix really was, she knew that Juan was just looking to find some side stuff, and with his being as good looking as he was, she was certainly willing to accommodate. She only hoped that she could end up with him. He was everything she wanted in a man, both physically and financially, and he was a widow.

Now she was calling her baby to see if she could get with him that night. She needed to feel his loving. She was thinking about what she was going to do with him when he picked up the phone.

"What are you doing after work, lover boy?" she whispered in her sexy voice.

"How are you doing? I'm glad to hear from you. It has been a long time," he said.

"You're with someone I guess?" she asked. She could tell because he was acting somewhat professional. "I want to see you tonight. I need you." Phoenix was really hoping that he would say yes.

"Sorry, I won't be able to keep that appointment because I have another engagement tonight. Try to get with me some other time," Juan said. "It was good to hear from you. Thanks for calling."

Phoenix was so disappointed. *He must be with a business associate, because he was talking out the side of his mouth, like I was a long time friend trying to get him out for drinks. Now what am I going to do? I don't want to go home to sit and watch television while Devante does crossword puzzles.* She thought, *For a salesman, Devante sure was boring. I wonder if he bores his clients.*

She picked up the phone and pressed the button for extension 2134. “Megan girl! You want to go to Club Illusion?”

“I was sitting here myself, trying to think of something to do. I just didn’t want to go home and sit in front of no television, especially on a Friday night.”

Phoenix said, “I’m going to call Devante and let him know that I’ll be working late. Hey Megan, ask Patches and Denver if they want to hang out with us.”

“Don’t ask Denver ass anything! She ain’t in this clique with her non-dressing unprofessional ass.”

“Girl, you need to stop tripping. She’s okay. She’s just out of touch,” Phoenix said laughing.

“She always tags along like she is part of this team. But she is not my type.”

“Well, I am going to ask both her and Patches to go.” Phoenix was trying to get Megan to soften up a little, but it was to no avail.

“Whatever! We’ll leave for happy hour right after work,” Phoenix said.

Once they arrived at the club, they found seats near the dance floor. It had taken a lot to get Denver to go to the club, especially since they never invited her out with the group. But she finally agreed to go for a couple of hours. Megan, with her bold self, even asked Jerickca to go, but she turned her down, gently reminding them that she didn’t party on Friday night because it was her Sabbath. It was written in Exodus, Chapter 20. She told them it was God’s Law to remember and honor his day and to keep it holy from sundown on Friday until sundown on Saturday. Yet everyone knew that Jerickca wouldn’t party even without that Sabbath stuff.

They had a good time anyway. Megan, with her crazy butt,

laughed at everyone who walked through the door. There was a lady who walked in with this sheer outfit on, looking like a stuffed turkey because she was overly thick in the waist, her arms were too fat, her sleeves were too tight, her butt was too wide, and her skirt was too short. Also, she had the biggest, widest feet, and it looked as if she had forced all that fat into her clothes. Megan christened her with the name Big Foot. They laughed all night. Megan even pointed out this older guy who walked into the club with his beautiful lady on one arm and a cane in the other, wearing a red pinstriped suit. She immediately told everyone that he looked like a red rooster.

Denver laughed so hard she spit out her wine, and Patches just shook his head and kept saying, "Girl, you are crazy." When everyone stopped laughing to go to the dance floor and get their bump on, it was their chance to finally cool down from so much laughter. Once everyone was back at the table, Megan would start up again. It was over for everyone when the young brother walked in with a black suit on and a black top hat when it was damn near 100 degrees outside. Megan pointed and whispered, "There goes the Penguin!" With all the liquor and heat, everybody fell out laughing.

They were having such a good time. It was times like these when they were having so much fun that Denver enjoyed her coworkers the most. At times like these, they were one team with one goal, and that was simply to enjoy each other's company. They were having a ball.

Patches was getting horny, and he had not seen anyone he wanted to take home, so he looked at Denver who was getting drunk and thought about how it would be to get with her. But as quick as the thought entered his mind, it left just as fast. *It would feel too much like incest,* he thought. When he put his rum and coke down, a beautiful black woman wearing a black sleeveless summer dress with black leather sandals asked him to dance. He looked her up and down and smiled. "Sure," he said, and he got up and walked to the floor with her. Once they were dancing to the song "Country Grammar" by St. Louis's own Nelly, Patches whispered, "I'm McNary, but everyone calls me Patches."

The beautiful woman with the gorgeous smile and the badass body mouthed, "I'm Jessica." They danced all night. On the slow jam, Patches pulled her in real close and held her tight. It felt so good. After the second slow jam, they retreated to the opposite side of the room, away from his co-workers, and took another vacant table. They talked the rest of the evening. He found out that she was an attorney with a local firm. He was impressed. He told her about his occupation as a social worker and a high school football coach.

They exchanged telephone numbers, and he walked her to her SUV. She was driving a Ford Explorer, Eddie Bauer model. It was a 2001, and she looked good sitting in the driver's seat. He knew one thing, and that was he definitely wanted to see her again. She was a classy professional and she looked marvelous.

When Patches walked back over to the table, Megan was jamming hard with an older man who was wearing tennis shoes without socks. He was doing the splits and jumping around like Fred "Rerun" Berry from that old television show, "What's Happening?" It was ironic, because earlier, Megan, Phoenix, and Denver had said they would never dance with that fool, but I guess when no one else came knocking, they did what they had to do. At least that is what Phoenix told Patches when he sat down.

"Who the hell is Megan dancing with?" Patches asked.

"Hell, if I know," Phoenix laughed.

"He's our dance partner, and I know he's tired because we have danced him right out of his socks." Denver said while pointing to his feet. They all laughed. When Megan returned to the table, she was sweating missiles, dripping and slinging sweat everywhere.

"He danced my ass out!" She said while getting her purse. When she pulled out her wallet, Denver said, "I thought we were leaving after that dance."

"We are, but he asked me to buy him a drink."

"Girl, stop lying," Phoenix said while staring at the guy as he stood back, waiting for his money.

"I know he didn't," Denver reflected.

"That man danced all night with all of us and gave us a hell of a lot to laugh at. He deserves a drink and ya'll should pitch in, because ya'll wouldn't have been dancing if it wasn't for him," Megan said while turning to hand the man a five-dollar bill.

"This was so much fun," Megan said while putting her arms around Phoenix. "We should do this more often."

"You're right!" Phoenix and Denver said at the same time.

Patches just laughed. He wasn't thinking too much about what they were saying. He was thinking about Jessica so much that he got horny again and pulled out his cell phone and called Toi.

"You want to get together?" He needed this booty call.

"Yeah, pick me up, because my sister is here with my kids."

"I'll blow the horn for you in ten minutes," he said.

Chapter 20

Jerickca was lying in bed, thinking. When she glanced at the clock, it was 2:00 a.m. She could not sleep. She had too much on her mind. It was time for a cost of living increase and she had to decide who would receive a merit raise. She was worrying about her sister Pammie and trying to plan a surprise party for Lula Mae. Soon, she would be turning sixty-one, and she wanted to do something special for her mother, who had been so supportive.

She looked over at Anthony and her heart warmed. He was so boring, but she loved him. She always tried to stay busy, because then she didn't have to think about how routine her life had become. He was such a great provider and family man, and he loved being home, sitting in his traditional leather armchair, right in front of his fifty-two inch big screen Magnavox color television.

Jerickca needed to be stimulated, and she wasn't getting it at home. Anthony seemed pleased with their sex life. He never complained. That was the thing about being successful at work. She realized that you couldn't have it all. So she basically just accepted the fact that this was her life and it only got better at work. Anthony was a sweetheart, and she was doing her best to inform him of her unhappiness. It never crossed her mind to leave him because she loved the life he afforded her. She had diamonds, pearls, gold, and silver. She wore a Rolex and a Movado and had at least ten other name brand watches.

When she went shopping yesterday, purchased two new Jones of New York suits, and handed the salesperson her Visa, the girl called the manager to ask her if they took these kinds of cards. The manager told her that she had never seen a Visa like that but to run the purchase through and see what happened. They both asked her if that was a new card and Jerickca said no. Inside she was smiling. *This is a platinum card. Doesn't everyone have one?* Jerickca thought.

That was why Jerickca loved Anthony. He knew how to make their money work for them. She lived a comfortable life and had no financial concerns. But she longed to be romanced by the man who used to make her insides shake.

She got up and went into the bathroom to relieve all the water she had drunk before retiring to bed. She grabbed her book by Terry McMillan and decided to read a couple of chapters of *Another Day, Another Dollar*. Terry was such a great writer. She wrote about human emotions, and once you picked up her book, you didn't or couldn't put it down. Jerickca had met her when she took all of her books to a signing that the poet Eugene Redman pulled together. Terry was very friendly and had taken some time to talk personally to Jerickca and Daphnie.

Finally, Jerickca fell asleep, and when she awoke the next morning, she removed her book from across her stomach where she had laid it before closing her eyes. She got up, showered, and dressed. Today she was going to take the thirty-minute drive to go visit her mother. This was her day for church, and she always spent her time at the church and at her parents' home with her entire family, especially her mother and sisters. This was their time together to laugh and update themselves on happenings in their immediate and extended family lives.

After she dressed, she looked at Anthony who was still sleeping. She hated the fact that after twelve years, he suddenly stopped going to church without giving any explanations. She prayed that God would lead him back or that he would become inspired by her and Daphnie leaving and attending so many church functions. Unfortunately, he still hadn't returned to the church he had once shown so much love for. Taking another quick glance at him before walking out of the bedroom, she wondered, *Why can't he express his love more openly to me?* She would just have to work harder at helping him to become more expressive about his feelings. Otherwise, if he didn't, she would die from a lack of romantic stimulation.

When Jerickca arrived in East St. Louis, she decided to stop by the office to pick up her briefcase. The office was usually open to serve the community. People who were affiliated with any local organization could request to use the facility to have baby or wedding showers, birthday parties, or some other celebration, as long as they hired the janitor and did not bring liquor on the premises. Once she secured her briefcase, Jerickca drove straight to her mother's house.

After her family attended church, everyone gathered at her mom's house except her sister, Barrington, who didn't attend church on this day. Their mom was not able to prepare dinner the night before, so they decided to go to a restaurant. As Saturday Sabbath-keepers, this was something they were totally against, because they were breaking the sixth commandment, which stated: Remember the Sabbath day and keep it holy. But they had to eat. In the future, they would try to refrain from breaking the commandments and try to work hard to do what God had instructed his people to do.

As soon as Jerickca pulled into her mother's driveway, Pammie and her partner parked behind her. They greeted each other and walked into the house.

Pammie asked, "What's to eat?"

Lula Mae answered, "Nothing. We are going out to dinner."

"Where are you guys going? Maybe we can go too."

"We haven't decided, Pam. Anyway, don't you have to go to the doctor to get rid of that cold?" Jerickca inquired.

"Yeah, you're right. I guess we'll have to catch you all on the next trip. I don't want to break my appointment," Pammie said. Jerickca was so happy that Pammie and her partner would not be sharing dinner with Lula Mae and her, because she wanted to discuss some private stuff with her mama and it was only for her ears.

After chatting awhile with Pammie, Jerickca and Lula Mae got into the car and Jerickca drove over to her baby sister's house to drop off her niece. Once they arrived on Godier Drive, Jerickca got out of her car to walk her niece into the house and to ask Barrington if she wanted to go with them. She enjoyed talking to her middle sister, who was a manager at Dillard's Department Store.

Barrington was five years younger than Jerickca and had only attended one year of college before getting pregnant and dropping out. Since her baby's daddy didn't marry her, she went on to get herself a job, bought a small three-bedroom, ranch-style home, and was dating up a storm all across the metropolitan area.

Barrie, the name her family called her, had a great personality and a sexy walk that attracted men from every direction. To top that, she wore a size 5/6 dress. She had a perfect hourglass shape with curves in all the right places. She thought she was the most beautiful person who had ever walked the earth. She was very attractive, with beautiful dark eyes, thick, Brook Shields eyebrows, and hair that reminded you of Oprah Winfrey. Jerickca was disappointed that Barrie couldn't spend Saturday with her and Lula Mae, but Barrington told her that she would meet them later.

Jerickca decided to take her mother on the Casino Queen Riverboat for dinner. They didn't go to gamble, but to enjoy the food. They had some of the best food around. They walked into the dining area and chose a table close to the deck so that they could view the Mississippi River. Once seated, Lula Mae gave Jerickca the update on her other children.

She told her that Pammie and her partner were getting a new car and new furniture in their new home. Jerickca breathed harder and harder, because she just couldn't believe what was happening for her sister. She was a drug abuser who had hit a major payday because she had found someone to love her in spite of her faults.

Jerickca told Lula Mae that she only hoped that Pammie didn't break Jamie's heart. She had a bad reputation for trying to get over on people, and Jerickca feared that this was what she was doing to her partner. Just trying to find an easy way to survive had been Pammie's M.O.

Lula Mae discussed Barrington. "I think Barrie is being hit by that big-headed boy, Michael."

"What makes you think that, Mom?"

"For one thing, she had a black eye, and when I asked her what happened, she said that she walked into a door." Lula Mae asked the waiter for more napkins. She picked up her salad fork and proceeded to take a mouthful of salad.

Jerickca asked, "Did you notice anything else about her that could indicate abuse? Like does she spends as much time with you as she did before meeting Michael? Or does she worry about what he thinks about stuff she enjoys doing?"

Lula Mae rested her hand on her face and thought about her daughter's situation. She had noticed that Barrington seemed tense and jumpy lately, especially when she thought Michael was coming over. "Jerickca, she has been acting different lately. One morning, I saw her sitting in her car in the driveway and she was crying, and when I asked her what the problem was, she was about to tell me when Michael walked out the door. She seemed frightened, now that I think about it."

"I'll just have to talk to her, and hopefully she will be honest with me. Please don't worry. I'll talk to her as soon as I can. Now, back to my marriage. How do you know when you have fallen out of love?"

"You can tell the difference by comparing how you felt earlier in the marriage to how you feel now. For instance, when you think about him, you get excited and maybe lose your appetite because you can't wait to see him or you get all tingly inside when he's near you. You want to hold him and be held by him. You want to feel him inside of you even when you are not around each other. When you fall out of love, you care for the other person like a brother or sister. You are not sexually attracted to him. You don't want anything to happen to that person, but he gets on your nerves or something that he does seems gross or stupid," Lula said.

"Mom, maybe we shouldn't discuss this topic today, but I'm so troubled."

"Go ahead, baby. You have to clear your heart, no matter what day of the week it is. You can't celebrate God's blessings if you can't think or talk about your problems."

"Well, I love my husband but I'm bored to death. I want romance and excitement and to spend money in Paris, buy Gucci, and Chanel. And all he wants is to save money."

"Child, what are you talking about? And who or what is Gucci?"

"A famous designer."

"What they make?" Lula said with a quizzical look on her face.

"Purses, shoes, clothes, and other things. The purse you are carrying that I gave you for your birthday last year is from the designer's line. Anyway, that's not the point, Mother. I want to do stuff that's exciting, romantic, and spontaneous, and he acts like he is sixty years."

"Watch yourself, baby, because I am sixty plus and I love to do stuff. You just need to talk to him and let him know how you feel. He is a reasonable man, and I'm sure he will do what it takes to make his marriage work."

"What is Jeremy up to?"

"You don't want to know. That boy is going to be the death of me," Lula chuckled.

"Why, Mom?"

"The other day, I guess it was on the first—you know, that is the day the State pays almost everyone whose name falls in the alphabet from A to F—well anyway, Jeremy got his social security check, and at least four drug dealers showed up for their money, saying that he owes them for crack they gave him on credit."

"I can't believe that. Are you saying they came to your house for money?"

"They sure did, and I had to pay because they said they'd kill him if he didn't pay. They said something about they gotta teach him a lesson so that others won't try to do that to them. So I cashed Jeremy's check and paid all of them. He didn't have but a hundred twenty dollars left. Now, how he gonna pay his house note and utilities with that?"

"Mom, you can't be talking to drug dealers. Don't pay his debt. I don't like that. Please tell them he doesn't live with you. Mother, are you okay financially?"

"Yes, everything is all right." Lula Mae smiled, thinking about how special her daughter always made her feel. She looked at Jerickca and remembered that she had always worried about her more than her other children.

"If you need anything, let me know, but take this check and buy something special, just for yourself." Jerickca looked at her mother and wanted her to have everything that her heart desired.

"You are so good to me."

"Mom, you and dad have been married for thirty-six years.

How did you make your love last?"

"It was hard because we were so different from each other. I went to church and your dad stayed home. I went out and your dad stayed home. Every now and then, I would take a drink and he would become so angry that he called me an alcoholic, a drunk, or any name he could to discourage me from drinking. But he is a good man who took pride in providing for his family. After about ten years, the fire died, but I still loved him. You have to work hard to make your marriage last, and that includes keeping your sex life active and exciting." Lula Mae had a thought-provoking look on her face as she told Jerickca how to keep her sex life thrilling.

Lula Mae continued teaching Jerickca how to keep her man happy. "Child, buy you a long wig, and a new negligee and a bottle of wine and surprise him when he gets home from work. The purpose of the wig is to whip him with it. Swing it all around his body and pretend to be a burlesque dancer. Make that man think he's with a different woman," Lula Mae said with a laugh. She continued, "Excite him and entice him."

Jerickca looked somber and said. "But what if I'm the one who needs the stimulation? Mom, I'm so bored. I have tried to do things to please him, but I still feel left out. Why is the woman the one who always has to do the pleasing?"

"Honey, men believe those statistics that there is one man for every ten women, so if you mess up, they can basically go get the other nine."

Jerickca frowned and leaned over to her mother and said, "I hope the other nine slapped the heck out of that brother." They both laughed and continued to eat their food. It was always nice to have someone to talk to and to share a good time with about life issues.

Jerickca thought about Patches and how fine he was. She

fantasized about making love with him. She could almost feel his tongue lightly flick, lick, and suck her nipples. They would respond by becoming hard pebbles as the sensations traveled down her body like molten lava. She squeezed her thighs together to control the passion threatening to erupt in her. Jerickca realized that she would never cross her set imposed boundary with her employee. It would never happen, no matter how sexy he looked. She shook that young boy off her mind with a quick shake of her head. Thinking about her husband, she wished he could make her feel sexy again. Jerickca knew that she would have to do something to get back in the groove with him. He was a kind and wonderful man. He seemed uptight about some things, but he was a basically good guy.

She knew one thing: she was glad that she had a man, because when she was dating before she got married, she hated it. She never knew if the guy would become obsessed with her and kill her in a rage or if she would end up with some type of sexual disease. People didn't care about each other like they used to, and she was glad she didn't have to take chances in the dating field. She made up her mind that she would work hard to love and be loved by the man she had promised to love until death did them part.

As Jerickca and her mom prepared to leave the restaurant, Jerickca's thoughts returned to her mother and her encounter with the drug dealers. She said, "Mom, don't pay any more drug dealers. I will talk to Jeremy. This is going to stop, okay?"

"Sure baby. I don't like it either."

They both left a tip on the table and walked out of the restaurant together, with their arms lovingly around each other's waist.

Chapter 21

Megan walked through the front door of her home and passed quickly through the living and dining rooms. She pulled out the oak wood chair at her kitchen table and tossed the mail so hard that it soared through in the air. She was sick and tired of being sick and tired, and she was so horny. It had been a while since she had been sexually intimate, and she was frustrated.

She chuckled to herself, thinking that if she were with a man now, she would probably kill him while they were having sex, because she would ride him to death. She could almost visualize the poor man pleading with her to stop loving him so hard and so long. She decided to call an ex-lover and invite him over. She picked up the phone, dialed his pager number, and waited on him to call her. The phone rang three times before she was able to pick it up and whisper in her deep sexy voice "Hello."

"Megan," Cecil said.

"Hey Cecil, what's up?"

"You girl! It's been a long time since I heard from you. How have you been?"

"I have been doing fine; just thinking about you. What are you doing tonight?" Megan asked.

"Hey I was just chillin' at the house tonight."

"You wanna come over and get into something?" Megan hoped he would answer yes.

"You still live in the same place?" Cecil inquired.

"Yeah. How long would it take for you to get here?"

"Hey baby, I'll be there in about twenty minutes," Cecil said, whispering, as if someone had walked into the room and made him uncomfortable.

"Cool. I'll see you then."

Megan had met Cecil in high school. They had dated on and off for twenty years. They were "friends with benefits." She decided to shower and change into something sexy. She went and pulled out a bottle of Cristal, grabbed a bucket, and filled it with ice to chill the wine.

In less than fifteen minutes, she heard a car door slam. She went to the large bay window and pulled back the burgundy drapes to take a peep. As Cecil walked toward her door, the timer light flickered on, and she saw that he had kept himself in shape. He had a bald head, and he looked damn good. She started getting tingly all over, and he hadn't even walked into the house yet.

After she let Cecil in, they sat down on the French provincial couch and Megan took two crystal wine glasses and filled them with the tasty liquid she needed to enjoy this evening. As they drank the wine, they both began to get comfortable. Cecil reached for her, pulled her into his arms, and gently kissed her. She grabbed his head and tried to steal his tongue from his mouth because it felt so good inside hers. She was so hot and ready for him. He lifted her up off the couch, pulled her toward the bedroom that he was so familiar with, and stripped her out of her negligee. Once on the bed she grabbed and stroked his penis gently and felt his hardness. She knew he was ready to take her, but she didn't want the night to end too quickly, so she slowed it down. She kissed his ears, face, and stomach and went back up to his face where she continued passionately kissing him. Cecil grabbed her by the butt, pulled her on top of him, and whispered, "I missed you so much."

"I missed you, too," she whispered as she kissed him deeply on the mouth.

“Where is your raincoat?” Megan asked in a low, sexy voice that sounded as if she were weak with desire.

Cecil reached toward the nightstand, pulled out a condom, and opened it. As he tried to put it on, Megan grabbed his penis and began to lick it. He moaned softly as she deep throated his organ. Cecil was moaning and massaging her sensually, all over her body. Finally, he pulled her under him, spread her legs, slid down her body, and buried his head in her treasure island. As he dug deeper with his tongue to find her jewels, her body temperature began to rise, and she tried to back up toward the headboard. She wanted him inside of her when she had her orgasm. She grabbed the back of the headboard in an attempt to get leverage to help her escape from him but he was so determined to please her that he followed her every move. When she backed up, he crawled to her.

“Please put it in me now!” she begged him.

Cecil reached up, pushed up towards her face, and kissed her again. “We have all night,” he said. “This time I don’t want you to forget me.”

Suddenly, she felt the hard pressure of him as he jammed himself inside her. The throbbing between her legs was so loud she could record a song without a microphone. His loving was so hot and hard that she had multiple orgasms. Cecil was so good at what he did. After sleeping for a little while, Megan woke him again for round two. He was a keeper. She didn’t want the night to end, but she knew that it would because he had to go back home to his wife and children.

Chapter 22

"Hey, good-looking," smiled Precious. "Think we can get together tonight?"

Patches responded, "Hell no! If you keep getting into my business, you will never spend another night with me."

"What are you talking about? I haven't been in your business."

"We'll talk later," he said as he headed toward the back room.

Patches walked down the long hall toward the closed door and wondered what they were discussing this time. As he turned the knob, he announced, "Big Daddy is home." This was the name that Patches called himself.

"You are just the person we wanted to talk to," Megan said as she snickered. She continued, "We were just discussing Afro-Americans participating in anal sex, and we were wondering what your take was."

"I don't have a take Megan. That's not me. What you into freaking now?" Patches frowned as he spoke and looked as if he smelled something funky.

Megan looked at Patches as if she didn't believe him. You could tell she was thinking Patches was lying by the way she lifted her eyebrows and stared at him. Finally, after a few moments of silence and a look at Patches, she said, "Stop lying. You are a Scorpio, and everybody knows about the people born under that sign."

"Megan, I didn't say I never tried it, because I have, but I didn't like participating in the act, especially with someone I cared about," Patches said, looking down at his shoes.

Phoenix joined in and asked, "Then why did you do it to this woman you claim you cared about?"

Denver interjected, "Yeah, why did you do it, Big Daddy?"

"I only did it because she had already been exposed before I met her and that was her preference."

"But Patches, you did it anyway, right?" Phoenix asked.

"Yeah, I did and it was okay, but I had a bad feeling about it, especially since someone else had done her. It felt okay, but really, I was kind of grossed out thinking about her being with someone else."

Megan re-entered the conversation and said, "But you did it anyway, and I think you are saying it felt unnatural, right?"

"Yeah. But for a lot of African Americans, it seems from what I'm hearing, they are trying it," he said.

"That's the same thing I'm hearing, especially from the young people. They are doing things that we never would have done," Denver concluded.

Just as Megan was about to say something, the door opened and Jerickca walked in.

"Hey, how's everyone doing?" she asked.

"Fine," everyone said simultaneously.

Megan looked at everyone quickly and smiled a devious smile. "Jerickca, we were talking about young people and African-Americans getting involved with anal sex and other things that they never used to do. What do you think about the subject?"

Jerickca had an "I-can't-believe-she-asked-me-that look on her face," but responded anyway. "If you are asking me if I participate in that type of activity, the answer is no. Do I approve? No, again. The way I figured it, God gave us nine holes in our bodies and each has its own function."

"What are the nine holes?" Phoenix and Megan asked at the same time and laughed because they were both on the same note.

"Well, you have two ears, two nostrils, vagina or penis, anus, mouth, and two eyes. The anus is only for removing waste. You know, expelling, not taking in. So I'm not sure why people are into anal sex now, particularly since AIDS was first identified as being a disease from the gay community. I'm not sure why people would participate in something that is so unclean. Now don't get mad, but that is my opinion." Jerickca added, "Maybe we can have a seminar on AIDS, HIV, and other sexually transmitted diseases. After all, knowledge is power, and we need to educate the African American community, because now more than fifty percent of the current people who are getting HIV and AIDS are heterosexuals and from our race."

"Why is that?" Patches wanted to know.

"I'm not sure, but I believe that our young people don't think that it can happen to them. The other part of it is that it is probably transmitted from our men having bisexual relations. So many of our men have been in jail and may have had sexual relations with other men, and they come back out and pass their diseases to their girlfriends and wives. Also, there is a new term for men who are having sex with both sexes but keep it a secret. They are on the down low. Believe me, I am not an expert, but I've read so much on the subject, I probably could do a presentation on it."

"I've heard of men on the down low. It's just a new term, but we all know it's the same as homosexuals in the closet," Megan added.

"I feel sorry for our people, because we are so trusting and naïve. We believe anything," Phoenix said sadly.

"Yeah, and when our women get involved in something with a brother, they always try to get another brother to do the same,"

Patches said.

"Don't try that Patches, you know that you like it, too. You said that you wanted your women to be willing to try new things," Megan declared. "You know you like anything they do to you," she continued.

"You're right, but I want to be the only one she tries things with," he laughed.

"You are wrong! How many women do you know that are pure and untouched? There's not many, so don't complain when they come already exposed."

"Now you are tripping, Megan. I don't want my women busted from the back by anyone. As a matter of fact, I don't want to know about stuff like that," he acknowledged.

"Well, don't do anything to someone else's woman that you don't want done to yours," Phoenix declared passionately.

Jerickca stood up and began walking towards the door. As she reached for the door, she turned and said, "That's my note out. Let's plan a workshop on that subject this quarter. We'll plan it at our next staff meeting." She pulled the door closed.

Patches turned and whispered, "Megan you are a fool, girl. I can't believe you asked Jerickca that question."

"I told you all that Jerickca is cool like that. Trust me. We can talk about anything."

Denver and Phoenix just glanced at each other as if they were saying that Megan ought to quit perpetrating. They both were thinking, *Megan isn't that cool with the boss.* They seemed to be getting tired of her exaggerating about her relationship with their boss.

Patches was sitting at his desk, thinking about the conversation.

He picked up the phone and whispered, "Precious, what are you doing for lunch? Meet me at my car, okay?" He was wondering if he had any raincoats in his car, because all that sex talk was getting to him.

Even though Patches had said that he would never have relationships again with women that he worked with, he couldn't seem to keep his promise. He knew one thing, and that was that he loved good-looking, fine women. No matter what he said, seeing a beautiful African-American woman was his major weakness.

Chapter 23

Phoenix was sitting at home, talking to Devante. Sometimes when they were together in the quiet of their home and spending time with their daughter Simone, she could feel the strong love he had for his family. This was the time she felt the most secure in her life. She had been fortunate enough to meet Devante, but he was a very quiet and unexciting man. She never doubted his love for his family, but she wanted more. She wanted everything life had to offer, including great sex. Why couldn't she have it all?

If only her husband would try to meet her halfway, things could be different, but since he wouldn't take one step, she wasn't about to take two. Now, all she had left was a troubled heart. Until she met the exhilarating Juan DeFrance, her world had been lifeless. He was everything a woman could want in a man—stimulating, sexy, handsome, and electrifying. He met all her qualifications for the ultimate life with a fantastic man.

She couldn't continue to sleep with both her husband and Juan, because it was becoming increasingly difficult to balance both relationships. Plus she was almost caught by her co-worker, Megan, who had the gift of the gab and would broadcast her business throughout the professional community. This would definitely get back to Devante, and the last thing she wanted to do was to cause him embarrassment. One way to prevent a catastrophe was to get Megan on her side by confiding and begging her to keep this secret if they were really best friends. Megan bought it like a child buying French fries from McDonald's restaurant.

After putting Simone to bed, Phoenix decided to talk to Devante about their sex life. She wasn't looking forward to having this conversation because they always ended up in an argument, but she was willing to do anything to try to salvage her marriage. After all, she had an infant. And what could be better than allowing her to grow up with her father?

Devante walked into the den and sat on the green leather couch. He grabbed the remote control and searched for something to watch on cable TV. Phoenix entered the room and sat next to him.

"Honey, we need to talk," she said.

"What is it about?" he asked.

"Our marriage." Phoenix shifted and propped her legs up on the couch so she was sitting in an Indian style.

"What seems to be the problem with our marriage?" he inquired. "Because I thought we were doing fine."

"Well, we are doing okay if you like having a boring sex life."

"It didn't seem boring last night by the way you screamed out in pleasure when we were in the act," he said angrily.

"I can never talk to you because you always get an attitude. I want more, Devante—a good sex life and a larger home."

"You know what, Phoenix? If you are so unhappy because you don't have a good sex life and you're too poor, why don't you just leave?" Devante threw the remote control across the den. It hit the mirror over the stereo system and broke it into small pieces. The remote tumbled to the floor and broke apart. Devante stormed into the kitchen, grabbed his keys off the table, and walked briskly to his black Navigator. He jumped in and burned rubber out of the driveway. Phoenix bowed her head and cried. After crying until she could release no more tears, she picked up the phone and called Juan.

"Juan."

"Phoenix! Hey baby, how are you?" Juan asked cheerfully.

"Not too good," Phoenix replied.

"What's wrong, sweetheart?"

"Devante and I just had an argument about our relationship. He doesn't seem to understand my needs and I'm so frustrated," she said while trying to refrain from crying.

"Phoenix, try to be patient with him. Maybe you both need counseling. Believe me, it's not that I don't want to be with you, but I don't want any guilt from this relationship, either. Talk and make him understand before you do something rash."

"Juan, can I see you tomorrow?"

"Phoenix, honestly, I think we should stop seeing each other until you work out your problems. Our relationship is probably hindering your marriage, and I think it is best that I step out of this and let you work this out with your husband," Juan said boldly.

"Fuck you!" Phoenix said as she slammed the phone in his ear. "How dare he just drop me like an egg when he knows that I love him?" she said to no one in particular. "I don't need his ass, and I don't need Devante," Phoenix cried as she ran upstairs to pack and get Simone. She did not know where she was going but she knew she was leaving Devante. She had been married five years, most of them spent pleading with him to change and accommodate her sexually, and he always refused. There was no way in the world she would stay another day in a relationship that made her so sad.

Chapter 24

"Spencer, hey how are you?"

"Jerickca, what's up? I haven't heard from you all week. What's been going on in your life?" Spencer inquired, happy to hear from her friend.

"Girl, same old thing," I was thinking about coming to see you in July when I attend this conference. After it's over, I plan to stay a few more days. I need a break from work and family stuff, and I want to talk to you about something."

"Are you sure everything is okay?" She wanted to know. "How is Pam doing?"

Jerickca laugh and said, "Girl, Pammie is doing okay, probably getting more sex than the both of us."

"You got that right," Spencer said. "My client is here, but call me to let me know the day you plan on coming and your flight information, and I will pull together a weekend agenda. I look forward to seeing you, girl. We'll have a great time. Talk to you later. Okay? Bye now."

"Bye," Jerickca said, happily.

Just as Jerickca placed the receiver on the hook, Patches walked through the door. "Jerickca," he said. "Do you have a moment?"

"Sure, what can I do for you?" she said while closing her agenda book.

"I have a client who needs food because she sold her food stamps to pay her light bill. Since they have that new link card to decrease fraud, instead of the food stamps, she basically took someone to the store and let them select what they wanted to purchase and she used her card to pay for it. I've already counseled her and looked at all her bills and helped her to set up a budget for the next four months, but honestly, I told her she needs a job to help her stay afloat. She agreed to job search and look into going back to school. But for now, she needs food," Patches said.

"Did she contact any agencies to assist her with her utilities?" Jerickca wanted to know.

"Yes she did, but they helped her out before, and she would have to wait another three months before she can receive additional help."

"I see. She's had assistance within the past six months, which excludes her from help for another three months. Go ahead and submit a form to me for specific assistance, take her to Schnuck's grocery store with the corporate card, and let her buy one hundred dollars worth of food and toiletries. I hope that she understands that she will have to help herself by becoming employed or she will remain in this cycle."

"I'm working closely with her and her three children, and she does want to do better," he responded, as he stood up and walked toward the door. "Thanks," he said. "Jerickca, can I ask you a question?"

"Sure, what is it?"

"Have you ever dated someone who worked for you?"

"No, why do you ask?"

"McNary took a deep breath and said, "I just wanted to know if you would ever consider dating someone who worked for you?"

"Actually, McNary, I wouldn't. It would be a disaster. It could never work. Why, are you interested in someone here?"

"Yes, I am but she is married and she is an executive here." He smiled and lifted his left eyebrow, waiting on her to figure it out.

"Well, I'm sure that I … I mean, whoever it is wouldn't do something so unethical."

"So you are saying there would not be a chance for a relationship between too consenting adults in positions like yours and mine, right?"

"Yes, that is what I'm saying."

Just as Jerickca was about to say something else, her phone buzzed.

"Ms. Parker, you have a call on line 2150," Karen said.

"Thank you."

"Are you finished McNary?"

"Yes," he said and walked out the door.

"This is Jerickca Parker. How may I help you?"

"Jeri, this is Jeremy. Can I borrow a fifty?" he asked.

"I don't have it," she said to her brother. "Anyway what do you need it for?"

Jeremy said with hostility, "You don't have to ask me what I need it for. Either you have it or you don't."

"I don't have money to give drug dealers," she stated.

"You don't have to go there. I need to pay a bill. Anyway, everybody knows you got money and you can give it to me without this hassle."

"I don't just give money away. By the way, please don't have your dealers stopping by Mama's house for your monthly check.

You are putting her in danger with that stupid shit!" Jerickca raised her voice because she wanted him to get her point.

"I don't want to talk about that shit. Are you gonna spot me or not?"

"Did you tell me what you need it for?" she asked again.

"I told you that I don't have time for this stupid shit. Fuck you!" Jeremy slammed the phone down hard.

"What the hell! He actually slammed the phone in my ear!" she whispered as if she couldn't believe what had happened. Just as she was hanging up the phone, Megan walked into her office.

"Do you have time to go over the banquet details for the families?" Megan wanted to know.

"Not right now. Ask the selected committee members to meet today at 1:00 p.m., and I will attend. At that time, we can go over everything together," Jerickca replied.

"Can we make that at 2:00 p.m.? Phoenix and Denver are both in the field and will not be back until after 1:30."

"That's fine," Jerickca said, still smarting from her brother's response to her not giving in to him.

After Megan walked out the door, Jerickca picked up the phone and called Deborah at her office. "May I speak to Attorney Dennison, please?" Jerickca asked.

"Hello, this is Attorney Dennison."

"What are you doing for lunch today?" Jerickca wanted to know.

"I'm going to be in court today. But I'll call later in the week. Okay?" Deborah said coldly.

"Are you okay, girl?"

"Yeah, I'm fine, but we'll talk this weekend."

"Hey, you're my girl, and if you need me for anything, just call me and you know I'll be there in a second. You do know that, don't you?"

"Yes, I do, and you know I will call if I need you. I'll talk to you later. Bye." Deborah hung up the phone.

Now I want to know what is going on, Jerickca thought. Then she picked up the phone and dialed Deborah's home. After five rings, Danny picked up.

"Danny, is Deborah home?"

"Nah, she is in court today," he said.

"All right. I'll call her this evening."

"No, as a matter of fact, stop calling here at all. She doesn't need some nosey bitch getting into our business, so please leave us alone," he said.

"Danny, nothing is going to keep me from my best friend, and you can take that shit to the bank and deposit it." Now it was her turn to hang up the phone, and she did—hard!

The nerve of him! Does he think I am going to let him alienate her from her friends so that he can manipulate and beat her? Because if he does, he's got another thing coming, she said loudly. *This has been a day*! she thought. "What in the world is going on with these people?" she asked.

"Hi Jerickca," Kelvin, the janitor, said as Jerickca walked down the hall to the ladies' room.

"How are you today, Kelvin?"

“I’m fine,” he responded.

“Good,” she said as she walked toward the back of the building. Just as she turned the corner, she heard loud laughter. As she listened, she heard Megan ask Phoenix if she had heard about Denver and Jerickca discussing the new contracts. Phoenix told her that she didn’t know what she was talking about. Just as she completed her last word, Jerickca pushed the door open.

“Hello everyone,” Jerickca said as she moved inside of the wooden door.

“Hi.” Everyone seemed to say in unison.

Jerickca wanted to confront the question she had heard Megan asking Phoenix about the contracts. “I was walking down the hall and I heard Megan inquiring about the contracts. What seems to be the concern?”

“Nothing,” Megan quickly said.

Jerickca looked at Phoenix and asked her, “Are you sure you have no concerns?”

“Not really.”

“All right, then, I guess I will leave. But as I told you guys in the past, if you want to know something, please ask me.” Jerickca walked out the door.

“She is such a bitch with her think-she-is-all-that ass.” Megan said with her top lip twisted up as if she could smell Jerickca shit.

“You didn’t say shit when she was in here, so don’t start now,” Patches said.

“Fuck ya’ll, she was just testing to see if I’m discussing what she told me.”

“You need to quit Megan, ’cause Jerickca ain’t told you shit about nothing.”

Just then, Denver walked into the room. “Hi all,” she said, smiling.

“Hi your own ass. What can we do back here for you?” Megan wanted to know.

“Just stopped through to chat.”

“Well, sorry Denver,” Megan smiled. “We are really busy and don’t have time for chatting today.”

“What’s on your mind, Denver?” Patches asked. He was tired of the group alienating Denver.

“Nothing, I’ll come back later when you all don’t have so much to do.”

“Yeah, you just do that,” Megan said without so much as even trying to make Denver feel accepted.

“Come back whenever you feel like it, Baby Girl.” Patches smiled.

“I will,” Denver said as she walked out of the office.

Patches turned to Megan and the rest of the gang. “You guys need to stop tripping with that girl. She is a nice person, and you all treat her bad for no reason.”

“I just don’t like her!” Phoenix and Megan snapped at the same time.

“You’re only doing that to her because of Megan.” Patches got up to leave the room.

“I don’t need Megan’s approval for nothing.”

"Are you sure? Because that is not the way it seems to me."

Megan hunched her shoulders and completed her case notes.

Patches just shook his head and glared at both women before walking out of the room.

Chapter 25

Jerickca cleared her desk and grabbed her black leather organizer. She picked up the phone and pushed the intercom button. "Karen, please hold all my calls. I'm heading to a meeting in the conference room."

"Okay," she said. "Should I hold the calls for the rest of the staff?"

Jerickca responded, "You have to check with each of the staff. They may have calls from clients that they are expecting."

"All right, I will talk to each of them," Karen stated.

As Jerickca walked toward the conference area, she was met by Megan, who wanted to talk.

"I need to talk to you."

Jerickca started walking slowly and Megan tracked quickly behind her.

"It's important."

Jerickca stopped and walked into the storage area. Megan followed.

"I'm sorry I haven't said anything and I certainly didn't want to tell on my coworkers, but I think the families in our program deserve the best and unfortunately, I haven't had much help from my peers. They haven't followed through on anything. I can't do this by myself. I mean I could, but I shouldn't have to," Megan whined.

Jerickca was surprised that Megan was reporting her peers, and she was shocked that Megan had even told her, because usually she would make reference and not come straight out to make her complaints when she felt someone else was not doing their part. "Well,

I will bring it up in this meeting," she said.

"I would prefer that you not do that unless you let them know without disclosing that I said something. After all, I have to work with them and they can get pretty angry." Megan thought about the last time her peers had become angry with her, and she didn't feel like going through all that drama again. *No,* she thought, *I definitely don't want to go through that again.*

Jerickca understood what Megan was saying, and she said, "I'll bring it up my way."

"Thanks, Jerickca. I knew that you would be able to handle that because you are an excellent director who really knows how to talk to people."

Jerickca smiled, because whenever she talked to Megan, she never failed to brown nose. As a matter of fact, Jerickca didn't mind at all.

Jerickca walked to the conference room and Megan followed. Once inside, she placed her organizer on the table, took a seat, and patiently waited for everyone to arrive. At exactly 2:00 p.m., Phoenix, McNary, and Denver walked through the door, followed by several other workers.

Jerickca started the meeting by informing everyone that she wanted to get an update on the banquet to ensure that everything was in order. She began by polling each person. "Phoenix, can you give me an update on the entertainment?"

"Sure," Phoenix said. "I have two parents who will be singing one solo each, and one of the fathers will be reading a poem. I have also asked McNary to read a poem, and Karen will be saying the welcome. Jerickca, you are also down for the occasion. I'm working on other things that I haven't quite finalized yet."

"You must have worked hard on that today, because yesterday

you didn't have anything," Megan stated with a surprised look on her face as she turned to look at Jerickca.

"Dang," Patches said. "How you gonna bust a sister out?"

"I didn't mean anything by it. I was just surprised that's all," Megan said defiantly.

"Okay, what about you, McNary? Have you finalized the transportation list?" Jerickca inquired.

Patches looked at Jerickca and smiled, "I got that under control. Don't worry about it. Patches knows what he has to do," he said cockily.

"Well, I would like to see the list by Friday," Jerickca said.

"What list? I know that my people are not on any list because you didn't ask me anything," Megan said boldly.

"Girl, you have issues," Patches said to Megan as if he could knock her out of her seat. "As I said, the list will be completed by Friday."

"Very well," Jerickca sighed.

"Denver, your report please," Jerickca said.

"Well, I'm not sure what I was supposed to do."

"I know you are kidding, girl. You have to be kidding," Megan said with her shoulder hunched up.

"Well, I don't remember what it was."

"Denver you were supposed to get the keynote speaker, remember? Your friend, the big-time football player, Marshall Faulk," Megan said as though she didn't believe her.

"I'm sorry if I said that, but I know he won't be able to come to the banquet because they are in training now."

"I knew that wasn't going to happen," Megan laughed.

"Well, do you have any suggestions, Megan?" Jerickca asked.

"Why don't you do it, Jerickca? The clients don't see you that often, and it is way too late with the banquet being next week for us to ask someone else. You speak better than those other people do anyway."

"That's a great idea," everybody said in unison.

"I guess I can do that, and one of you can do the occasion," Jerickca said looking at Patches.

"We'll get that together," Megan said as she turned to her peers. "We can get together briefly after this meeting."

"Okay, then this meeting is over. By the way, the banquet will be catered by B and F Soul Food cafeteria."

"Good job, people. We'll get back together in three days to confirm everything," Jerickca said as she walked through the door. She could hear the room buzzing, and she knew what was about to happen.

Patches turned to face Megan, "You are a trip. Why did you dog us like that? What were you trying to do, bust us out? You need to get a grip on yourself," he said angrily.

"I wasn't trying to bust you all out. I was just surprised that all of a sudden you all had information, but when I asked you all earlier, none of you had done anything. But let Jerickca come in here and ya'll act like you been working hard," Megan said with disgust. "Ya'll know me, and I don't like anything I work with to be messed up, so you all can get mad at me if you want, but I just want the banquet to be the best for our parents. You know how I feel about them."

"Megan, you are full of shit," Patches said.

"Whatever, but I guarantee that we will have a great banquet," Megan said as she stood to leave. "What's for lunch?" They were eating lunch late today due to their heavy schedule.

Denver and Phoenix said that they wanted some fried chicken from Popeye's.

"I'll pick it up. I should be back in twenty minutes," Megan said. "I will get your food and you can pay me when I return. You all want the usual?"

Denver and Phoenix both responded with a yes. Patches walked out without saying a word. Megan just stared at his back. She knew that he wouldn't stay mad long, because he never did.

After the meeting, Jerickca informed the staff that she would be leaving the office for a couple of hours. She walked to her office, grabbed her purse, and informed Karen that she was going to be out of the office for a while but she could reach her by cell.

Once she arrived at St. Clair Square Mall in Fairview Heights, which was approximately twelve minutes from the office, she parked and walked into the Famous Barr Department Store. As she browsed through the women's department, she bumped into Deborah.

"Deborah girl! What's up?"

"Nothing," she said as she turned around to face her friend.

"What happened to your eye?" Jerickca asked loudly.

"Nothing, I bumped into a door." Deborah said in a low voice, trying to hide her face as if she didn't want anyone to notice her.

"It looks like someone socked you in the face. Did Danny hit you?" She asked.

“No,” she said coldly.

“You can discuss this with me. You know I would help you in any way that I can. Please let me help you.”

“Jerickca, I don’t need any help. Just stay out of my relationship and we will get along just fine,” she said as she stormed off.

Jerickca just stood there staring long after Deborah had walked away. How could a lawyer who knows the ropes, allow something like this to happen to herself? Jerickca was perplexed. *I have to help my friend*, she thought.

When Jerickca arrived home, she went straight into the living room. Standing in front of the fifty-two-inch television, she said, “Anthony, Deborah had a black eye and she wouldn’t talk to me. I know Danny hit her.”

“I’m trying to look at the news and you are blocking my view,” he said.

“My friend is being abused. Did you not hear what I said?”

“Yeah, I heard you but that is her business. If she allows a man to knock her around, there is nothing you can do about it, so please let me look at the evening news.”

Jerickca walked away frustrated. Fucking men!

Chapter 26

Phoenix pulled up in front of the house and thought about how she had almost lost Devante when she ran out the house last week. It didn't take her long to find out that she didn't have anywhere to go and she didn't want to show up at her mother's little house. Once she walked out the door with Simone, backed out of driveway, and left her subdivision, she realized that she didn't have any money or a place to rest her head. Juan had made it clear that he wanted her to work on their marriage and that he was willing to step out of her life if need be.

She was very hurt and felt abandoned when he told her that he would let her go so easily. Since that time, she had started to see Juan only when she wanted to. Now she was working intensely to make her husband love her. She wasn't complaining nearly as much and had agreed in her own mind that rather than getting left out in the cold, she would just suffer. It was better than being without money and a nice home. Once she could convince Juan that she would be good for him she would make her move.

As she sat in her car in deep thought, she noticed that the heavy burgundy curtain was open. Devante was on the phone looking out the window. He was a good husband and a great provider. It wasn't his fault that she wanted more than he had to offer. It wasn't that they didn't have money—they just didn't have enough. They were just the typical all-American family, and that wasn't what she dreamed she would become. Her dreams were of lavish parties, expensive designer clothes, and fast, exclusive cars. She wanted to mingle with the rich and famous, not the meager and barely surviving.

As she got out of the car and walked through the house, she noticed that Devante was smiling as he hung up the phone. She walked toward him and kissed him on the lips, "Hi sweetheart," she said.

"Hi, Phoenix," Devante said as he grabbed his car keys and headed toward the door. "I gotta make a run and I'll be back later. Don't cook anything for me. I'll grab a bite later."

"All right. See you later." Phoenix didn't worry about where Devante was going because he was as straight as the Nile River.

After cooking dinner, eating, and putting Simone to bed, she picked up the phone to call Juan. "Hey, baby. What's up?"

"You, baby," Juan said. "Are we still going to the Ozarks next weekend?"

"Yeah, Devante is going to keep Simone," she said. "I can't wait. I have never been there. What is it, about three hours away?"

"It is just about that many hours or less. There is so much to do there with swimming, horseback riding, boating, and dancing. That's why I like it—because of the variety of activities they have to offer."

"I can't wait. I miss you so much. I just want to touch and suck your body all over," she said while smacking kisses through the phone.

"You really turn me on. I couldn't stay away from you if I wanted to."

"I love you Juan."

"Don't do that, Phoenix. I am not in love with you. I do care about you, but I don't love you. Remember, I am not about to get emotional with anyone right now."

"I can handle that but it doesn't stop my feelings," she moaned.

"I'll talk to you later," Juan said as he hung up the phone without waiting for Phoenix to respond.

Phoenix looked at the phone and slammed it back into its cradle. "Just wait and see, I'll get that nigger," she said out loud.

As she stood to walk to the kitchen to retrieve a glass for her sparkling white wine, the phone rang.

"What's up dawg?" Megan shouted.

"Nothing but you, girl. What's up?"

"I called to ask you something. What did you think when Denver came in to work with those stretch pants on with that little ass top?"

"Megan, girl, you are a fool and you know it."

"I know, but she ought to be ashamed of herself, wearing those little bitty ass clothes with her flat ass. Aren't those stretch pants for women with shapes? What is on that girl's mind?" Megan said, as she laughed.

"I don't know what's on that girl's mind, but I know one thing: she sure is a space cadet. How in the world does she have so much book sense and no street sense?" Phoenix said, shaking her head as if Megan could see her.

"I don't know," Megan stated, "but she is stupid. She really needs to change the way she is dressing. I don't care if she is in her twenties, she should dress more professional. I wonder why Jerickca hasn't said anything to her about her attire?"

"You know Jerickca ain't gone rub her feathers since Denver helped write that proposal to get us all employed," Phoenix interjected.

"Well, eventually I'm going to say something to her trifling ass. It doesn't make sense that we are out here teaching people how to get a job, and then they come to the office, they see someone with stretch pants on making good money," Megan said bitterly. "You know our people. They think they can wear stuff like that and get away with it on a job."

"Hey, did you see Precious and Patches leave for lunch the other day?" Phoenix asked.

"You know they were having sex, with their funky asses. They ain't seen an ounce of water. You could tell what they had been doing. They had that look. Patches' pants were pulled up to his waist and his breast nipples were pronounced," laughed Megan.

They both were laughing so hard and finally Phoenix said, "You are too crazy, girl. Only you would notice some shit like that. Precious was looking like she hit the jackpot or something. She was so glad that she was seen with Patches."

Megan countered, "You are right. One of these days Patches gonna put that penis in somebody and all their shit gone explode."

"Boom! Boom!" Megan said loudly as if she was a firecracker in a Fourth of July fireworks display.

"Girl, shut up! Just shut up! Who ain't that boy fucking?" Phoenix said laughing intensely.

"He ain't doing me, though sometimes I wondered about his bedroom tactics. The boy must have some skills." Megan said as she visualized Patches naked.

"Girl, if you got hold of that boy you would kill him," Phoenix laughed.

"You are right. He wouldn't know what hit his ass. Girl, I have to go. I have another call coming in," Megan said. "I'll see you at work."

"Bye, girl." Phoenix said as she hung the phone up.

Chapter 27

The banquet was beautiful. Megan and her committee had decorated the Shrine of Our Lady Restaurant banquet room in red and white. The tables were covered in white sheer and lacy material. There were a total of twenty-five tables with ten chairs and silverware sets at each one. The tables had crystal bowl centerpieces, filled one quarter with water so that the lighted candles would float without the water overtaking them. The tables were lined in processional order, with a slight slant toward the front where the podium stood.

At the head table sat the keynote speaker Jerickca, along with Megan, two parents, and two federal reviewers from Washington, D. C. They had been invited after they finished reviewing the program to ensure that compliance goals had been met. They wanted to participate in the banquet to show their support. There were two organizations from the community and two business vendors who had donated furniture and clothing to the families.

Megan had again demonstrated to everyone that she had great organizing skills. Everyone was in his or her appropriate place, dressed as sharp as stainless steel knives. Megan had pulled the troops together and, as always, they were smiling as if they had just hit the Illinois lottery jackpot. That's how it always happened. Everyone would be furious with Megan because she worked and pushed too hard. Then the night of the activity, they would be standing around shaking the guests' hands and graciously accepting all the compliments about how professional and elegant everything looked. During these times, they truly loved Megan. They would stand around smiling and catering to Megan's needs because they were so proud of her. Megan would just float around greeting everybody, smiling, and looking pretty.

She was good with this kind of stuff and watching the people's faces made her feel like she was the executive director. Jerickca wasn't flashy. She mingled with others but had such a quiet persona. She didn't need to be in the front. She didn't seek awards because she had been so fortunate in her life that she felt she had already received her glory on Earth. She was only seeking another kind of glory, and that was one that surely wasn't earthly. This gave Megan the floor to be brassy yet polite, pretty but not conceited. Jerickca stood back, proud. She really did have an extraordinary staff. They really excelled when they collaborated, organized, and worked together to have successful activities.

One thing that did not surprise Jerickca was that Megan handed out the most awards for her families. Her families received awards for most successful, hardest worker, most achieved, highest paid, and most professionally dressed. Patches, Phoenix, and Denver had one parent each who received awards for most responsible, most respectful, and most reliable. All the other participants received awards for successfully completing six months of the program. The staff stood proudly as the families approached the head table to accept their awards and to shake the extended hands of the prominent guest.

The highlight of the evening was the keynote speaker. Jerickca Parker was great. She had written a speech that was powerful, inspirational, and encouraging. Her speech entitled "Knocked Down but Not Out" emphasized that we all have struggles, but it's how you handle your life that makes you a champion. She talked about stepping out into the darkness with God as your lantern. She told them that the only failures in life were those who stopped trying. She spoke with such elegance and strength that several times during her speech she received loud applause.

Finally, Jerickca told the audience about herself: how difficult math had been for her and how she would sit at the table and cry with her mother right by her side, rubbing her hand because she didn't have the education to help her, but she wanted her daughter to know that she would stand by her, even in the most difficult times in her life. Jerickca finally said that it was those who had your interest at heart that would not lead you astray, and that people should pick their friends wisely. Her last words were, "Just the way my mother sat with me at the table when I thought I was in my darkest hour and showed me that she would be there even during the rough times, that is what we, this agency, want you to know: when you feel at your lowest, like giving up, pick up your phone and call us, because we are here for the long haul. For those who may not have access to a phone, stop by our office. We welcome you." Megan had tears running down her face, and Phoenix laid her head on Patches' shoulders, too emotional to move. Jerickca saw tissues being passed around and people wiping their faces. The clapping was so loud that it sounded like thunder, and people were leaping to their feet, smiling. As Jerickca walked back to her seat, everyone at the head table grabbed and hugged her and said how inspirational her words had been to everyone.

After the awards had been given to the parents and all the remarks and presentations made, the families who rode on the bus were loaded and taken to their destinations. The staff stayed around to congratulate Jerickca on her speech and to thank each other for such a wonderful banquet. That night, everyone went to bed happy and feeling proud to be a part of Jerickca Parker's staff.

Chapter 28

Denver kissed Lathan on his nose, his eyelid, and finally those supple, sweet lips. "Lathan," she whispered. "Wake up, sweetheart, I want to talk." Lathan turned over and kissed her gently. "What's on your mind, girl?"

"Do you think I dress too casual for work?"

This was not a conversation he wanted to discuss with her. All his life, he had stayed away from questions that women asked him about their clothes and their weight. "How do I look, Lathan?" "Do I look fat, Lathan?" Over and over, these were the questions that if you answered wrong you would be in the doghouse forever. He wasn't about to get trapped tonight, not now when he wanted to push Denver's legs over her head and give her the best loving she ever had.

"Do you hear me, Lathan?"

"I heard you, but I'm not on your job and I certainly don't know what you wear, but it doesn't stop me from wishing I could see your sweet ass every day."

"Megan said that people were talking about me and how I wear stretch pants and big shirts and that it wasn't professional. She told me that if I wanted to move up and make more money, I should dress the part."

"Why do you all let Megan stress ya'll out? Why is she so powerful?" Lathan asked.

"I don't know, but she is something else. She just gets to me and everyone else there."

"She's only as powerful as you all allow her to be. Ignore her ass and she will go away. People like her are powerful because you let her say anything and do anything."

"Maybe, you're right. But she made me feel so insecure because she said everyone was talking about me. I like my peers and don't want to feel uncomfortable around them," Denver whined.

Lathan grabbed Denver and kissed her hard and passionately. "Does Megan have someone who can make her feel like this?" he asked.

Lathan pulled Denver under him and kissed her aroused nipples. Then he allowed his tongue to slither down to her navel, then back up to her lips again. Denver gently rubbed his nipples and licked his left ear. Lathan was so aroused that he grabbed Denver's butt and squeezed her lovingly. Then he whispered how much he wanted her. At that, she arched her back and raised her hips to receive him. Denver rocked her hips hard and used her kegel muscles to grip Lathan as tight as she could. He moaned out loudly.

"I love you baby," Denver screamed as her body began to weaken. Just as she was about to say something else, Lathan hit the spot and Denver felt tingling all over, and as she gripped Lathan's taut love tool, stuff started happening to her body that felt so good, she cried, smiled, and screamed as her heart felt like it was having spasms that were shutting out the intense beating. *Oh Lord, please don't let me die,* she thought as a single tear rolled down her right cheek.

Lathan tried hard to keep up with his young lover but she was whipping his butt with her slender hips. He tried to hold out by trying to control his stroke, but this girl was like a wild animal chasing him with her goodness. He tried to pull out so that he could slow the rhythm, but it was hard. His pores had become liberated and out spurted a plethora of sweat that flowed from him and dripped onto her velvety skin. He couldn't control his groans. "D- D- Den- Denver," he stuttered. Just as he said her name, he released his love juices inside her. Denver grabbed his butt and held on as his organ increased and decreased in size.

Lathan kissed her again and rolled over. He had so much on his mind. He was beginning to really care about this young, beautiful girl. She always seemed so needy to him, unlike his woman at home who seemed to have the strength of Sampson. He had started to think about Denver incessantly. When he was with his woman sexually, he was really with Denver. He wanted her desperately. But he was scared. He wasn't going to be falling all in love with someone so young. He didn't want to hurt this woman, because he truly did love her. This had to be the last time he would see her. He couldn't risk his feelings overpowering his common sense. Tonight was goodbye.

Chapter 29

Patches had finally contacted Jessica. Ever since that night at Club Illusion, she had made like a magician and disappeared. Not being able to mesmerize her as he had so many others made him want her with a great intensity. She had played him the way Jordan had played the NBA. Finally, after practically begging her for a date, she conceded. He took her to the Royal Dumpe, a well-known restaurant and dinner theater in the city of St. Louis. They really enjoyed themselves. Jessica was a classy lawyer with an enormous amount of self-confidence, and she wasn't desperate for a man. Her career was her bed warmer. After their first date, he took her back to her house and kissed her. She kissed him back and slowly walked backwards toward her front door. As she walked back, he grabbed her fingers and kissed them. Jessica thanked him for a nice evening, walked in the house, and closed the door.

Since the first date, he had seen her every other week and he was nowhere near sleeping with her. Once he told her he wanted her and she said she wasn't a one night- stand. She didn't have to tell him that. He already knew that after the first date. He had never allowed any woman to walk away from him before he'd sampled her goods unless it was he who did the walking. But this attorney was nailing him. He wanted to see her so much that he was spending less time with his hood rats. Usually, they were all that he needed to make him realize that he didn't want to be tied down to one woman. But when he took Jessica to the family barbeque and saw how easily his family members talked to her and how gracious she was under pressure, not only was he impressed, but he was beginning to fall in love with her. The worst thing for him that day was when his mother Sinclair told him that she liked his date and was glad he had finally met someone who didn't have a child. She didn't think anything was wrong with a lady having a child, but every time she met anyone that he brought home, she either had a child or was from the projects. She would get attached to the child and then suddenly he would dump the woman, and she would be the one feeling the pain. So she wanted Patches to find someone who he could start a family with so that she could have a grandchild of her own. She wanted him to settle down with a smart, independent woman, and Jessica had it all—the looks, body, smarts, and manners.

Patches had been spending a lot of time with Jerickca and was lusting after her. She was smart and independent, just like Jessica. These were two women whom he admired, and neither was letting him taste their goodness. He found himself telling her about his life, his problems, and how he wanted to change and stop seeing so many women. He wasn't bragging, but he was downright tired. He trusted Jerickca. He wanted to confide in her about his desire for her but didn't want to risk getting fired. So he would bring her lunch and volunteer for special projects. He even offered to train with her because she had expressed a desire to lose weight. He could tell that Jerickca wouldn't mind cuddling up to him, because he made sure that she knew that he was experienced and preferred older women. He told her how he selected whom he was going to sleep with. "I just open my black book and look up who I haven't been with in a period of time and call them," he said.

Jerickca was amazed, "Just like that and they sleep with you?"

He knew he had her going. "Just like that, because I have skills," Patches said as he held her eyes intensely.

He could have kept her going if Megan hadn't walked into the room.

"Every time I look up, you are all up under Jerickca. What's up with that? You know she married and don't want your broke ass."

"Get out of my face, Megan. You talk too much." As he stormed out of the office, he looked back at Jerickca and saw the way Jerickca looked at his backside. *I want you too,* he thought.

Whenever he got too tense and angry, he would just intercom Precious and ask her to do him a favor. “I’m stressed. Can you do a brother a favor?”

“I’m going to ask if I can leave early because I’m sick. Where do you want me to meet you?” Precious was so excited. She really liked this man.

Precious asked Patches, “Could we go to your place?”

“No!” he said angrily.

He wasn’t about to spend one dime on her going to a hotel, either, for all he cared. She could do what he wanted her to do in the parking lot, in his car.

Later that evening, Patches called Jessica to ask her out, but she refused stating she had an early appointment with a client. Patches found himself begging her for just a little time.

“McNary, I really can’t see you for a while. You want too much of my time, and I’m not ready for that.”

“Well, I thought you liked me as much as I do you,” he said feeling hurt.

“I do like you, but it’s bad timing. I have too much on my plate. Maybe we can get together some other time.”

“Are you saying that you don’t want to see me?” Patches was so disappointed.

“No, that is not what I’m saying. I just think we should cool it.”

Patches slammed the phone down and said loudly, “No bitch rejects me!”

Chapter 30

Jerickca was packing her clothes to go to the conference when Daphnie walked in to talk. "How's my baby girl doing?"

"Fine. When are you coming back from Chicago?"

"I will be back in five days."

"Why do you have to go?"

"I'm going to a conference and to see Spencer."

"Why can't I go?" Daphnie wanted to know.

"I can't take you out of school! Maybe this summer I will take you to Chicago to visit your relatives. Okay? You know that we paid a lot of money for you to attend the Summer Institute. You only have two weeks left to attend and then I will take you to Chicago."

"Well, bring me something back."

"You know I will." Jerickca said as she bent down and kissed her lips.

"Jerickca!" Anthony screamed, "You have a telephone call."

"I got it," she said. "Hello, this is Jerickca."

"Hey Jerickca," Deborah said. "I got your messages and I'm ready to talk."

"Where can we meet?"

"I'll be leaving the house around 6:00 p.m. I can meet you half-way so neither of us has to drive so far," Deborah said.

"Let's meet at Cristo's off Riverview Drive at 6:30 p.m. then."

Deborah hung up the phone and thought about what she was going to say to her friend. They hadn't talked in weeks, even though Jerickca continued to call her. Jerickca had decided that she would keep calling Deborah and sending her "I miss you cards" so that her friend would realize that she had people who cared about her.

The one thing that Jerickca knew for sure because she was a social worker was that domestic violence was a series of syndromes that abused women went through. For instance, when she first started trying to help Deborah, she was unsuccessful because she was in the Honeymoon Syndrome, which was also known as the Hearts and Flowers because the abuser did everything they could to bribe the person to get them to stay or return. All of this could have been avoided because Jerickca tried to warn Deborah when she was in the pre-battering state, which was when the abuse first started with the throwing, breaking things, verbal abuse, and making threats to her.

She watched her dear friend go through the beginning level of abuse, like when Danny first grabbed Deborah around her neck and pushed her into the wall while restraining her to keep her from getting away from him. Now Jerickca needed to talk to her friend to help her get out of the situation.

Jerickca walked downstairs to the living room and told Anthony that she needed to leave. "I finally have Deborah wanting to see me," she said happily.

"Well, don't push her too much or she'll just retreat back into her shell. I know you want to help her, but if people want to accept bad stuff then there is nothing you can do. You be careful. You are not God and you can't help everybody," Anthony reminded Jerickca.

"I know I'm not God, but Deborah is my friend and there is no way that I am going to let some tack-head man destroy her self esteem and her ability to look in the mirror and respect herself."

"Just remember, she is a lawyer and she knows the system. I am really surprised that someone so smart allowed this to happen," Anthony said, shaking his head.

"From all the reading I've done, it doesn't matter how smart you are when your heart is involved. Plus you have to remember this is something that can slip up on you if you are not aware of the signs."

Jerickca grabbed her purse and keys and kissed Anthony on his cheek. "Would you mind getting dinner together for you and Daphnie?" she asked.

Jerickca opened the door by pressing firmly down on the pad inside the garage. She eased into her black Lexus and drove through her subdivision towards the highway. She drove two miles on the highway before exiting off 270-East. Listening to the music playing on her specially recorded CD with all the number ones songs, she thought of how to give the information to Deborah without alienating her from the one person she had been able to count on for over twenty years. She had previously contacted one of her associates and obtained information on domestic violence, and tonight she would share all the contents of the red folder. She closed her eyes briefly to offer a small prayer, and then she quickly opened her eyes so that she would not venture into the next lane causing an accident. Jerickca always closed her eyes when praying, because she didn't feel that it was appropriate to do anything different to show reverence to God. "Lord, please help me," she said out loud, "to help Deborah. She is such a good instrument of your love, and we need her strong and confident to help other lost souls. Please give me the words that will help her tonight. Thank you, Jesus, for blessing me. Amen." Now she felt solid strength as she pushed down on the accelerator to move just a little faster to her destination.

Once Jerickca existed off 367 on to Riverview Drive, it took her only ten minutes to get through the signal lights and stop signs to reach Cristo's. Once inside the restaurant and after being seated with Deborah, she told her she missed the times they spent together.

"I missed you too, and I'm so sorry that I didn't return your phone calls, but I was so ashamed of myself for allowing something like this to happen to me, the attorney," Deborah said with an embarrassing smile.

"What happened to you is something that so many women go through, no matter what their social position or economic background. It is such a cycle that it takes professional help to get out. Don't ever be ashamed of anything with me because we have been through so much together and will go through much more while we go through life's ups and downs. Just promise me that we will love and help each other to stay the course and do everything we can to support and assist each other, no matter what." At that, they both stood up and hugged each other. "Now," Jerickca continued, "let's order our food. I'm famished."

They reviewed the domestic violence literature as they waited on their Chicken Cordon Bleu dinners, which included a glass of wine, cheese ball & crackers, soup and salad, rice pilaf, and vegetables.

"I can't believe this stuff. It says that each year three to four million women are beaten by their husbands or partners, and it's still the most common yet least reported crime in the country," Deborah said with amazement. "It further states that when mothers are battered, the father is about three times more likely to be a child abuser. Thank God I don't have children by Danny."

"Based on the information in this brochure, it's says that boys who witness their mother's abuse are more likely to batter their female partners as adults than boys raised in nonviolent homes. So maybe Danny saw his mother being abused and he needs counseling," Jerickca said. "However, he is really not my concern at this moment."

"Why didn't I see his problem before now?"

Jerickca thought for a second, and then she responded. "Probably because you were too close to the situation and you loved him and wanted it to work. Plus there are so many characteristics of a batterer that it is difficult to see them all. They have low self-esteem, blame others for their actions, present dual personalities, and are very jealous, which could have made you feel that he really loved you. But the worst part of this is separating, because you face more danger since the batterer may escalate his violence and retaliate against the woman to coerce her into reconciliation and staying with him."

"What do I need to do now?" Deborah asked.

"We need to contact the Women's Crisis Center and they will take you through all the necessary steps," Jerickca said with a quizzical look on her face. Finally, looking at her friend, she said, "You know, it's amazing how hard he tried to keep you isolated from your friends, all because he wanted to have power and control over you. When we met him that day at the Black Expo, I really thought he was a nice man, but I now understand how they have that dual personality. I'm so glad that you are taking the steps to get help. I love you and couldn't bare the thought of him hurting you any longer."

"Thank you for not walking away from me when I put him first. I love you Jerickca. You have always stood by me. I'm so glad we met." Deborah wiped the tears off her face with a napkin and smiled, because she knew that her life was going to improve.

"Danny is going out of town for his company tomorrow for a mandatory meeting. I will wait until I see him get on the plane and go and pack my things and leave for the shelter. But first, I have to talk to an attorney who specializes in this so they can get an order of protection and let the senior partners know that I have to take an emergency leave of absence. I need to go to the lounge and make a quick call and I'll be right back."

Jerickca watched her friend walk to the lounge, bent her head, and thanked God for helping her to stick with her friend. She was glad that she had been home when Deborah called and not in Chicago. She was leaving for the big city in two days. It was perfect timing to help her friend.

Chapter 31

Ever since Phoenix and Devante had had that huge argument about their sex life, she noticed that he had become distant and was staying away from the house for long periods of time. It hadn't occurred to her that he might be doing the same thing she was doing. Since she had returned from the Ozarks with Juan, he seemed even more distant. She noticed that he hung up the phone quickly whenever she entered the room and he was taking more and more business trips. She even noticed how he was exercising and dressing sharper. Why hadn't she paid close attention to his actions earlier? *No wonder we have such a poor sex life. He is seeing someone else. This makes me livid,* she thought as she gnashed her teeth. "Wait till I catch his ass," she said out loud.

Since that last scene, three months had passed and he was still walking around ignoring her, but she had a plan. She wasn't going to let him get away from her, and no other bitch would benefit from all her hard work. She would burn the house down before some other freaky bitch got her man. The more she thought about it, the more she began to scheme. I need to catch him in action.

She picked up the phone to call his office and asked for his extension. "Devante, what are you doing for dinner?"

"I have a meeting and will be home late."

"Where is the meeting, because I want to see you and I'll wait until the meeting is over?"

"What are you doing? Checking up on me?"

Phoenix hesitated. "Do I need a reason to check up on you? After all, you are the one who suddenly has so many meetings to go to that you don't have time for Simone or your wife. So are you seeing someone, Devante? Because if you are, I want to know."

"I think that's a stupid question. I think I spend more time with my daughter than you and I don't appreciate you calling my job and acting stupid," he said furiously.

"Oh, I'm stupid now because I want to be with you? Is stupid what you're calling me now?"

"I didn't say you were stupid. I'll be home after the meeting." Devante hung up the phone.

"That is the last time that bastard is hanging up on me," Phoenix said as she grabbed her keys and went into Simone's room to dress her. She was taking Simone to her mother's house, because it was time to visit her dear husband's job.

Chapter 32

Jerickca arrived at O'Hara Airport in Chicago at 10:00 a.m. She quickly found her limousine and headed for her hotel. While traveling on South Michigan Avenue, she spotted the Ebony Magazine office. The limousine pulled up to her hotel and the bellhop politely took her luggage out. As she walked into the Congress Plaza and Conference Center to register, the attendant put her luggage on a cart and waited to escort her to her room. She registered, went to her room, and quickly changed clothes. Then she called Spencer at her office.

"Hey girlfriend, I'm here safe and sound," she said.

"It's so good to hear from you and have you in my corner of the world. I haven't seen you in a while. What's on the agenda for today?"

"Well, this evening around six there is a reception that I plan to attend, but I'm free after eight," Jerickca said while glancing over the conference materials she had received last week.

"I'll tell you what. I'll come over around 8:30 to see you. You are at the Congress Center, right?"

"Yes. It is a beautiful old hotel that's very regal," she commented.

"Yes it is, and a lot of people come here just to stay in that hotel," Spencer stated.

"I'll see you at 8:30. I'm hungry, so I need to get a bite to eat," Jerickca said as she picked up the menu.

"Okay. I have a patient coming in about fifteen minutes, so I'll see you tonight. We are really going to have fun. I'll talk to you later."

Jerickca said goodbye and put the telephone receiver back into its cradle. She quickly scanned the menu, dialed room service, and ordered a fruit dish. Then she took out her conference agenda again and reviewed it to make sure that she had all the information correct. After she hung up her three suits, she grabbed the remote control and scanned the television stations to see what was on while she waited for her meal.

Just as she began to relax, there was a knock on the door. She jumped up and looked through the peephole to see who was there. She slid the chain and opened the bulky door. "Hi!" She said. "You can bill that to my room." Jerickca handed the room server his tip.

"Thank you and have a great lunch," he said with a smile.

Jerickca sat down, prayed over her fruit, and quickly ate all of it. Then she undressed, bent over the toilet and forced the fruit back out. She then took a shower and lay across the bed to take a quick nap, because she planned to talk to her friend and didn't know when she would be able to catch enough sleep again.

Jerickca slept for four hours. She was so tired. The plane ride had zapped all her energy, even though the ride was less than fifty minutes. She was so frightened sitting on that plane that it took every ounce of her strength to stay mellow and calm. Jerickca had flown more than 100 hundred times but still could not adjust to being that high in the clouds. She felt like she was out of control flying in the air, unlike when she was driving in a car. She felt that if the plane was about to crash, she had no options to try to save her life. If she was in a car, she could avoid an accident or jump out of the car and still survive. But how many times had someone survived a commercial jet that fell from the sky? She could only recall one little girl being saved. So she spent most of her flight uncomfortable, praying, reading the Bible, and trying to find the courage to have faith that God would protect her.

At 4:30, she got out of the bed and showered again. She

dressed in her navy blue suit and slid her freshly pedicured feet into her navy blue Anne Klein pumps. Jerickca glanced in the mirror one more time to make sure that her braids were still in the French roll. She sat down and watched the five o'clock news while flipping through her conference binder to find out which room the reception would be held in. She had more than twenty minutes before the reception would start. After confirming that she looked great, she picked up her black leather portfolio, grabbed her door key card, and walked to catch the elevator down to the reception room.

Jerickca mingled with so many familiar colleagues and met a lot of new ones. She was just about ready to leave when a young man gently grabbed her arm and introduced himself. "I'm James Thurgood. I'm one of the conference facilitators."

"Hi, I am Jerickca Parker from Missouri. I'm with the East St. Louis Department of Adolescent and Children Resources."

"Nice meeting you," he said.

They chatted for more than an hour. Jerickca was all in this fine man's face. He was very handsome. He had the sex appeal of Denzel Washington and the body of actor and professional wrestler "The Rock." Dressed in black pants and a perfectly ironed and starched white shirt with a black and white swirled necktie, he looked good enough to eat. His eyes were dark, his skin a smooth mahogany, and his lips thick and kissable.

When she realized she was staring at the man's mouth, she quickly shook his hand and left. James quickly caught up to her and asked her to have dinner with him. She declined because she was lonely and didn't know what she would do with this handsome stranger. He said maybe they could see each other tomorrow. She smiled and walked into the open elevator. Jerickca couldn't believe that she was all into this man that she had just met. She got off the elevator on the third floor and walked to her room. She put on a pair of loose fitting jeans, a large sweatshirt, and some flat walking shoes and waited for Spencer.

She heard a light tap on the door and peeped through the hole. She started screaming as she swung the door open and quickly grabbed her friend in a tight bear hug. Jerickca was so happy to see Spencer that tears flowed down her face.

"What's wrong, honey? I thought you would be happy to see me," Spencer said, joking.

"I am, but I'm so stressed out."

"Well, let's sit down and talk. Maybe we can stay in tonight and order something." Spencer held Jerickca's head up by putting her fingers up under her chin. "You have a lot on your mind and need to release it. We can tour and do other things tomorrow, but right now I'm all ears."

"I'm so frustrated with my weight, my family, my job, and my marriage. I need time out. I'm losing it, Spencer."

"You are dieting and walking, aren't you?"

"Yeah, but nothing is happening. I've only lost five pounds in the last two months."

Spencer smiled and congratulated her friend for losing five pounds. "It's a great accomplishment. You didn't gain. You have to take little steps. Didn't I tell you that fine things take time like fine wine? So you have to take small steps, because when the weight comes off at a reasonable rate, it will stay off. You look great. Don't give up. You are doing great. Keep exercising, and you will see better results in the next months. Is Anthony complaining?"

"No, he never says anything. It doesn't make any difference to him. If I were money, maybe he would notice me more. Other than that, he just accepts me. At least I think he does."

"Well, if he is not complaining, continue your plan. It's a great one and sanctioned by your doctor, so work with it, girl. You will be surprised at the results you will get. But you have to remember, it took time to put the weight on and it will take time to get it off. Now what's this I hear about your family?"

"You know I told you about my sister, Barrington. Well, anyway, I heard that she has been acting strange. Momma said that she had a black eye and I think she is being beaten by that knucklehead. I don't understand these women. Why do they let these men hit them?" Jerickca said perplexed. "I just don't get it. If a brother or anybody else attempted to hit or harm me, I would clock that ass. What gives? Why are women so weak?"

"Many of them suffer from low self-esteem. For some women, it is a familiar scene. Jerickca, self-esteem issues are powerful, and when you don't believe in yourself, you will allow others to do almost anything to you."

"Why can't they wake up and help themselves?" Jerickca looked at Spencer, needing answers that she already knew but needed to hear again.

"Sometimes they need help to make that move, and most of them are afraid to leave for a variety of reasons."

"You know that I just helped Deborah get away from that crazy bastard that she was with. She had to leave so that she could live, but I miss her terribly."

"I know how you feel, but you should do the same thing with your sister that you did to help Deborah. I really don't feel like you would have a difficult time with Barrington, because she is not stuck on one man. So talk to her. Now tell me what about your job?"

"It's the gossiping that bothers me. I have the best and most competent workers any one company could ever dream of having, but they gossip too much and I am totally tired of hearing that kind of negative stuff. I don't feel satisfied."

"Jeri, girl, everybody gossips. It's what they do with the gossiping. That is the question or problem, depending on how you see it. In my opinion, there are two types of gossipers: one is malicious and the other is for informing. You must ask yourself whether the gossiping is helping others to become better or giving others negative information that can destroy people's lives. You see, sometimes the only time that others listen or are willing to receive information is when it comes to them in the form of gossip. Otherwise, you're not able to get information to those who need it the most. Most people only want to hear information when they think it's about someone else. The other question is whether or not a person is sharing in defaming someone's character by spreading lies they heard and know are not true. You must ask your staff why they are gossiping and whether or not what they say is to inform or to hurt. But don't quit jobs because of gossip, because no matter where you work or play, you are going to find people who enjoy gossiping and those who love to hear it."

"You are so right. I have never quite looked at gossiping that way. Spencer girl, you go deep, don't you?"

"Life is for living and getting the most out of it. We all have our faults, but its how we handle them that gives us strong characters. You take life seriously with a touch of salt. It is sour to the taste buds, yet sweet to the mind. You have to live, learn, and let God help you through prayer. Then you can live a full life. Most African Americans have a problem with getting help when we need it. We worry about how others will perceive us if they knew we went to see a shrink. We worry about what our current or potential employers would do to or with us if they knew we sought mental health counseling. Yet Caucasians brag on how many therapists they see like it's a badge of honor. We should do the same thing and maybe we can lose some of the baggage many of us carry around."

"You're right. I know I need counseling, but I have held those same stereotypes in the back of mind. I guess I have been all lips and no action."

"Now, tell me. What's going on with you and Anthony?"

"I need a glass of wine to discuss this. Let me get your gift first. I brought this Dom Perignon for you, but I think I need a glass now. This is difficult for me to talk about."

Jerickca took the two water glasses and poured the wine into them. Just as she reached to give Spencer her glass, the phone rang. "Hello," she said. "Hi baby. How was school today?"

"It was fine. What are you doing?" asked Daphnie.

"I'm sitting here talking to Spencer."

"Tell her I said hi."

"What are you and your dad doing this weekend?" Jerickca asked.

"He said that we were going to a movie," Daphnie said with excitement. "I want to see 'You Got Served.'"

"I'm sure your dad will make sure that it is rated PG-13. Let me speak to him."

"Hi, Honey. I miss you."

"Mhmmm," said Anthony. "Jerickca, when you come home we need to prepare for our summer vacation. Daphnie is too excited about going to Florida. She wants to get to that amusement park so bad; otherwise, I would have taken you all to Hawaii."

"We'll get a chance to go to Hawaii later."

"When are you coming home?" Anthony asked. "Your daughter misses you already."

"Does she miss me or do you?"

"Both. Please don't waste money while you are there."

"Anthony, don't start that shit with me. I love you."

"Me too." Anthony quickly said, "Bye."

Jerickca took a sip of her wine, walked over to the bed, and sat down. "Spencer, that man knows that he love him some me, girl. He can't stand for me to leave him and I can't stand to sleep without him. I feel so empty when he goes on business trips."

"So what's the problem between you two?"

"Satisfying sex and communication. It's always about sex. Either you are getting too much sex, not enough, or not correct, or somebody's G-spot is not getting tapped. In this case, it's mine. I'm not sexually fulfilled. I love my husband, but kissing and foreplay went out the window four years ago. I feel like I'm married to my brother. There is no fire, but I love him dearly."

Spencer looked at her friend and asked, "Have you talked to him about this?"

"Spencer, you know I have. But he's says that there isn't a problem and that he is satisfied. He basically said that he's happy. I asked him to go to counseling but he told me to go since I was the one unhappy. He will not bend on that one because he is so private."

"Then you go. Counseling will give you the guidance that you need to talk to Anthony. But if I were in your situation, I would probably just jump his bones."

"I tried that but he always says, 'I'm tired, just give me some now." Jerickca said in a deep manly voice, "He has the equipment but he doesn't know how to use it."

"Well, it's difficult to counsel a friend on an issue like this one but I strongly feel that you should seek counsel. I will give you some referrals and their numbers. I encourage you to call and talk to each therapist to see whom you feel you would be comfortable meeting. I'll make sure you get the numbers before you leave." Spencer got up and hugged her friend. "You have a man who cares about you. Try to work this out because you guys still love each other after all these years, and that's rare in these times."

"I'll try. I always wondered why people have affairs and now I know. It's not that the heart stops loving. In most cases, sex dies or communication stops. Someone always gives up, and I'm not old. I'm still sexy and want good loving, and I know my husband does to. He just doesn't want to give it up. I feel better since talking, but girl, I want action when I get home. You know there is this fine facilitator here and I was definitely feeling some vibes from him. He asked me to go to dinner with him. I even thought about trying to get with that fine brother. But I guess I'll keep my legs closed and my heart warm for Anthony."

"You'd better," Spencer said laughing. "Let's go to Spago Restaurant on Dearborn Parkway. They have fabolicious food and the atmosphere is great."

Jerickca and Spencer spent a lot of time together. They visited the Sears Tower, the world's tallest building. Spencer took her to Robie House to look at the exquisite glass windows and doors. They went to Buckingham Fountain to see the light and water show, and finally they visited the Art Institute. She learned a lot about Chicago and shopped in their great stores. They shopped in the Loop, and at the Magnificent Mile and visited Marshall Fields, Ann Taylor, Neiman Marcus, Saks Fifth Avenue, Bloomingdale, and Nordstrom. They shopped at the Louis Vuitton Store, Hugo Boss, where they picked up something for Anthony, and the Coach

Store, where she purchased a purse for Daphnie.

She bought something at each of the stores. Anthony was going to have a fit, but Jerickca didn't care. "What was the use of having money if you couldn't enjoy it?" she always said. Jerickca and Spencer shopped until they almost dropped. They enjoyed touring the city of Chicago together. Spencer was excited that her friend had got the chance to see how she was living.

Jerickca enjoyed Spencer's company so much that she hated leaving her friend. At the airport, Jerickca took her hand and thanked her for her hospitality. "Thank you for always being in my corner, Spencer. You are such a good friend. Most so-called friends would have told me to seek pleasure outside of my marriage, but you want my family to stay together. I thank you for not encouraging me to sleep with James, the conference facilitator. It was so clear that he was interested in me. It's so hard to find good friends, but I thank God that He led me to you."

Spencer smiled and said, "I love you, too, and when I come to visit in the fall, I want you to show me around Missouri, the Show Me State. I had a great time with you."

"Girl, you know I will show you all the hot spots. You think Chicago is the bomb? Wait until you get to St. Louis! There is so much to do. We can cross over the Mississippi River and we are back in the state of Illinois. So baby, you get two treats for the price of one. Well, they are calling my boarding number. Smooches, love you, and thanks for bringing me to the airport." Jerickca grabbed her friend and hugged her tight.

"You are welcome. Call me when you get home. Have a safe trip."

"Bye now."

"Bye." Jerickca shouted as she walked to get on the plane. She turned and mouthed the words "I love you."

"I love you, too," Spencer responded.

Chapter 33

Patches closed his eyes and tried to think about Jessica. He missed her. He had to see her, because he couldn't function without seeing her. In a short time, she had captured his heart. He was having a hard time keeping a hard on. Toi was sucking his penis like a trick trying to catch a payday to purchase some crack, but all he thought about was how she disgusted him. He would never have Jessica on her knees on the ground while he stood next to a car. He cared too much for her and would never allow a woman he loved to be outside in the dark, on her bare knees on the heated concrete, sucking his dick.

"Toi, get your ass up, girl."

Toi ignored him. She was trying hard to turn him out because she wanted more from Patches. She wanted to be his one and only gal. So she wanted to give him pleasure that only she knew how to give him, but tonight was different. He couldn't keep a hard on and she was working it but to no avail.

"Toi, I said get your ass up," Patches said as he pushed her head back.

""What's wrong, baby? I'm not making you feel good?"

"Nah! I can't do this with you anymore. Get off your knees."

"What do you mean? You know I love you," Toi whined.

"Didn't I tell you that I don't roll like that? I ain't in love with you, and you know that."

"Why are you here then, letting me suck your damn dick?"

"I'm outta here." Patches said as he zipped his pants up and walked toward his car.

"You yellow bastard!" Toi said as she picked up a large rock, threw it at Patches' car window, and missed it by inches. "I hate you!"

Patches turned around and walked briskly toward Toi. He tried to grab her by the waist but she took a step back and smacked him hard. Finally grabbing her by the arm and twisting it back gently, trying not to hurt her but giving her a message, he said, "You will never get a good man like me by sucking dicks in a parking lot. Get some class and stop giving up your ass." He dropped her arm and walked toward his car, got in and burned rubber, leaving her standing there looking stupid.

He picked up his mobile phone and dialed Jessica.

"Hey baby girl, how are you?"

"I'm okay, and you?"

"Missing you, that's all. Can I come over?" Patches asked.

"It's too late, and I have to be in court early tomorrow."

"Are you afraid of me?" Patches wanted to know.

"No, I'm afraid of what we might do when we are together. You know I'm not a one night stand."

"I know that, but we have been seeing each other for five months and you and I haven't touched second base yet."

"Is that all you want from me? Sex?"

"Jessica, I really like you and I'm thinking about you every second of the day. I just want to hold you tight."

"Come on over," she whispered.

"I'll be there in ten minutes."

When he walked up to the door, he knocked lightly while he adjusted his shirt. Jessica opened the door wearing a white negligee with a long matching robe. He grabbed her and kissed her hard as he shut the door and locked it. The kiss was so powerful that his knees buckled. She pulled him to the couch and they kissed, touched, and hugged for more than an hour. Jessica took Patches' hand and walked him into her bedroom. There she removed his shirt and kissed his nipples. She gently glided her hand across his chest and planted kisses on his cheek, nose, ears, and finally, his lips.

"Are you sure you're ready for this Jessica?" he asked.

"Yes, I am. I couldn't be more ready."

Now it was his time to take the lead. He wanted this to be special. He wanted to please her the way he had never pleased another woman. He wanted to be gentle with her.

After laying her across the bed, he kissed every inch of her body as he strategically removed her nightclothes. Her body trembled as his tongue glided over every inch of her body. He lingered longer on her perky breast as he gently suckled each one. Moving his head and tongue from her chest down to her stomach, he kissed and stroked every inch of her body, savoring the taste of her skin. Finally, he tenderly pushed her legs apart and licked her like he was trying to reach her soul. Within minutes, she screamed out as her body shook while she pressed his head down deep into her being. Jessica grabbed the headboard on the bed and screamed, "It feels so good."

Patches stood up and lovingly looked into her eyes. "I love you," he said. This was the first time that he uttered those words and really meant them.

"I love you, too," she responded.

With that said, he lay down next to her and kissed her for ten minutes. He felt no need to rush, and he wanted to remember this night forever. He studied her body as she moved toward his manhood. As she tried to lick him, he pulled her back up against him and kissed her. He knew that if she took him in her mouth, he would not last very long and would release his liquid into her. Plus he remembered that Toi had been sucking on him and he didn't want Jessica to taste the remnants of her saliva. He had to regain control, so he massaged her clitoris until he had her full attention. When she was very moist, he eased into her. Jessica tensed up and tried to move her body away from him. The more she tried to scoot back, the more he moved into her. He thrust himself deeper and she moaned loudly in pain. "Jessica, you're a virgin?"

"Yes," she shyly whispered.

He kissed her hard and entered her gently. It was the sweetest feeling he ever had when they climaxed together. He knew that he would marry her.

The next morning, he walked into the office singing because he was so happy. He decided to go to the lounge area to get a cup of coffee. When he walked into the back room, everyone was sitting down, laughing, and talking about sex.

"Ya'll tripping this early in the morning?" He laughed as he looked at Megan. "What's up?"

"No, you are the one who just walked in talking that crap. Why you giggling like a little pussy?"

"Megan, I know that you didn't go there. I'm not going to let you take me out of this mood. I feel too good to let your stupid ass mess with me this morning."

Megan jumped up from behind her desk and swiftly walked toward Patches. She screamed in his face, "I know your yellow, silly ass didn't call me stupid, did you?"

"Girl, you better step your ass out of my face. Your ass can dish it but you can't take it. You best to move it!"

Megan stepped back. She didn't know whether Patches was serious or not because he had never talked to her like this. "What's your problem, Baby Boy?"

"Baby Boy is in looove," he sang.

"No shit," Megan said with a big smile on.

"Who is the lucky girl?" Phoenix wanted to know.

"Ya'll remember that night we went to Club Illusion? Well, I met this attorney named Jessica there, and we danced and talked most of the night. She was very nice and all that. We kinda hit it off slow but we kept seeing each other."

"She didn't up that coochie, did she?" Megan laughed.

"I don't roll like that. I get my needs taken care of," Patches said as he lifted his chest up like he was a muscle man.

"You can get off your high horse, 'cause once Jessica finds out about your no-good butt, she's gonna send you packing anyhow."

"Megan, you're always so negative. But true this. I really like this girl, and once I get her info to check on her credit status, I'm going to ask her to marry me."

"Real." Denver chimed. "She must have really turned you out."

Patches paused as if he was reminiscing and smiled showing those pretty teeth, "Yeah, that sister turned the brother out," he said dragging out his words.

"Well, you have never talked like this before, so maybe it's true. But why do you have to check her credit and all?" Denver looked Patches in his eyes and said while sucking her teeth, "Explain that, will you?"

"I want to make sure her credit is A-1. I don't want to marry a woman and she isn't responsible enough to take care of business. I want too much—a nice home and furniture just like the next person, and a person with bad credit stops you from doing so much. Plus it's a window into someone's life, their future, you know."

"Well, if all men were checking women's credit history, most of us would be left out in the cold," Phoenix said as she walked over and hugged Patches. "Congrats, Baby Boy!"

One by one, everyone hugged Patches. He stood straight and tall, smiling happily like he had won the Illinois State Lottery.

"If she says yes when you propose, whatever you need, we'll definitely help out," Megan said as she kissed Patches on his cheek.

"You got it, dog," he said affectionately.

Chapter 34

Phoenix pulled into the lot of Devante's job and parked near the rear by the entrance gate. She wanted to see what her husband was up to and bust him if she could. As she listened to Mary J. Blige, "No More Drama," she quickly glanced around the parking lot. As she bent down to retrieve her cell phone, she turned her head and saw Devante walked out with a young lady who looked to be about thirty. She was very attractive, and as she walked, her long hair swung back and forth. They walked toward a pearl white 2002 Maxima, and she saw Devante kiss the young lady on her lips as they got into her car and drove off.

Phoenix was paralyzed by what she had seen and couldn't believe her eyes. Shocked into a fixed position, she was unable to collect herself in enough time to follow the two kissing bastards. Dazed, she started crying, because she felt that the husband who was supposed to be all that was a no-good, two-timing bastard.

Not knowing what to do, she drove directly to Megan's house in East St. Louis. Knocking on the door, she was crying so hard it was as if the Mississippi River had released its floodgates and poured water out into the surrounding communities, overtaking everything in its path.

With a broken heart and unable to control her tears, she banged on the door. Megan sneaked a look out the peephole to see who was banging on her door so hard that it sounded as if the Fourth of July had returned. Opening the door she shrieked, "Phoenix, what's wrong?"

"Devante is having an affair," she cried.

"Come in, baby." Megan put her arms lovingly around her friend and hugged her. "Let me get you some coffee, and you go sit down in the living room by the fireplace."

After Megan made the coffee, she walked back to the living room and found Phoenix sniffing and blowing her nose. Megan knew that while she was making the coffee, her friend would have time to collect herself. "Take this and be careful. It's very hot. Where is Simone?"

"She is with mama." Phoenix said as she put the cup to her lips and tried to sip the steaming hot coffee.

Megan looked at Phoenix and asked, "Tell me how you know that Devante is having an affair?"

"I saw his ass with some young woman about thirty years old. They were kissing in his parking lot at his job."

"What makes you think she was so young? Girl, she is about two years younger than you, and you are an old ass." Megan was trying to make Phoenix laugh.

"You are right. Bitch is about my age. I guess I was too upset to think," Phoenix said as she sat her cup back on the coaster.

"I know you were upset you when you saw him kissing that stank whore, but I have a question to ask you, and I hope that I don't offend you. How do you think he would feel if he knew you were seeing Juan?"

"What's the difference? It doesn't change what he's doing."

"There is no difference because you both are doing the same thing. So the way I see it, you are very hurt because your husband is seeing another woman, and he would be equally hurt if he knew about you."

"But I keep my shit tight. He would never catch me."

"That's not the point. You are still having an affair with another man who is not your husband."

"What is your ass, some kind of head doctor?" Phoenix looked at her friend with a disappointed face. She came here to find someone to join her in beating down her two-timing husband, not someone who wanted to talk about her indiscretions.

"I wish I was. Then I could analyze my own damn self. But I want you to really look at this picture, because I think you and your husband need to see a marriage counselor. It's obvious you still love him if seeing him with another woman upset you so badly that you drove over thirty miles to come here."

Phoenix held her head down in shame. "I was fucking Juan for money because I wanted things that we couldn't quite afford. I just didn't anticipate falling for him. I do love Devante and can't imagine my life without him. I want him to be there for his daughter and to support me forever. He's my life, and I guess I took him for granted.

"I should have talked him into going to counseling because of the sex problem. I want him to get his freak on. Lick me all over my body and put me in positions that only a pretzel could understand, but he seems so uptight. Juan loved to experiment and do things you only dream about."

"Girl, you have to train your man. Like dogs train their puppies where to live and eat, you have to do the same thing. Maybe he wants to try different things but is afraid you wouldn't be interested. I bet that whore is sucking his dick right now."

"Woman, you supposed to make me feel better, not worse," Phoenix said as the tears started again.

"What I'm trying to tell you is to go home and suck your man's dick and let him know you love him. Trust me girlfriend, it ain't nothing out here. These men don't want to be responsible for no women. I certainly don't see Juan asking you to marry him, and he's single right."

"Yeah, by death of his spouse, but he doesn't want me. He just wants to fuck whenever he has the urge."

"Well, I'm glad you came to your senses, because you need to work out your problems and get counseling," Megan said shaking her head. "There ain't a man out here better than the one you have at home. Trust me, I know this."

"You are right. I am going to salvage this marriage even if it kills me."

While they sat there talking, the doorbell rang and Megan got up to answer the door. It was Cecil. He looked great and she would love nothing better than to kiss his lips, but she had her friend here and she was in a crisis. "Come back later."

"How much later you're talking about?"

"Like tonight around 10:30. Can you pull that off?" She whispered in his ear and gently bit the bottom where his diamond stub was and said, "I want to suck your dick." She knew that would make him come back.

"Megan, who was that?" said Phoenix.

"That's the married dude I told you about. See, married people end up being boring and cold in the bed. They look for someone to stimulate them and wake up the dead in their needy bodies, when all they have to do is talk to their spouses and get help when words are no longer coming out. I don't have a spouse to work it out with since Richard died, so I messed around with other women's husbands, because the wives stopped talking a long time ago. Marriage is based on commitment and trust, and when you lose that, you allow enough space between you and that man so that a woman like me can slip in and ruin everything, when all you had to do was talk."

"Megan, you are kind of deep."

"It may not seem like it, but I'm for marriages staying intact as long as I can get a piece every now and then," Megan laughed. "Now you go home and work on your marriage. Leave Simone with her granny and go get your man."

They both stood up and hugged each other. "Thanks, Megan. I really needed someone to be honest with me. Most women would have been like 'girl, take him to court and take everything from his ass.' But you're different. I never expected this out of you."

"I'm like that. People don't know how to take me. But remember that I would never lead you wrong."

"I'm outtie. Thanks so much."

"You are more than welcome. Go get that man."

Megan watched her friend get safely in the car and then she walked toward the bathroom to run a bubble bath and get ready for her night of passion.

Chapter 35

Denver had just stepped out of the shower when she walked into the bedroom and found Lathan, naked and lying across the bed, looking at her photo album. It was clear in her mind what she had to do. Tonight she would have one great night of sex and let him go home to his wife. She had thought long and hard and knew what she had to do to make herself happy. She was moving. She was going back to school to get her medical degree. All her life, she had dreamed of being a doctor, and now she was going to take the steps necessary to fulfill that goal. Her mother Diane could forget about her becoming an attorney, because she was going to do what she wanted to spend the rest of her life doing—serving people and making them better.

She gently grabbed the photo album from Lathan's hand and pushed him on his back. She straddled herself over him, bent down, and kissed him. First, she teased him by kissing him lightly and then she kissed him with brute force. He grabbed her by the waist and held her tightly while whispering to her about how beautiful she was. Denver smiled and positioned herself over his penis. She grabbed him and tried to help him enter her. She wanted him badly. She had long ago fallen in love with him, even though she knew that it was wrong. As he entered her with one hard thrust, he tried to lift his weight off the bed but fell backward. "My chest," he whispered.

"What?" she said while straining to hear him. He grabbed his chest while falling back on the bed.

"My God!" she screamed as she snatched the phone and dialed the emergency number 911.

Denver didn't know what to do as she waited for the ambulance. The look on Lathan's face scared her, and he couldn't seem to catch his breath. Finally, there was a knock at the door. Denver let go of Lathan's hand and ran to let the paramedics into her apartment. Right after she called 911, she quickly dressed and put Lathan's underwear on, because she didn't want him to feel embarrassed. As the paramedics worked on her lover, she grabbed her purse to ride in the ambulance with him. She wasn't about to allow him to go to the hospital alone.

Once at the hospital, everybody started asking her questions that she could not answer. They wanted to know if he had insurance, how old he was—questions she was too shook up to answer and many she didn't know the answers to. Finally, she admitted that she was not his wife and told them to check his wallet for information.

After checking, the hospital contacted his wife and she rushed to the hospital. Denver saw her with the doctors. She looked sad, and tears were streaming down her face. She saw his wife take out her cell phone and make a call. Then she disappeared. Denver walked up to the nurse to ask about Lathan, but they said that they could only release information about his condition to his immediate family members. This frustrated Denver, and she walked back to the waiting room, sat down on the couch, laid her head on the armrest, and cried. She didn't know how long she had been there when she felt a hand softly touch her head. When she looked up, she saw Lathan's wife.

"Hi, I'm Donna. Thank you for bringing him to the hospital and telling the nurses to call me. I wouldn't have wanted him to be alone. What is your name?"

"I'm Denver Anderson. How is he?"

"Lathan died. I have contacted his fiancé and she is on her way to the hospital."

Denver couldn't believe what she heard. As if she was a zombie, she said, "What did you say?"

"Lathan died of a massive heart attack," Donna said again.

Denver became hysterical and just stood there crying and calling his name. Then a young woman walked in and Donna went to her and held her in her arms as the lady cried. Denver was so confused. *Who is that woman and why did Donna say she was his fiancée?* she wondered as she stood there trying to figure out what to do. Finally, after what seemed like hours but actually was forty-five minutes, Donna and the other woman walked over to her.

"Denver," Donna said with compassion in her eyes, "this is Carol Perry, Lathan's fiancée."

Denver looked at them both with a look of shock on her face. Her mouth fell open and she stammered, "What are you talking about? Lathan told me that you were his wife."

Carol stood there, too frozen to say a word. Finally, Donna said between sobs, "I was for about fifteen years, but we separated five years ago. We remained good friends because of the children. Lathan has been engaged to Carol for two years, and they were planning on marrying in two months since our divorce was finalized.

Denver was screaming and becoming more hysterical. "Why are you lying to me? He said you were married."

Donna covered her mouth and sobbed heavily. "That's true. We were married, so that wasn't a lie. I think he forgot to tell you we were divorced and there was someone else. We both know what you two were doing when he had the heart attack," Donna said.

Denver looked at Carol, who suddenly came out of her frozen state and started screaming and flinging her arms at Denver. She had an angry and disappointed expression on her tear-stained face. The way she looked at Denver made her feel dirty. Before she could say anything, Carol asked her a question between gut-wrenching sobs.

"Are you a prostitute?"

"No, he was my lover, and we planned to get married after your kids got out of school."

Carol and Donna both laughed and cried harder. Then Donna said, "My children are grown."

Denver was humiliated. She couldn't believe her ears. Carol looked at her and said, "You are a dirty whore and a murderer. You killed my fiancé." Everyone in the waiting room waited to see what would happen next. She was crying and slinging snot and tears while she balled her fist and hit Denver hard in the face, knocking her to the floor. Denver was crazy with pain and anger. She picked herself up, swung wildly, and kicked Carol on the leg as hard as she could. Then she ran and stumbled toward the exit. She could barely see as she ran down the stairs, not having any place to go. She didn't even have a car. She was alone.

After pacing and crying for over an hour in front of the hospital, she opened her purse and took out her cell phone. She dialed the only person she felt could help her.

Listening to the phone ringing, she asked God to forgive her. Finally, someone said hello.

"Jerickca?" she asked, weeping.

"Yes, who is this?"

"It's Denver Anderson."

"Where are you?"

"I'm at Barnes Hospital. Can you pick me up? Please, I need you."

"Are you okay?"

"No, please come."

Jerickca asked her, "Do you know where the front of the hospital is?"

"Yes," Denver sniffed.

"Go there and wait for me. I will be there in thirty minutes. You do know that I am thirty five miles from the hospital, right?"

"Yes."

"Give me time to get there," Jerickca said, worried that Denver would become impatient waiting on her. "I will be there soon."

Denver hung up the phone and walked over to the brick bench in front of the hospital. A security guard asked if she was okay. She told him yes, and he walked back over to his post. While sitting there, she had time to think about her love for Lathan. *Why did he lie to me?* she wondered. *I really trusted him. If he was divorced and engaged, that meant he never loved me.* While thinking about this, she started crying again. When she looked up, a black Lexus was pulling up and she saw Jerickca. Before she could get out of her car, Denver ran over. Before she could get in Jerickca jumped out and walked over to the passenger side. Denver started crying again after seeing a friendly face. Jerickca held her in her arms and allowed her to cry. Finally, Jerickca told her to get in and she drove in silence. "Do you want to go home?" Jerickca asked.

"No, please take me to your house. My married lover had a heart attack there and I can't ever go back to that place."

"Is he okay?"

Denver cried harder, "No, he died. The cheating bastard died, and now I can't get any answers."

"I'm sorry," Jerickca said.

"His ex-wife came to the hospital and told me that they had been separated for five years and recently divorced and he was engaged to someone name Carol. Then the bitch shows up at the hospital and asks me if I was a prostitute. How could he do that to me? I guess I wasn't good enough for him because he lied to me and made me think that the only reason he couldn't marry me was because he wanted to wait until his children were older. Guess what, they are grown."

Jerickca almost laughed thinking about that scene at the hospital. Boy, she hoped that she'd never experience something like that. She reached over and lightly touched Denver's hand. She didn't know what to say to make her feel better. She risked her own heart messing with a married man. She always tried to tell young women that the men who messed around on their wives were not worth having, and that they never seemed to have good intentions for the women who allowed them to have access to their bodies with the promise of a future life. But as usual, they never listened. So she drove to her house, took Denver to her guest room, and made her comfortable. She told Denver they could talk in the morning unless she wanted to finish their conversation now.

Denver told her that she wanted to sleep and thanked her for coming to her rescue. Jerickca decided to let her go to sleep, because she didn't know what to say to her. She left Denver in the guest room, went to hers, crawled into the bed, and went to sleep, hoping tomorrow would better for everyone.

Chapter 36

"Hello, whom am I speaking with?"

"Who are you calling?" Megan hissed. She hated when people called, didn't identify who they were, and then had the nerve to ask whom they were speaking to. First, they should inform the caller of who they were. This was the protocol for people who made the call in the first place.

"My name is Bertha Macklin, and I keep finding your number on my caller identification box, and also on my husband's pager. We have two children, so I wanted to talk to the lady who is having an affair with my man."

Megan hesitated, because she was feeling pissed off that this woman would stoop so low and call her. If she couldn't keep that fine man of hers home and satisfied, it wasn't her fault. After all, when she finished giving his ass the best loving he ever had, she always sent him back home. Now, here she was talking to someone by the name of Bertha. Anyway, her name sounded so familiar. *Exactly where had she heard that voice before?* she wondered. While trying to figure out the voice on the line, she was also trying to decide how to respond to this hussy. "Let me explain something to you. You sound like you're young and inexperienced, so before you ever call another woman—the so-called mistress, as you say—make sure you understand the consequences. First, don't ever go looking for trouble, because what you seek you will find. Next, it takes two to tango, and you should be discussing this with your man. So don't ever pick up that damn phone to call me or any other woman to talk about your man." Megan wanted to continue to read her the riot act but decided it wasn't worth it.

Bertha sucked her teeth and asked, "So I guess you're saying I should let some whore who can't find her own man just have my husband, am I right?"

"First of all let me explain something to you about a real lady. A real lady does not look for dirt, because if you go digging a hole for one, you better dig one for two." After a long pause, it finally hit Megan who she was speaking to. "Is this the Bertha Macklin who attends the Department of Adolescent and Children Resources parenting classes?"

"Yes," Bertha responded. "Whom am I speaking to?"

"This is the counselor from the department, Megan DuPree. Girl, I know damn well you ain't calling me accusing me of sleeping with your husband. Why in the hell would I stoop that damn low to sleep with some public aid recipient? I ain't having nothing like that. Take that shit somewhere else. I pick people off the ground but I don't take them home."

This pissed Bertha off and she would just report this woman to her boss. She wasn't even worth talking to and she was tired of her putdowns. Bertha decided to tell Ms. Dupree that she would talk to her later, but Megan said the conversation was over. "Ms. Dupree, thank you for talking to me. I will handle this professionally."

"You just do that and get some class, girl," Megan hissed. She couldn't believe she had slept with that woman's husband. She jumped up, ran to the bathroom, and tried to scrub herself clean until she broke her skin. The soap stung her broken skin and she jumped up and down trying to let the water in the shower spray the pain off. *How could I be so stupid, sleeping with a man who is married to someone on public assistance?* she wondered. Tears flowed freely down her face. She was so lonely that she had taken the first lover who came on to her, even though she knew he was married. She would have to be careful or she would lose the reputation that she had worked hard to build. After showering, she went to bed feeling disgusted with herself.

When Megan arrived at work the following morning, she immediately headed to the backroom. "Phoenix, girl, you ain't going to believe this shit." Just as she was ready to spill the whole story, Patches and Denver walked in.

"Good morning," Denver said.

"To hell it is!" Megan responded. "Let me tell ya'll the scoop. Ya'll ain't going to believe this. The married man that I was seeing is Bertha Macklin's husband."

"Your client?" Patches asked.

"Yeah! That's the bitch."

"Boo, you better be cool with calling people names." Patches hated when Megan dissed her clients.

"What do I care about these people who don't want nothing out of life? All they do is suck up all our tax dollars. We have to beg them to work, and they still don't amount to nothing. They are fucking disappointing leeches in this society."

Just then, Jerickca walked in, heard what Megan was saying, and asked to see her. She had met with Bertha earlier and she wanted to discuss this matter with Megan, but now she was upset. She would no longer tolerate this disrespect for their program participants. "I need to see you now," she said with more agitation.

After Jerickca walked out, Patches said, "I told you about that."

"Damn! I hope she didn't hear me," Megan said, concerned about her job.

"I think she did. She was very calm but extremely angry." Phoenix turned to face Megan and said, "You have some apologizing to do."

Megan walked out the door and went straight to Jerickca's office. "You want me?"

"Yes, I do. I spoke to Bertha this morning about her concerns, but that is irrelevant now. I heard what you said about our participants. That attitude is not accepted here. Please retrieve your purse from the office and leave. You will be contacted later."

"Are you firing me Jerickca, after all I did for this program? I made it successful. It is my caseload that gave you all those great statistics you report to the feds." Megan was so angry that she was pointing her finger in Jerickca's face and screaming loudly.

Jerickca calmly said she would contact her later. Patches walked in and escorted Megan out. "I can't believe she fired me. I don't need this job. I can wrap her ass a hundred times in my money and still have some left over to slap her fat ass."

While waiting for Megan to come to her office, Jerickca called Personnel and had them to send a security guard to her office. She was going to fire Megan and she wanted to make sure there were no problems. They said they would send someone right away to clear her desk out. Patches and the security guard escorted Megan to her car as she screamed horrible accusations about Jerickca.

Patches told her to go home, forget about this place, and volunteer her services elsewhere. He knew that Megan just didn't fit in.

Jerickca called a staff meeting and explain to them what was going on. She discussed three issues with them: respect for the clients, commitment to their jobs, and teamwork. It was a good meeting, and the staff agreed to be more supportive of all their clients. Finally, they split Megan's caseload. From now on, it would be a new day at the office. No more putting down those who needed the services of the program the most.

Chapter 37

When she arrived home, Jerickca walked through the kitchen door and spoke to Anthony. "We need to talk now," she told him hastily.

"Jerickca, please, we will do that later. I just got home and need time for myself," Anthony replied.

"That's the problem. It's all about you, and I am fed up with that attitude. This relationship has two people in it, not just you. I want to talk now." Jerickca grabbed the kitchen chair, sat down, and started talking. She knew she had about an hour before Daphnie came home from the game.

"We need counseling. I am not happy in this marriage. You only think about yourself when it comes to sex. There is no romance in our marriage. I can't take this anymore. I need romance, conversation, and a man who at least act as though he thinks I'm special. You don't even want to talk to me when we come home from work."

"Jerickca, you know that I love you. I take care of all the finances, and you don't have to worry about household problems, bills, or anything. I am working hard so that we can have a comfortable future," Anthony said while rubbing the right side of his head near the temple.

"I realize that you have taken care of the family, but relationships are about more than finances. It's about living now, not only for the future. Anthony, we don't know what the future holds, so we should strive to enjoy our lives today. I want to be happy and spontaneous, the way we used to be. I'm not going to lie to you. I love being financially secure, but I want other things too. I want the passion back. You know, like when we used to call each other at lunch and go straight home to bed because we couldn't wait a whole day to see and touch each other. Every time I try to discuss this with you, there is a blockage. You won't even try to improve our marriage."

"That's not true. I just don't think anything is wrong with our marriage or our sex life. I'm happy and you should be too. You are being unrealistic. You want all that romance like you see on TV. This is real life. Most of the time, I'm tired from dealing with the problems at work. When I come home, I want to put my feet up and rest and think. I'm not worrying about sex and romance. I'm a man with more things to contend with than trying to have sex. Don't get me wrong I enjoy sex. But face it, I'm getting older, so its not as important as it was when I was young and trying to get with anyone who had a slit between their legs. I'm happy with you and sexually satisfied. There's more to life than sex. It's good and all, but when I'm tired, I want to rest."

"What about me and what I need? I need romance and I need foreplay, which you don't seem willing to do much." Jerickca held her head down and began to cry. Anthony felt bad. He realized that Jerickca needed more, but he also knew that he had been selfish. If she decided to leave him, he would certainly fall apart. She had been his strength when he was weak and his anchor when he was sinking. He wanted to make her happy. That's why he worked so hard to have financial freedom. However, if his behavior was making her unhappy, maybe he could at least meet her halfway.

"All I want is to make you happy. What do we need to do?"

"We need counseling and we need to work on pleasing each other and to not let our passion and love die."

"Jerickca, when do you want to see a counselor?"

"I've schedule an appointment for next Monday at 3:00 p.m."

"Give me the information and I will be there." Anthony got up, walked over to Jerickca, and tenderly kissed her. "I really do love you," he said. With that, he grabbed her gently and pulled her out of the chair while kissing her forehead. Jerickca looked into his eyes and tilted her head up while Anthony bent down and planted a kiss on her lips. Then she caressed his neck while kissing his eyelid, his forehead, and finally, his lips. They walked to their bedroom, stripping their clothes off. Jerickca pushed Anthony down on the bed and tore his Perry Ellis white long-sleeve shirt open. The buttons popped off in every direction. She straddled him and gently licked his nipples. Playfully, she licked his ears and his neck, and took her tongue and circled his lips. Then she kissed him passionately. Anthony started removing her clothes while caressing and gently squeezing her breasts. He kicked his shoes off and lifted his hips up high enough to remove his pants and underwear. Anthony's penis stood erect. But Jerickca wasn't ready. She lay on her back while Anthony teased her with his tongue. He licked her hard nipples and used his lips to kiss a trail down to her navel. He lingered there, knowing that was her hot spot. Then he shocked her when he plunged his tongue inside her vagina. He hadn't done that in years. He was skillful. He licked and gently sucked her clit. She moaned and gently rolled her hips. He stayed there more than ten minutes. He was intent on bringing her pleasure. He kissed and licked until she could take no more. Finally, she rolled her hips fast and screamed out his name. He could feel her skin, which was very hot to the touch. Her vagina had become juicy and wet. She whispered, "I can't hold back." He didn't want her to. She lay their shaking until Anthony turned her over and pulled her to the end of the bed. He was ready to do it to her doggy style. He entered her from the back and thrust his penis deep inside her. It felt so good. He couldn't believe he had put sex on the back burner. He wanted to please her but didn't realize how much pleasure he had missed. His legs were getting weak as he stroked her pussy. Finally, her hips began to rock faster and her moans increased, and he could not hold back any longer. They both released their love juices and held each other until the shaking of their bodies subsided. Anthony gently smacked her on her ass and told her how good she was. They kissed passionately and were ready for a second round when they heard the garage open and knew that Daphnie was returning from school. They quickly dressed and she whispered, "I love you." He responded by smiling and saying, "Me too."

When Daphnie arrived home from the game, she told her mother that her friend had to leave school to go to the hospital for treatment. She said, "She was pretending to eat, but the teachers caught her throwing food away. She wasn't fat but she wanted to be really skinny. I am so glad that I'm happy with myself. It's more work trying to avoid eating."

"I'm happy you have a healthy self-esteem, because that's what causes so many young girls to look in the mirror and see themselves as fat, ugly, or whatever in between." Just as Jerickca started to say something else, the phone rang.

"Hello," Daphnie said as she answered the phone. "Mom, it's Jeremy. Pick up the phone."

"I have it. Hey Jeremy, what's up?"

"Nothing. I want to come over until I go into treatment. I need to stay with you for about two weeks until a bed is ready," he said.

Jerickca hesitated, because what she was about to say would hurt her as much as her brother. It had to be said. For too long, Jeremy had sought refuge at her home after he didn't pay back drug dealers. She had allowed him to stay with her for months at a time with the hope that he would return to treatment after the three-day detoxification. But it was all a game.

Once he had lain around the house getting free cigarettes and eating everything he wanted, he would leave with the pretense of going to the treatment center, only to detour back to a drug house. She couldn't take it any longer. Every time he came to her house, he took some of her soul with him when he left. She wanted him to stop using and change his life. He had always tricked her in the past, making her believe that this time he would follow through.

But this time she had to tell him no. Her sanity depended on it. He wasn't a teenager. He was a man, and it was time for him to start thinking like one.

"Jeremy, you can't stay."

"Why not? I told you I was going to treatment."

"Yeah, you always say that. But do you ever go? No, you don't, so don't call me until you are in the treatment center. I will not allow you to continue to play with me. Don't call mother, either. You have to make a decision about becoming clean and do it. Just like Bo Jackson said—just do it! Stop kidding yourself. You are a drug addict and you need help. Another thing, next time your drug dealers show up at Mom's for payment, I am calling the police. Let them explain to the cops why you owe them drug money."

"Fuck you Jerickca! You think you're better than everybody, but you ain't shit." With that, he slammed the phone down hard.

Jerickca found herself getting weak, and she began sweating profusely. She was dizzy and felt nauseated as she dropped the phone. She was having a panic attack that was quickly causing her heart to beat too fast, which made her feel as if she would pass out. She reached over and turned the fan on to get her some air. Slowly, she breathed in and exhaled. She laid her head down on the table, closed her eyes, and tried hard to concentrate on something else. Finally, she regained control and the symptoms quickly disappeared.

She picked the phone up off the floor and placed it back into its cradle while saying out loud, "Lord, bless my brother and help him to want help. He needs your help and your blessings."

Jerickca finished cooking dinner and finally sat down to enjoy the rest of the evening watching television. She watched CSI, one of her favorite shows.

That night upon retiring to bed, Anthony stroked her like a guitarist stroking his guitar. Jerickca moaned and they made the most beautiful sounds together. She hadn't received love like that in years. Now he was ready for round two. She could only thank God. She was sure that this man loved her, and she loved him even more now than she had in a long time. She knew that their future looked brighter.

Chapter 38

Denver called Jerickca and thanked her for coming to her rescue last weekend. Jerickca was so special. She never made you feel silly or stupid. She just let you cry on her shoulders without any demands. Jerickca told her to take some time off from work because she had suffered a terrible loss. Although, she felt better, her heart still ached.

Denver had been so heartbroken that the only thing she could do was to call Diane. She was on a flight immediately to comfort her child. She loved her and only wanted the best for her only child. She calmed Denver down quickly and made her feel secure with her words. She truly loved her daughter and had only wanted the best life for her that she could possibly have. That is why she had put so much pressure on Denver to achieve at her highest capability. Diane knew that men played dangerous games and that you always had to be prepared for their immature, game-playing asses. She had planned to talk to her daughter and allow her to live her life without her interruptions. She felt Denver's pain, because she truly loved her child. She decided that from this moment on, she would no longer pressure her sweet Denver, but would allow her to be what she wanted to be, no matter what. She told her daughter she would meet her at her house in four hours. She had two hours left on the flight, and once it landed, she would head straight to her child.

Once Diane arrived at Denver's home, her baby told her about the whole ugly ordeal. Diane just held her and silently cried with her. No words were needed. Her baby needed comforting. This day, they bonded as mother and daughter. Finally, after they had been in the same position for over an hour, Denver told her about her plans for the future.

"Mom, I don't want to be a lawyer. I want to go to medical school. I always wanted to be an internal medicine specialist. I just never said anything because you kept saying you wanted me to be a lawyer. I have already applied to Washington University and I have been accepted to start in the fall."

"I never knew you wanted to be a doctor. I don't understand why you never said anything. I just wanted the best for you because I knew you had the potential. Since you have made a decision to follow your dreams, I guess I should tell you that you can now have control over your trust fund."

"What trust fund?"

"Since your dad's family never did anything for you, his Grandma Justine decided to leave you her money."

Denver smiled and happily asked her mom, "How much did she leave me?"

Diane laughed. "Well," she said, "Let's just say that you can go to medical school without financial pressures, get an apartment and a new car, and still have spending money. You see, I invested it well in secured stocks and bonds. Grandma Justine was the only one in that family who supported me."

"Really!"

"How did you think I was traveling so much? She was good to me."

"Mom, tell me more about her."

"I'll do that later, but first, I need you to accept my apology. I love you so much."

"I love you too."

Wiping the tears from her eyes, she said, "Mom I forgive you. Let's spend more time together?"

"That's a deal. Now, get up, baby, and let's go eat." Diane was so happy. Her strategy had worked. It was hard on her not talking to her baby and hanging the phone up on her. All she was trying to do was make her baby strong. Now, Diane could rest because Denver would be all right, just like her mother.

Chapter 39

Patches walked out of the club with Toi following quickly on his heels. He was heading to see Jessica. Toi was pissed. He had ignored her and she hadn't heard from him in months. She wanted to show him how much she loved him. She grabbed his arm.

"What's up baby? Long time no see."

"Hey Toi!" He said as he continued to walk.

"Wait!" She screamed as she ran to keep up with him. "I miss you, Patches." She grabbed him and kissed him. Patches pushed her away and told her that he didn't roll like that.

"I'm through with it!"

"Let's do it one more time for the road," Toi suggested, thinking that if she could have sex with him, he would remember how it felt to be together.

"Toi, I have a girl and I love her."

Toi grabbed Patches penis and squeezed it. He pushed her away.

"What is wrong with you?" she asked.

"Nothing. Just tired of this stuff." Patches jumped into his car and sped off toward Jessica's house. He knew that he wanted her. Ever since he met her, his habits had begun to change. For instance, club hopping was not the same with his boys, because he spent his time missing his girl. Why should he go to a club and ask others to dance with him when he could be in Jessica's arms?

As Patches' mind raced, he turned the corner without looking and a transfer truck veered quickly to the right to avoid hitting him. Patches swerved too quickly to the left and his car tumbled over. Patches did all he could to take the impact but he felt his head hit the steering wheel hard. When he regained consciousness one week later, he was wearing a cast on his broken arm, his head was bandaged, and his leg was in traction. He was in so much pain. He felt someone squeeze his hand and tried to turn his head toward the person he felt near him, but when he turned it slightly, he had to stop. The little movement he made was excruciating.

"Sweetheart, I'm here for you," she whispered.

"Jessica, what happened?"

"You were in a car accident. The police think you lost control of your car and it rolled over twice leaving you in this condition. The doctors said that you are one blessed man."

Patches moaned. He tried to shift his body, but it was useless. He wasn't going anywhere. "Where's Sinclair?"

"Your mom is in the cafeteria with your dad. They took a break to get something to eat. They will be back in a minute or so." She bent down and kissed his lips. Patches closed his eyes and succumbed to the pain pills. Patches' parents would stay at the hospital until he was out of danger. They refused to leave their only child.

Days later, he was released from the hospital and taken to the McAfee's home. There, his parents tenderly cared for his every need. Every day for one month, Jessica came to visit, and Patches found that he missed her when she was not there with him. He found himself looking forward to each day, because he knew that she would come over after work. When she walked through that front door, his mouth would spread into the biggest smile.

Friday was a great day, because Megan, Phoenix, Denver, and Jerickca all had come to see him. They had a ball laughing and talking. Megan wanted to know why he tried to run into a transfer truck. She told him he was not Hercules. "What were you thinking about? Jessica?" she playfully asked. He told her that he didn't remember, but he smiled and looked into Jessica's dazzling eyes. He felt so good being near her. After his friends and co-workers left the house, he pulled Jessica into his arms and gently kissed her lips. Earlier during the week, he had informed his parents that he really loved her and wanted to marry his sweetheart. McNary, Sr. had arranged for his favorite jewelry salesman from Zale's Diamond to bring out diamonds in the two-carat range, and McNary chose a princess cut.

Looking into her eyes, Patches breathed slowly before he spoke, "Jessica, ever since I met you, I have found myself changing to become a better man. I want you near me every day, all the time. I love you so much. Jessica, will you marry me?"

Jessica started crying, and then she looked up into his eyes and said, "Yes." Then she said, "I love you." They kissed gently, and when they opened their eyes, they looked right at his parents who were both crying.

After Jessica called her parents and told them the good news, she spent the rest of the evening with Patches and his family. Soon they would set a date and start planning their special day.

Chapter 40

Phoenix lay on the bed crying and wishing that things could be different with Devante. But it seemed as if it was too late. He refused to reconcile their differences. He said that he knew that she was seeing someone and that it had really destroyed his trust in her. He advised her to get help, because he wasn't sure he could ever forgive her for hurting him and their daughter, Simone. When she asked him about the woman he was with on the parking lot, he admitted that he had finally accepted her offer to go out two days earlier. He needed time to think about his life and time to decide where he wanted to be. They discussed how Phoenix never seemed satisfied with their lifestyle.

Devante cried when he told her how much he loved her and how hard he worked to make sure that she was happy, but every time she slapped him in the face with the words, "I'm not happy, I want more."

She tried to tell him that she really did love him and was just too selfish to see that life meant more than material things. She begged him to stay with her and their child. But Devante walked out with only one promise, and that was to seek marital counseling. Now she sat on the bed crying, unsure where her life would end or whether or not he would ever forgive her. She had been so stupid. Now, all she could do was pray that God would forgive her and open the door for Devante's heart to soften so that he would forgive her.

Phoenix was sure about one thing: if Devante would ever forgive her, she would never let him down again. She prayed that next Friday would come soon, because that was the day they had scheduled to talk to the marriage counselor. Until then, all she had was love and the hope that he would want to be with her again, too.

Chapter 41

Jerickca had a lot on her mind this morning. First, she had to call the caterers and plan a little dinner for her loyal staff. She wanted to reward them with special acknowledgements. She would also give them their raises for a job well done. They had found employment for more than eighty-five percent of their families. Some of their clients had married, and others had purchased homes for the first time. She wanted Thursday to be perfect, and she had three days to plan everything. More than anything, they needed some rays of happiness, because some of them were really going through a lot of trials and pain. She wanted to lift their spirits, if only for a day.

Jerickca was so excited that she found herself hyperventilating again. She did this often when she was upset or excited. She had gone to the doctor several months earlier and found that she was having serious panic attacks, which were treatable. Once she read as much as she could find on the subject, she learned to manage the attacks without medicine. She practiced controlling her breathing and staying calm and, to her surprise, they disappeared. She sat down, inhaled slowly, and took control of herself; and as quickly as the attack had started, it stopped.

Jerickca called her mother. She told her that she had talked to Barrington, who had a bad ear infection, which had caused her to lose her balance and walk into a wall. She had been treated by a doctor and was taking antibiotics to clear up the infection. Barrington had told Jerickca that she was afraid that something was seriously wrong with her, and that was why she was so secretive. Jerickca didn't tell her mother everything that she and her sister discussed, such as how Barrington had begun to scream at her children out of frustration but promised that she had quit doing that when she started treatment for the ear infection. Also, Jerickca and Barrington had planned a surprise for their mom's birthday and had kept it a secret for several months.

Jerickca told her mom that she and Anthony were in counseling and that life for her was definitely on the upswing.

Lula Mae said that Jeremy had gone without anyone's help to a drug treatment center in Mount Vernon, Illinois, and that he had passed thirty-seven days of sobriety. She also told Jerickca that Pammie had broken off with her girlfriend and moved to Chicago with Detective Byrd. However, after running and trying to hide from her feelings, she found that she really loved Jamie. So she returned, and she and Jamie made up and moved to Chicago. They were planning a summer wedding with their families. Jerickca thought that Pammie needed much prayer, because she seemed so lost and unsure of who she was.

Jerickca and her mom made plans to have lunch on Friday, when they would continue to update each other on everything. When she hung up the phone, Jerickca called her pastor and set up a date for counseling and Bible studies. She was sure of one thing, and that was that she needed a strong relationship with God. She wanted to make sure that she understood what God expected of her, and she wanted to live according to His will. It would take time, but she would share what she learned in her Bible lessons with all her family members. Maybe then they, too, could find the peace they were seeking.

On Thursday, everybody at work was talking about all the changes that their coworkers were going through. Denver had submitted her resignation and was going to attend Washington University Medical School. Patches was getting married. Megan had been fired but was still calling and asking questions about what was going on. Some days, she even showed up on the job, trying to be nosey and spreading gossip. She only came around when she didn't see Jerickca's car parked outside. This further alienated her from her old friends. She couldn't move forward because she was stuck in reverse. They wanted her to progress and be happy with her life, because that was the only way they could enjoy her company. They missed her, but they didn't miss the way she treated those she felt were beneath her. Phoenix and her husband were in counseling, trying to sort out their problems. The clients were continuing to progress.

When the meeting to plan the new fiscal year was over, the staff came out and headed to the backroom. Phoenix was the first to walk through the door. The room was decorated with balloons and streamers. Near the window in the far right corner was a long table filled with catered food. There was a pan of macaroni, seafood and pasta salad, green beans, cornbread, collard greens, chicken, ham, turkey, dressing, cakes, sweet potato pies, and a pecan pie. It was a beautiful sight, and all the food emitted aromas to savor. Phoenix asked, "Hey ya'll, what's going on? Who laid this table out with this food?"

Patches rushed over to the table and immediately started looking for the plates. "I don't know who did it, but it's for us since it's in our office. I do know this: brother is ready to eat."

Jerickca walked through the door and told everyone to take a seat. She had a table brought in so everyone would have a place to sit. Once all the staff was settled, she told them what today meant. "First of all," she said, "I want to thank each of you for your contributions to both the program and our clients. We have had an amazing year and have seen our clients excel at levels that were higher than we ever expected. The success of this program is you. You all made this happen, because you were diligent, patient, and motivated. I wanted to thank you so I planned this lunch meeting. In addition," Jerickca picked up some envelopes and completed her sentence, "I wanted to give you all a token of appreciation just to say thanks for a great year."

She called out the names. "Phoenix, Patches, and Denver, thank you for your support." She also gave Karen, Candy, and Kelvin their envelopes, as well as seven other workers. As they opened their envelopes, broad smiles spread across their faces. Phoenix was the first to say thank you, after which Candy stood up, walked toward Jerickca, and hugged her. "You are the best boss a person could ever have." Everybody followed and hugged her, but Patches kissed her cheek.

Phoenix immediately saw that moment. "Boy! Jerickca ain't one of your women on the street!"

Patches laughed. "Somebody is jealous." Everybody laughed and continued to eat.

As everyone finished their meal, Denver asked, "Who cooked this food?"

Jerickca responded that B and F located on 19th Street had catered the food. They all agreed it was very tasty. As usual, the staff started talking about current events. They discussed war, terrorism, dating, marriage, and raising children in these times.

Denver said, "I'm sure going to miss the talks that we have shared back here."

Phoenix stated, "Yeah right, like you participated in them all the time. You rarely came out to talk."

"Sometimes I felt uncomfortable. You know, Megan made sure that you all didn't get too close to me. She really confused me. There were times when I felt very close to her, and then she would rip into me and treat me like I wasn't important. But I still liked her. She was so animated and full of life."

"I know what you mean," said Phoenix. "When Devante and I were going through so many problems because of me, she really helped me to pull myself together. She told me that the grass was not green on the other side—it was actually burnt! She told me to work out my marriage problem, and to go home and fight for my husband because there was nothing in the street but other women with no men on their side. She was so cool. Everything she told me really helped me to get through my ordeal."

Karen laughed. "Then the heifer called me and asked me had I talked to you. Said I should call because you were having marital problems. I guess she couldn't help herself."

Jerickca jumped in the conversation. "It is possible that she wasn't aware of what she was doing? You do know that there are some people who can't see the pain and problems they cause others. They keep pushing until someone snaps. It is already too late to do anything about her. She was a good worker, and she had great statistics. It was the way she treated her clients. I have never seen anyone who talked about clients as bad as she did but would break her neck trying to make sure they were okay. Talk about a double-edged sword! Yet her clients were progressing and most of them did whatever it took to become economically self-sufficient."

Patches looked up from his cake, "You would, too, if you were on her caseload. I think she really did care about them, but she was too shallow to see how her actions hurt."

Just then the phone rang, and Phoenix picked it up. "It's for you, Jerickca."

"I'll take that in my office."

When Jerickca picked up the phone, it was the doctor returning her call. She told her that she needed to make an appointment because she felt that she had an eating disorder. She told the doctor that after eating her food, she would be forced to vomit. She then admitted that she had been putting her finger down her throat to throw up but had stopped because she feared that she would burst her esophagus. Since she stopped months ago, her body was doing it on its own. The doctor said that she needed to see her next Monday and would discuss a treatment plan. When Jerickca hung up the phone, she called Weight Watchers. Just as she hung the phone up after getting the date, places, and meeting time, she turned because she felt someone standing there.

"Deborah!" Jerickca cried.

They hugged each other, and Deborah told her that she had come back to practice law. She said that Danny had accepted a position in New York City and was marrying a model. Jerickca told Deborah that she needed to clear up a couple of things at the office and they could leave together. She excused herself to go to the backroom.

As she walked down the hallway, she could hear Kelvin, the janitor, telling everyone in the backroom the story about the gorilla at the St. Louis Zoo. "The Gorilla," he said, "saw a woman that he wanted to get with and he said, 'Damn that woman is fine!' So he grabbed her from the outside of the cage and pulled her in. He was hugging and kissing her and trying to find where to put his tongue in the woman's mouth when she started screaming, 'I'm not a gorilla you fool.'" Everybody waited on the punch line. Finally, he continued. "The gorilla said, 'You are a damn gorilla. Look at you! You're hairy and black like me, you are big and wide like me, and you sure is ugly like me.' He grabbed the ugly woman, started kissing her, and said, 'You sure can kiss!' Then the woman slapped me so hard, I dropped my bananas and ran out the cage." The punch line was that Kelvin was the gorilla in the cage. Everyone started laughing, including Jerickca, who had stepped into the room to tell them that they could take the rest of the day off. Before heading for her office, she took a detour to the bathroom.

When she walked out of the bathroom and passed the backroom, they were still in there talking about sex. She walked back in, listened, and laughed for about five minutes.

Then she said goodbye to them. "I tried to give you all the day off, but I guess you all love this room so much you want to stay."

"We are just chillin'," Patches reflected.

"All right. I will see you all tomorrow." With that, she walked back to her office.

Phoenix had walked up to the front to ask Jerickca a question without knowing that she was in the ladies' room. When she walked through the door, she saw Deborah Dennison.

"Deborah!" she said, "where have you been? I have looked everywhere for you. I wanted to thank you for helping me through college. I never got a chance to tell you how much I appreciate what you did for me. Thank you so much, because without you, I couldn't have made it. Please forgive me for being such an asshole."

They hugged and updated each other on their lives. Deborah told her that Jerickca was her best friend. This didn't surprise Phoenix at all. She told Deborah that Jerickca was so cool. Jerickca walked in on the "Get Reacquainted Party" and opened the file cabinet to get her purse. She grabbed her coat and walked toward the women, who were talking. Phoenix excused herself, and Deborah told Jerickca that she would update her later on that conversation.

When Jerickca walked out the door, she turned to look back and saw that the staff was finally leaving the backroom. Jerickca laughed and thought, *When information is needed that will help you grow or that may hurt your soul with pain, go to the backroom, the place where information can be dangerous or helpful, depending on who gives it, how it is given, and how the receiver handles what he hears. Backroom Confessions. Sex. Love. Pain. Success.*

www.ingramcontent.com/pod-product-compliance
Lightning Source LLC
LaVergne TN
LVHW091034080826
845145LV00002B/486

* 9 7 8 0 9 7 5 3 6 3 4 1 6 *